Maine Men Book One

Finn's
FANTASY

K.C. WELLS

This is a work of fiction. Names, characters, places, and incidents either are the product of the author's imagination or are used fictitiously, and any resemblance to actual persons, living or dead, business establishments, events, or locales is entirely coincidental.

<u>Maine Men</u>

Levi, Noah, Aaron, Ben, Dylan, Finn, Seb, and Shaun.

Eight friends who met in high school in Wells, Maine.

Different backgrounds, different paths, but one thing remains solid, even eight years after they graduated – their friendship. Holidays, weddings, funerals, birthdays, parties – any chance they get to meet up, they take it. It's an opportunity to share what's going on in their lives, especially their love lives.

Back in high school, they knew four of them were gay or bi, so maybe it was more than coincidence that they gravitated to one another. Along the way, there were revelations and realizations, some more of a surprise than others.

And what none of the others knew was that Levi was in love with one of them….

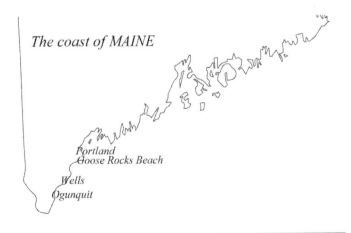

The coast of MAINE

Portland
Goose Rocks Beach
Wells
Ogunquit

Chapter One

April

Finn Anderson only had to glance at Teresa Young as she weaved her way through the tables—*Hey, scratch that. She's Teresa Cyr now*—to know she was on a mission. Guests called out to her, and all they got was the merest flicker of a smile in their direction, her determined stride not faltering for an instant.

"Quick, guys. Duck. The bride's headed this way," he said in a stage whisper. The others pretended to search with great urgency for the exit as she approached, like he'd known they would.

Teresa came to a halt behind Ben's chair, her hands clenched into fists, resting on her satin-and-lace-clad hips. "Don't even think about it." That earned her a ripple of chuckles. She glanced at Finn and the seven men seated around the table, her sculpted brows arching. "Well, what do we have here? Someone put you guys all together. Go figure."

Dylan rolled his eyes. "Gee. Who do you think did that?"

Finn was amused to note Dylan was the only one still wearing his tie. The others had loosened or removed theirs.

Teresa batted her lashes. "No clue." That glint in her eyes told a different story.

Seb's eyes sparkled. "Is it our turn for a grilling—I mean, our turn with the bride?" When she gave him a mock glare, he gave her a sweet smile. "That's a beautiful dress, Teresa."

Ben bit back a smirk. "Suck-up," he muttered.

She performed a slow turn, her arms held wide. "Thank you." Seb was right. It was a gorgeous low-backed dress, with a V-neck and Empire waist. The white satin hugged her slim figure down to her hips, where it flared out at the back. Lace added a filmy layer, covering her shoulders and spreading from knee point behind her in a train, its scalloped edges embellished with delicate embroidery. The fluted lace sleeves were cut to leave her hands free.

Seb rubbed his scruffily bearded chin. "Those sleeves, though…"

Teresa narrowed her gaze. "What about them?"

Finn struggled to suppress his laughter. Seb could always push Teresa's buttons, even when they were kids.

Seb shrugged. "A bit impractical? I mean, they're pretty and all, but you're lucky there's no soup on the menu, or you'd be constantly dunking them in it."

Levi cleared his throat. "Don't listen to him, Teresa. I think it really shows off your body." She blew him a kiss. Levi looked her up and down. "It kinda reminds me of something I saw on *Downton Abbey*."

Teresa's eyes gleamed. "Oh my God. Yes, *exactly*." She beamed at him. "Thank you for noticing." She glanced at the friends around the table. "Actually, I came over to thank Finn for the wedding present." She gazed warmly at Finn. "The rocking chairs are beautiful. You made them, didn't you?"

Finn gave a half bow. "I'm glad you like them." He'd

spent several weekends working on the ash chairs with spindle backs, and he was delighted with the result.

"One would have been enough, you know."

Finn shook his head. "You need two. They should be on your front porch, side by side, so you and Ry can sit together in the evening, like an old married couple." Then he realized silence had fallen around the table, and he gave his friends a quizzical glance. "What?"

Seb folded his arms. "Sure, make us all look bad, why don't ya?"

Finn frowned. "Huh?"

"I thought I'd scored pretty high, giving them an Instapot. But *rocking chairs*?"

From across the table, Ben chuckled. "At least an Instapot shows some imagination. I gave them a gift card." There were murmurs of *me too* from Levi, Noah, Dylan and Aaron. "And *you* can *afford* an Instapot, Mr. Teacher. *Some* of us don't earn as much as you."

Shaun grinned. "I got your gift cards beat. *My* gift card is for the restaurant. For those nights when Ry can't stand the idea of Teresa's cooking."

"Hey," Noah piped up. "Be nice. She might have improved since high school."

"*Might* have?" Teresa gaped at him. "And what's that about high school?"

Noah laughed. "Didn't they use one of your bread rolls as a baseball?"

Her hands were back on her hips. "Who told?"

Levi cackled. "That would be your husband, Mrs. Cyr."

Teresa whipped her head around, her eyes narrowed to slits as she stared across the ballroom to where Ry stood, chatting with guests. "Wait till I get him alone."

"You know, that's *supposed* to come across as sexy,

not menacing," Aaron observed, his lips twitching.

Teresa blinked, then burst out laughing. "You guys crack me up."

Finn laughed with her. Teresa had changed little since they'd graduated high school, thank God. Her temper still died down as quickly as it flared up.

Ben raised his glass of champagne to her. "Congratulations, Teresa. You make a great couple. And it's about time, considering you and Ry shared your first kiss in ninth grade." His eyes twinkled.

Shaun's eyes widened. "Hey, I'd forgotten about that."

"Did you also forget that Teresa told everyone how icky it was?" Ben glanced at her. "That *was* what you said, right?" He grinned. "Maybe it's taken you till now to marry him because you were waiting till he got better at kissing."

Amid the laughter, Teresa folded her arms, her pale pink nails long and curved as they rested on her lace-covered upper arms, the fluted sleeves hanging down. "Should you be drinking that? Because *I* don't think you're old enough."

Ben rolled his eyes. "Real funny. If I wasn't at your wedding, I'd tell you to…" He mouthed *fuck off*, and Teresa gave a mock gasp. Ben chuckled.

Levi put his arm around Ben's shoulders. "Aw, he can't help it that he still has the cutest baby face." He pinched Ben's cheek.

Ben growled from the back of his throat. "Knock it off. Christ, you've been doing that since eighth grade."

"He could always kiss it better," Seb suggested with a gleam in his eye. "He's probably a better kisser than Ry." That earned him a glare from both Ben and Levi.

Teresa deliberately turned her head in Seb's

direction. "You have *not* kissed Ry."

Seb's enigmatic smile reminded Finn why he fucking *loved* his friends. Put them all together, and the snark increased a hundredfold.

Teresa walked over to where Seb sat, and he pushed his chair back as though to stand. She pressed her hand to his shoulder. "You stay put, pretty boy."

"Pretty boy? I'm flattered." He shut up when Teresa sat in his lap sideways, her arms looped around his neck. A moment later, Seb laughed. "Go right ahead, Teresa. Get comfy."

"Consider this punishment for making me think you and Ry kissed."

Seb leaned in close and said in a loud whisper, "What happened between us will go with me to my grave." When Teresa gasped and tried to pull away, Seb held onto her. "Chill, sweetheart. Nothing happened. He's not my type. I'm not into jocks."

"That's not what I heard," Noah murmured.

Seb merely arched his eyebrows. "Which part?"

Teresa relaxed, her fingers laced, effectively locking her arms around him. Seb put his hand on her waist, and she smiled. "I figure I'm safe enough. It's not like *you're* gonna grope me, like Ry's creepy Uncle Al. And at least with *you*, I know for certain I'm not your type." She grinned. "So, Seb… Met any hot guys in Ogunquit lately?"

Finn laughed. "From what I hear, Seb's working his way through every guy he meets at MaineStreet, the Front Porch, and let's not forget the gay section of the beach. Which is probably where he's planning on spending the entire summer vacation."

Seb speared Finn with a look. "Just what are you implying?" There was no rebuke in his tone, however.

Ben whooped. "Dude, he ain't implying—he's flat out *saying* it."

Around the table, Finn's friends joined in with the laughter, and Seb wasn't far behind them.

"Hey, Levi, how's your grandmother?" Teresa inquired. "I haven't seen her around lately."

Levi's smile lit up his eyes. "She's good, thanks. She sends her best wishes."

"Does she still bake? I remember when she taught you to make cookies in eighth grade, and she sent you to school with a box of them for your friends."

Aaron snorted. "I'm not surprised you remember that. *How* many did you eat?"

Teresa smoothed her hands down her slim form. "My cookie-binging days are far behind me."

"Not surprising," Noah commented. When Teresa jerked her head in his direction, he pointed to her dress. "You couldn't eat cookies *and* wear that. Unless it comes in a bigger size."

"And yes, Grammy still bakes," Levi assured her. Finn saw the remark for what it was, Levi's attempt to cut the snark. But that was Levi, always the peacemaker, even when they were kids.

Finn glanced over Teresa's shoulder at the approaching figure. "Uh-oh. Incoming. I spy a pissed groom." Ry Cyr looked as if he was on a mission too, not that he appeared all *that* irritated.

Teresa stilled as a loud cough erupted behind her. Ry ignored her and greeted the group with a polite smile. "Not to interrupt this little gabfest or anything, but have any of you seen my wife?" They all laughed. Ry placed his hand on Teresa's shoulder, gazing at her in obvious amusement. "I see you found a comfortable lap. Now, unless you'd rather spend all your time with these guys when there are other guests to talk to, or God forbid, your husband…"

Seb chuckled. "You can have her back now."

Ry snorted. "As if I didn't know exactly where she'd be." He held out his hand to her, and Teresa stood, smoothing her dress. Ry glanced around the table. "You guys having fun?"

"We're having a great time," Finn assured him. "This is a nice place." The Maine Ballroom ceiling was festooned with white lights and draped with long spans of chiffon that spread from the center to all corners, where they fell in elegant lengths. Beyond the French doors was the patio with its white-columned pergola draped with more chiffon, where the service had taken place.

"That was a nice ceremony too," Levi added.

Noah frowned. "It was so short."

"That's what I meant." Levi's mischievous grin took Finn back to the seventh grade, when Finn had first met him. Levi had always appeared to be up to something, even when he was behaving himself. *And when did Levi ever misbehave?* He was their own Little Goody Two-Shoes.

Ry gestured to the wooden floor in the middle of the room. "I expect to see you all dancing later. Only… don't dance with each other, okay? You'll scare my relatives. Some of them aren't as open-minded as me." That look of amusement was still present.

Aaron's eyes flashed. "Hey. One size does *not* fit all, okay?"

Noah cleared his throat. "That's Aaron-speak for 'We're not *all* gay or bi.'" He patted Aaron's arm. "Welcome to my world. Whenever I go bowling with Levi, some smartass from high school always thinks it's funny to ask when we're getting engaged."

"Whereas *we* all know neither of you is the marrying kind," Finn observed. He couldn't ever remember Noah or Levi going on dates, although things might have changed since Finn had moved to Kennebunkport. It wasn't as though he kept close tabs on his friends. They called one another, sure, but they hadn't met up like this since New Year's, which meant it was high time they had a chat and caught up.

Levi blinked. "I see." Noah wore what Finn thought of as his deer-in-headlights expression.

Ry put his arm around Teresa's waist. "I'll see you later, guys. Right now we have to mingle." He led her across to another table, and Teresa glanced over her shoulder at them, wearing an apologetic smile.

"I think Teresa would rather talk to us than mingle," Shaun said with a chuckle.

"And speaking of talking…" Finn inclined his head toward the French doors. "How about we get a refill, then take our champagne outside where we can talk? We gotta catch up."

Dylan glanced toward the glass, and shivered. "Fuck that. It's freezing out there. I vote we find the bar. The fabulous Village by the Sea has to have at least one bar, right? Let's claim a corner of it where we can talk, uninterrupted."

Ten minutes later, they'd located the bar and dragged enough chairs into a quiet corner, one table in the midst of them, its surface crowded with their glasses.

Ben gave a longing glance toward the ballroom. "I was gonna dance."

Shaun laughed. "Well, that would be one way of clearing the floor for the rest of us."

"What does that mean?" Ben's voice held indignation.

"It *means* you dance like a flailing Kermit, and don't bother denying it." Dylan grinned. "We have proof."

"What?" Ben glared at them. "What proof?"

Seb pulled his phone from his pocket, scrolled through, then held it up for Ben to see. "New Year's. Party. That *is* you, isn't it?"

Ben's eyes widened. "You dickhead. Delete it." Around him, the others laughed, and Ben was clearly striving to keep up the pretense of being annoyed.

Seb hugged his phone to his chest. "Uh-uh. I'm keeping this for when I need leverage." He glanced at Levi. "You still living at your grandmother's place?" When Levi nodded, Seb pursed his lips. "That must cramp your style."

"I suppose it would," Levi acknowledged. "*If* I was on the lookout for someone—which I'm not." He raised his eyebrows. "It's not like I'm the marrying kind, remember?"

"Not *everyone* is like you, Seb," Ben teased. Silence fell as they drank champagne.

Finn shook his head. "Do you mean, this is the first time we've met up since New Year's, and there's *no* juicy gossip? Nothing to report?" Seven faces stared blankly at him, and Finn sighed. "Well fuck. Eight guys—none of us remotely ugly—and not a love interest in sight. To quote the sheriff from *Blazing Saddles*, 'I am depressed.'"

"Who says I *want* a love interest?" Seb demanded. "I'm happy keeping it casual. No strings. No commitments. I like my life as it is. And so what if I hook up with guys from MaineStreet? There's nothing wrong with that."

"Nothing at all," Finn assured him.

Seb flashed him a grateful glance.

"Do you mean you're not lusting after any of the hunky guys on your work team?" Shaun teased Finn.

"Those assholes? One, they're all straight. Two, they yank my chain every chance they get. They love to embarrass me—well, they *try* to, at least. They don't get very far." Besides, there wasn't one of them who piqued Finn's interest.

The sole guy to do *that* remained out of reach, and the idea of approaching him was nothing more than a fantasy. It had only been two weeks since he'd first clapped eyes on the man walking his chocolate lab on the beach, and ever since then Finn had kept a surreptitious lookout for him.

"What are you working on right now?" Levi asked.

"We're building a hotel on Kings Highway. It's gonna have a great view of the beach." The kind of view Finn ached to have from a front window of his own, but hey, unless he won the Lottery…

"Goose Rocks Beach?" Noah inquired. When Finn nodded, Noah chuckled. "Wow. You have a long drive to work every day, don't you? How long does it take you to get there? Two, three minutes?"

"Yeah, funny guy." Finn sipped his champagne. "And I'll have you know I live two hundred feet from the beach."

"Ooh, two hundred feet," Seb taunted. "Walking to work must be a bitch."

"Jesus, you must have ice water for blood to live there. It's gotta be freezing this time of year." Ben gave an exaggerated shiver. "Hope you wear your long johns on site."

Finn guffawed. "Says you. Remind me where you

live again? Camden ain't exactly the tropics."

That got him the finger.

"Aren't the properties there nothing but rentals? You know, for summer people?" Aaron stretched out his long legs, crossing them at the ankles.

"Mostly." Finn was renting a two-bed cottage from Jon, the builder in charge of the site. It had seen better days, and had obviously been decked out inside by someone with an overwhelming love of pine cladding, but it was comfortable and it suited Finn. From his front door he could look right along Belvidere Avenue to the beach. The site was to the right along the shore.

Finn loved the bracing ocean air and the smells that came with it. He didn't mind the cold so much—he was used to it—and going for a walk along the beach was his way to unwind. He'd lost track of the number of times during a workday that someone would yell at him to quit staring out at the ocean.

Not that Finn was gazing at the waves *all* the time—sometimes he was watching a man and his dog. Or watching *out* for a man and his dog.

I got it bad, for a guy I haven't even seen up close. For all I know, he might be the Elephant Man. Am I that desperate? Jesus, how long has it been since I got laid?

Long enough that Finn had stopped counting the days.

"So why *do* you think it took Teresa and Ry all this time to get hitched?" Dylan asked, pulling Finn back into the moment. "Unless Ben nailed it, and she was waiting till his technique improved." He gave a little snicker.

Ben snorted. "I can tell you why. Teresa was waiting for Mr. Right, and when she finally figured out he wasn't gonna make an appearance, she settled for Mr.

Right Now. Although her mom might've have had a hand in it too. Word is, she's aching to bounce grandkids on her knee. And Teresa must be almost twenty-six by now."

"How come you know all this?" Finn didn't think Ben made it back to Wells all that often. Finn could understand that: out of all of them, Ben had encountered more than his fair share of abusive assholes in high school, and most of them had stuck around. With the exception of Aaron up in the Acadia National park, Ben was the farthest north, in Camden.

Ben gave a sly grin. "I have my sources." He glanced at Dylan and shook his head. "Dude, take off the tie. You're not working reception at that hotel. Chill."

Dylan laughed as he loosened his dark blue tie and then removed it. "So I like neat. Bite me."

"Whereas *Ben* wouldn't know neat if it bit him in the ass," Noah observed with a twinkle in his eye. Ben merely gave him the finger, amid laughter.

"You gotta learn another response, okay?" Finn told Ben with a cackle.

Ben gave him a sweet smile. "You wanna know what my response is?" He did it again. "Sit on it."

Finn grinned. "I would, but with the size of those fingers, I wouldn't get a lot out of it."

"You met any pretty girls in housekeeping yet?" Shaun asked.

Dylan arched his eyebrows. "With my hours? When would I have time to talk to them?"

"How's your dad, Shaun?" Levi placed his empty glass on the table.

Shaun's face tightened. "He's okay. His in-home nurse is with him this weekend. I almost didn't come."

Finn's heart went out to him. Watching dementia

nibble away at the dad Shaun had known all his life must've been torture.

"Well, I'm glad you did," Noah said warmly. He peered at their glasses. "We need to make a toast." When Levi's face flushed, Noah chuckled. "Here. Have some of mine." He tipped half his champagne into Levi's glass.

"Thanks." Levi gave him a grateful glance before raising his glass. "So, what'll we drink to?" He gazed around the table and smiled. "I know what *my* toast would be. To the best friends a guy could ever wish for."

Ben bit his lip. "To the friends who saved my ass more times than I can remember." He lifted his glass into the air, as did the others.

"To the friends who've had my back since junior high," Aaron added.

"To the friends who take me as I am." Seb's eyes sparkled.

"To the friends who've always been there for me, rain or shine." Shaun's usually quiet voice rang out.

"To the best role models a guy could have." The sincerity in Dylan's voice tightened Finn's throat.

"To us," Noah said at last, gazing at each of them.

"To us," Finn echoed. They brought their glasses together, and no one spoke as they clinked. Each man took a drink in the comfortable silence. Then Finn grinned. "Okay. Enough chatting. I want to watch Ben dance. In fact, I want to dance my feet off." Monday already beckoned, not that he dreaded going back to work. He loved his job.

But Monday morning would also bring the guy on the beach, walking his beautiful dog.

Will that be the day I finally get up the nerve to talk to him?

Finn doubted it. Why wreck a perfectly fabulous fantasy by discovering the man he found so alluring was as straight as an arrow?

Ben huffed. "Fine. I was gonna dance anyway. But only if you guys keep your phones in your pockets. You got that?"

"We got it." Seb gave him a reassuring nod. As they got up from the table, he caught Finn's eye, and waggled his phone. *Your turn*, he mouthed.

Finn stifled his laughter. He had the best friends *ever*. The best life, come to think of it. There was only one thing missing that would make it perfect.

Someone to love.

Chapter Two

Joel Hall began counting in his head as soon as his sister Megan stepped through his front door. He'd gotten as far as fifty before she launched her first salvo. Joel was impressed: she wasn't usually that restrained.

Megan looked around, nodding. "Small, but nice loft bedroom." She grinned. "You don't think you could've found a smaller place? I mean, if you tried really hard, you might be able to swing a cat in here. I'm sure the dog would love that."

"It's not *that* small a place, and *the dog* has a name," Joel commented dryly. "It's only two syllables, for God's sake. Bramble. Bram-bull. Think you can remember that?" He figured Megan's withering glance was all the response he was going to get.

Megan crouched in front of Bramble, who lay curled up on his bed by the fireplace. She rubbed his silky chocolate-colored ears. "Your silly daddy thinks I'm here to see him, but *we* know the truth, right, puppy?"

Bramble's soft *woof* was adorable. "He's telling you he's knows *exactly* why you're here, *Aunt* Megan," Joel remarked from his rocking chair on the other side of the fireplace.

Megan shook her head. "Look at you. Rocking away in that thing as if you're eighty years old." Her eyes twinkled. "And why choose the rocking chair when there's a perfectly *adorable* armchair covered in pictures of sailboats."

Joel knew sarcasm when he heard it. He narrowed his gaze. "Okay, so the decor is quaint. What do you expect from a rental? An Edwardian library chair? An Irish fireside chair? A solid wood dresser? And so what if it's not to your taste? *You're* not the one living here." *Thank God.* Thirty minutes or more lay between him and Portland where Megan and her partner Lynne resided. It wasn't *that* great a distance, but it was enough. He loved his sister dearly, but *Jesus*, she could try the patience of a saint.

Megan gave Bramble one last ruffle of his fur, then moved to the armchair. "Hey, this is comfy."

"Don't sound so surprised." Joel preferred the gentle, soothing motion of the rocker. He loved how Bramble would putter over to him and lie at his feet, his tail safely out of the rocker's reach.

Megan peered at him. "So, is it working? With Bramble, I mean."

It took a moment for her meaning to sink in. Joel gaped at her. "You were *serious*?"

Megan blinked. "Of course I was serious."

"I did *not* get a dog simply to meet guys. Talk about a harebrained scheme."

Megan gave him a superior smile. "You may laugh, but wait and see. A man and his dog? That's a magnet for gay guys. You watch." She got up and walked over to the window, staring out at the scene beyond. "I have to say… Even *my* amazing plotting might falter in a place like this."

"A place like what?"

Megan rolled her eyes. "You know what I see out

there? Trees. Nothing but trees."

"I happen to like trees." Joel couldn't suppress his ruffle of indignation. "Okay, so it's not as… busy as Portland."

Megan's eyes were almost out on stalks. "Not as busy? I'm waiting for tumbleweed to roll leisurely across the road. What was wrong with that place in Augusta? You weren't that far from the kids and Carrie, you had every conceivable amenity on your doorstep… Why on earth did you choose to live in the back of beyond? There's nothing but tourists here."

Joel narrowed his gaze. "I *like* it here. It's quiet. I can write. I can walk the dog." And as for being farther away from the kids… His chest tightened.

"But there are no *guys*," Megan said, wringing her hands. "There have to be better places in this state for a gay man to live." She sighed. "I'd die if I had to live here."

"You'd have died if you'd stayed in Idaho. You wouldn't have met Lynne for one thing."

He loved the warm light in her eyes. "True."

Joel had liked the quaint cottage the moment he'd laid eyes on it, from its white-painted steps leading up to the front porch, to the steep slope of the roof with its two skylights. One glance at the Adirondack chair on the porch to the left of the front door had sealed the deal. He could picture himself sitting in it, reading, or maybe with his laptop on his knee. On the other side of the door were two white rocking chairs. Joel had stepped through the screen door into the interior, then come to a dead stop.

It was exactly what he wanted, even if it had seen better days.

The living area gave way to the kitchen on the right,

with a door to the bathroom, and despite what Megan said, there was plenty of room. Light poured through the window at the apex of the roof, and an oak staircase led to the only bedroom, up in the loft. A single and double futon in the living area would accommodate Nate and Laura when—if—they visited, and that was perfect. The loft was charming, with just enough room for a queen-size bed beneath the sloping roof, and he could gaze down into the living room.

Okay, so it was small, but it suited him. And he hadn't chosen that quiet spot in Kennebunkport, a stone's throw from Goose Rocks Beach, because it was teeming with gay men. If he wanted to meet guys, there was Ogunquit. Not that he'd ventured as far as the gay bar—*MaineStreet? Is that the name?*—but it was on his to-do list.

Yeah right. *How* many times had he driven past the place?

It could wait. Right then, all he wanted was to get used to being on his own for a while, just him and his thoughts. And there sure were a lot of *them*.

Megan speared him with a look. "Wait a sec. You said *write*. Are you *still* thinking about that? I thought you gave up on the idea."

Joel shrugged. "I kick it around now and then." Not that he'd gotten as far as writing a single word. It was as if that blank screen on his laptop taunted him. *Go on. I dare ya. Type.* Ideas? He had plenty of ideas. All he lacked was motivation.

Maybe this place is exactly what I need.

"Has Carrie been here yet? Has she been in touch?" Megan's voice was suddenly gentler.

"We talk most days," Joel admitted. "And no, she hasn't visited yet." That was about to change, however.

"How is she?"

Joel grinned. "You can ask yourself." When Megan widened her eyes, Joel tapped his watch face. "She's coming over. She wasn't specific about the time, she just said it would be the afternoon."

"Thanks for the warning. I'll be sure to leave before she gets here."

Joel's scalp prickled. "Why? I always thought you two got along." At least that was the impression he'd gotten.

"Oh, we *do*. It's just…"

Joel got up from his rocker, walked over to her, and placed his hand on her shoulder, giving it a hopefully comforting squeeze. "Don't worry. There won't be any awkward silences or tension between us. It wasn't that kind of a divorce." He went on into the kitchen to put on the coffee. "You're going to stay long enough for coffee, right?"

"That depends on what time she gets here." Megan followed him, leaning against the column that supported the loft. "Did you tell her about David?"

Joel's stomach clenched. "I told her everything. It was about time." He had to smile. "Her first comment? 'I thought you were a virgin when we got together.'"

Megan smirked. "Well… technically, you were. With women at least." She stiffened at the sound of a car engine. "This must be her."

Joel peered through the windows. Carrie's Honda Civic was indeed parked outside. "Stay a while longer? You only just got here."

"This was always going to be a quick stop on my way." Megan kissed his cheek. "Don't worry. I won't let it go for too long before I come visit my little brother again."

Joel pulled a face. "Aw, did you have to spoil it? Don't I get a reprieve or something?" He grimaced when she whacked his arm. "Ouch. I thought you'd grown out of that."

"You wish." Megan picked up her purse, and Joel grabbed her coat from its hook. By the time he'd helped her into it, there was a rap at the door. Joel opened it, and Bramble chose that moment to make a mad dash for freedom.

Thankfully, Carrie was more alert than Joel was, and shut the screen door. She peered through the mesh at Bramble. "Where do you think *you're* going?" Joel grabbed hold of his collar and held on tight. Carrie caught sight of Megan, and smiled. "Hey, I didn't know you'd be here. It's been a while."

"Yeah, but unfortunately, I have to go. Nice to see you, Carrie." Megan patted Joel's arm. "I'll see you next weekend."

Joel couldn't resist. "So soon?" That earned him a final glare. He tugged Bramble out of her way.

Carrie opened the screen door for her, and Megan squeezed past. She walked briskly to her car. Joel got a wave as she pulled out of the driveway.

"Something I said?" Carrie rubbed her arms. "Actually, tell me inside. It's freezing out here." She glanced at Bramble. "Unless he needs a W-A-L-K."

Bramble's ears pricked up, and Joel groaned. "Christ, now he can spell too. If Bramble had his way, he'd have five or six of those a day." He stood aside to let her come in, accepting her kiss on the cheek. "There's coffee if you want some."

"Sounds great." Carrie closed the door behind her. "So what was up with Megan? She flew out of here like I was contagious or something."

Joel sighed. "I think she felt as though she'd be in the way. Plus, I got the impression she was expecting tension between us. Newly divorced couple and all…"

Carrie shook her head. "Put her straight, please?" Her eyes glittered. "Well, as straight as your sister can be." She stared at the interior. "I think whoever named this place Periwinkle nailed it. A cute name for a cute cottage." When she saw the fireplace, her eyes shone. "Can I light a fire? It's cold enough for one."

"Knock yourself out. There are logs in the basket." Joel gave her a speculative glance. "You do know how to light a fire, right?"

Carrie narrowed her gaze. "My grandfather taught me, if you must know. It's a skill I've never forgotten."

Joel left her to it and went into the kitchen. "*Now* I understand why you kept choosing to look at properties with fireplaces, when we started house-hunting." It seemed incredible that after twenty years together, there were still things he didn't know about her.

"Which came to nothing, when the house we both fell in love with didn't have one. And when did I have the opportunity to light a fire? It's not like we ever went camping." She chuckled. "Now, why was that? Oh yeah. 'Too many bugs.' 'A bear might eat the tent.'"

"Hey, bears do that," he protested.

Another wry chuckle. "How long have you had the dog?" she inquired. "It's Bramble, I think you said?"

"Yeah. A couple of weeks. I got him the first weekend after I moved in here. And be warned. He'll lick you to death."

Seconds later, a peal of laughter bounced off the high ceiling. "Bramble, that tickles. My ears are perfectly clean, thank you."

Joel grinned. "Ear-baths are his specialty."

"Sit. Sit. Let me make up the fire, needy puppy."

Joel chuckled quietly. Bramble was clearly enjoying meeting two new humans in one day.

"I like this place."

Joel smiled to himself. "You're right, it *is* cute. Go take a look, once you've gotten the fire going."

Carrie laughed. "Let me guess. You already cleaned up because you knew I was coming, so I'm not going to find anything incriminating."

"*Incriminating* implies something illegal or wrong. Wanna rethink that word choice?" Joel took two mugs from the cabinet and placed them next to the coffee pot.

Carrie walked into view in socked feet. "I'm sorry. You're right. It's just that you kept a huge part of you hidden, for so long. It got me wondering if you kept anything else hidden too."

"If you're *that* interested, my gay magazines are on the bookcase next to the rocker. They're in plain sight. And before you ask, we're not talking erotica, so I wouldn't feel the need to hide them when the kids visit." His throat seized. *If they visit.* There'd been little communication since he'd first moved out. *They blame me for the divorce.* That much had been obvious from the start. And as for leaving the magazines in plain sight, Joel knew that was a lie. He'd bury them under a mountain of laundry, rather than let the kids find them.

Maybe one day. But that day didn't look like it would arrive anytime soon.

"They'll come around, Joel." Carrie's voice was soft.

He glanced at her, noting the strong eye contact. "That obvious, huh?"

"I told them *I* was the one who asked for a divorce, but they seemed to take that as a sign—well, Nate did—that I was trying to get away from you, so *you* must have done something to warrant it."

"Of course. But he's not wrong, is he?" The coffee pot beeped, and Joel filled the mugs with the aromatic brew.

Carrie walked over and took one. She gazed at the kitchen with its round white table and four chairs. "This is plenty big enough for you." She laid a hand on his arm. "And yes, he *is* wrong. We got divorced because we'd grown apart. We were more like roommates than a married couple." Carrie wrapped both hands around her mug.

"And *why* were we like that? Because of me."

She inclined her head toward the living room. "How about we sit by the fire while we talk?" Her lips twitched. "That's if it's still going."

Joel snorted. "Aha. So you're admitting your fire-lighting skills might not be as good as you claim." They went into the living room area. Carrie hurried over to the fire, kneeling in front of it, and he chuckled. "Oops."

Carrie grinned. "Oh ye of little faith." She grabbed some of the kindling from the log basket, added it to the fire, then blew gently on it. The flames burst into life, and she placed a single log on top. Carrie gave a flourish. "Ta-da."

Joel was impressed. "Okay, I take it back."

She brought the armchair closer, then sat in it, warming her hands.

Joel sat in his rocker, and Bramble came over to him, his head resting on Joel's knee, his tail wagging. Joel stroked Bramble's sleek head. "Good boy," he whispered. Bramble's tail picked up speed.

"How far is it to the beach from here?" Carrie asked.

"Depends on which route I take. The shortest is past the fire department, left at Clock Farm Corner, and down Dyke Road, where the village store is. That brings me out at the southern end of Kings Highway, about half an hour—unless Bramble is really pulling, in which case you could knock off four minutes or so. I don't see many people when I go that way. The longest route takes me through the village, and once I get to the lower end of Wildwood Avenue, I can pretty much pick any street—they all lead to the shore." He snuck a glance in her direction. "You dating yet?"

Carrie flushed. "The judge only approved the divorce decree two weeks ago."

"Yeah, but I moved out in January. It's been almost five months, sweetheart. You telling me you've not been looking?" When the flush on her neck deepened, Joel knew he'd hit pay dirt. "I see. Who's the lucky guy?" *She deserves to find someone who'll make her happy, in all the ways I couldn't.*

"His name's Eric. I play tennis with him at the Tennis Association." Carrie bit her lip, and in that moment, Joel saw her at age twenty-two, the shy girl who'd worked up enough courage to ask him to marry her.

"Would I approve?"

Carrie's eyes sparkled. "He's forty-eight, very sweet, and very kind. He treats me like I'm a queen."

Joel wasn't crass enough to ask if they were getting it on. That was no one's business but theirs. He'd lay even money that they were, however. That light in Carrie's eyes said plenty. *She needs to make up for lost time.*

The thought did nothing but heap another load of guilt onto an already huge pile.

"Then Eric *is* a lucky guy. You're a catch in anyone's

book." She wore her hair shorter now, only reaching her shoulders. Joel gestured to it with a chuckle. "You finally had enough, huh?"

"Do you like it?"

He smiled. "Yes, but I think it's more important that *Eric* does." He cocked his head to one side. "You haven't told the kids, have you? About me, I mean."

Carrie shook her head. "We agreed. That would be when you felt ready." She sipped her coffee.

He gave her a speculative glance. "But you think I should tell them, don't you?"

She sighed. "I just don't feel they'll react as badly as you *think* they will."

Joel placed his mug on a coaster on top of the bookcase. "Really? Look at how they reacted to us divorcing. I'm suddenly the bad guy—at least, I'm pretty sure that's how Nate sees me." Laura's reaction had been more low-key. "How on earth do you think they'll react if I said, 'Hey, kids? I'm gay. I've always thought of myself as gay, but I didn't want to risk coming out, so I did what a whole bunch of other gay guys did—I got married and started a family, because that was what was *'expected' of us'*," he air-quoted. He sagged into the chair. "I stayed in the closet back then because I didn't want to risk losing my family. And I can't help but be afraid that I'll lose Nate and Laura if I come out to them." He swallowed. "If I haven't lost them already."

"Then wait, but don't wait too long." Carrie cocked her head to one side. "What if learning the truth helps them see our divorce in a different light?"

Joel had wondered the same thing, but he wasn't brave enough yet to try out the theory.

"You've lost weight," Carrie commented. "I'd say at

least thirty pounds."

Joel laughed. "Forty-five." He hadn't started on a new regime with the intention of pulling guys, but he couldn't deny the thought had been there at the back of his mind.

"Don't lose any more though, hmm? You don't want to be too thin." Her brow furrowed. "You were *trying* to lose weight, right? It hasn't just dropped off of you."

"Relax. My doc has been on to me for a while now to lose weight to improve my blood pressure, cholesterol, and my heart health in general."

"Ah, so it's not part of some plan to catch a guy. Unless, of course, you've already caught one." Carrie peered at him. "*Is* there anyone… special?"

"No. But to be honest, I haven't been looking." He grinned. "Bramble is part of Megan's plan to find me a man. She thinks the sight of me walking my dog will draw the gay gays like flies to honey."

Carrie laughed loudly. "That sounds like something she'd come up with. And what makes her the expert?"

Joel stroked his chin. "Maybe the fact she's a lesbian? You think that might have something to do with it?"

Carrie's eyes gleamed. "Inside knowledge, is that it?"

"I'd hate to burst Megan's bubble, but while I'm sure Bramble would make for a *great* guy magnet, the doc's suggestion of regular walks and getting a dog as a companion to improve my mental health might have had more to do with it." Despite his irritation at her scheming, it warmed him that Megan was looking out for him. "I think Megan just wants me to be happy."

She sighed heavily. "That's what I want, too. I can't help thinking that if I hadn't asked you to marry me, you'd have been better off."

"I said yes, didn't I?" Joel leaned forward, his elbows on his knees. "And don't forget, I asked *you* out." Carrie bit back a smile that piqued his curiosity. "What went through your mind just now?"

"Oh, I was recalling how we went from meeting to getting engaged three months later, and all that time I thought you were such a gentleman for not trying to get me into bed." Carrie narrowed her gaze. "I'm the only woman you've ever slept with, aren't I?"

Joel nodded.

"Our sex life wasn't much, was it? Frankly, I'm amazed we managed to produce Nate and Laura." Carrie stared at him. "Can I ask something personal?"

"After twenty years, you get to ask whatever you like." He'd expected more questions when he came out to her.

"How did you… *you* know… if you knew deep down you preferred men?"

Joel blinked. "Are you asking me how I could… *perform* with a woman?" When she nodded, his heartbeat quickened. "I'm not sure that's something you should hear."

Carrie widened her eyes. "Hey, I want to know. I was a part of it, remember?"

Joel drew in a deep breath. "Okay. When we were having sex… I was thinking about guys." His face tingled.

Carrie's breathing hitched, and she blinked a few times in rapid succession. "Well. I asked, right?"

"I'm sorry. I should've kept my mouth shut." The last thing he wanted to do was hurt her.

"Don't say that." Carrie's voice was firm. "I'd rather you be honest with me. Because after everything we've been through, we're still friends. Aren't we?"

Joel gave her a warm smile. "We are." She was his best friend, if it came to that.

"And I'd rather have the whole picture. The day will come when you'll come out to the kids, and I'll be there to answer any questions they have." She chuckled. "Any questions *Laura* will have, I should say. Because you *know* she'll be the one who wants to know everything."

"Of course she will. She's fifteen. Nate will *already* know it all, like any eighteen-year-old."

Carrie glanced toward the window. "Do you think we can take Bramble for a… you-know-what? I'd like to see more of the village. You get to choose the route."

Joel laughed as Bramble thumped his tail on the floor. "You said his name. Smart dog. He knows what's coming. And how about we do a circuit? One way there, the other back." He peered at her boots standing by the front door. "Thank God you left your heels at home."

Carrie laughed. "I can't drive in heels." She stood. "Well, come on then. A good walk and a chat sound like a great way to spend the afternoon." That twinkle in her eye was good to see. "As long as being seen with a woman won't cramp your style."

Joel rose to his feet. "That's okay. I'll tell anyone we meet that you're a friend."

Carrie's face glowed. "I can live with that." She darted a glance at the fire. "Hey. We can't go out and just leave it. We might get back to find the place has burned to the ground."

"There's a screen," Joel told her, pointing to it. "Put that in front of it."

He waited till the screen was in place, then they grabbed their coats and pulled on their boots, while Bramble dashed around them, jumping up and barking, his tail almost a blur.

Maybe she's right. Maybe the kids will take it better than I think they will.

He still wasn't prepared to put that theory to the test.

Chapter Three

Finn put down his load of boards and stretched. He was glad he had his heavy coat: now and again the wind off the ocean had a biting edge to it that made even the most hardened guys shiver. The joists supporting the second story had already gone in, and Finn, Ted, and Lewis were laying the floorboards, while four others worked on the joists above their heads. It was going to be a beautiful building when it was done: four stories, twenty-one guest rooms, two of them oceanfront suites, in the only waterfront hotel in town. They had a long way to go, of course—at that point the hotel wasn't much more than a mass of posts and beams—and it wouldn't be opening its doors for another year, probably. Finn knew once the structural part was completed, he'd be working on the interior.

He'd be happier when the walls went in. He'd be a hell of a lot warmer too.

Lewis put down his hammer. "Break time." He adjusted his package. "I need to take a piss too." He headed for the ladder that rested against one of the joists.

"If you're going out back, be careful not to trip over the yellow sticks," Ted called out to him.

Lewis paused as he carefully stepped onto the rungs. "What yellow sticks?"

Ted grinned. "That wind is so fucking freezing that when I took a leak, I had to keep stopping to break it off into two-foot lengths."

Lewis rolled his eyes and continued his path down the ladder.

Max whistled from above. "Well, he-*llo* nurse." Finn immediately scanned the road below, searching for whoever had attracted Max's attention. Sure enough, a woman was walking her Great Dane along the beach. She continued on her way, oblivious to his interest.

"One day, you're gonna forget to keep your voice down, and they're gonna march right over here, climb up that ladder, and knock you out," Finn said with a grin. "Or worse, slap you with a complaint for harassment. Just because you work on a site doesn't mean you have to stick to the usual stereotypes."

"Stereotypes? A dumb ole boy like me doesn't cope well with long words." His eyes twinkled. "Did you miss how stacked she was?" Max mimed an ample bosom. "Gotta love a girl with big hooters."

Ted cackled. "You sure do. Size is important."

Finn couldn't resist. "That's what your dad says every time I drop my pants." That drew the usual hoots and snorts. He'd worked with these guys before, and he knew what was expected of him. That was part of the reason he'd been happy about this job. When he'd seen the list of people working the site, he realized he'd be okay. They were all aware that he was gay, and about ninety-nine percent of them didn't give a shit. The only guy who wasn't happy about it had long since learned to keep his mouth shut: the others loathed haters with a passion, and the one time he'd made a negative comment, they'd stomped on him—verbally, at least. Which was not a bad thing. Lewis was a big guy with big fists, and Finn pitied the guy who ended up on his wrong side.

"Hey, Finn." Max tucked his thumbs into his work belt. "Is that what *you're* into? Older guys?"

Ted arched his eyebrows. "Hey, Max. Look up in the sky, way, way up high. You see that contrail?" He grinned. "That's Finn's joke, going over your head."

Max rolled his eyes. "Duh. But I'm being serious." He leveled an intense gaze at Finn. "Would you fuck an older guy?"

"Do you really wanna know?" When Max nodded, Finn beckoned him with a finger. "Closer." When Max's ear was within distance, Finn whispered, "None of your fucking business."

Max sprang away as though burned. "Aw, you don't have to be like that."

"Yes he does," Ted commented. "Why should he tell you? That's private."

"Oh, come *on*. You all know *my* type." Max remonstrated.

Ted cackled again. "Sure. If she's got a pulse, she's your type. And I'm not even certain about the pulse part." That earned him hoots of laughter, and Max gave a good-natured grin.

"Doesn't hurt to ask if Finn has a type," Max persisted.

"No need to ask," Lewis said as he climbed the ladder. "We already know." When Max gave him a puzzled look glance, Lewis caught Finn's eye. "You got a thing for dog lovers, don't ya?"

There wasn't much that got past Lewis.

Finn walked over to where he'd stored his bag and his Thermos. "Well if it's break time, let's take a fucking break." He unscrewed the cap, poured coffee into it, and took a drink, staring at the ocean. Thank God the guy with the dog was nowhere in sight. That would have been all the ammunition Lewis needed.

"Anyone want a cookie? The wife baked."

Finn eyed the box in Lewis's hands. "Only if you haven't touched 'em. We know what you were just doing, remember?"

Lewis guffawed. "A little piss won't kill ya."

Finn grimaced. "I'll pass, thanks." He sat on his toolbox and took another drink from his flask.

How's that for a view? He gazed out at the wide expanse of sand that stretched toward Sand Point Road, where the Little River began. Here and there were figures walking on the beach beneath a brilliant blue, cloudless sky.

In high school there had always been those who spoke of leaving Maine, of going to the West coast, New York, *anywhere* but Maine, but Finn had never been one of them. That was yet another thing he and his friends had in common—a love of the state. More than that, a love of the ocean, for none of them had ventured too far inland. In his own case, the coast… *pulled* him somehow, and he was never more alive than when he could walk on a beach or smell the sea air. He'd leaped at the chance to work on the hotel. Several months on a site overlooking the shore?

Heaven.

Lewis coughed loudly, and Finn peered at him in concern. "You okay?"

"I'm fine." Then he coughed again, and nodded toward the ocean.

Finn followed his gaze, and stilled. There was a tall man on the beach, walking a gorgeous chocolate Labrador.

He had no clue why this particular man should draw his attention. Finn knew nothing about him, except that he clearly adored his dog, judging by the way they interacted. As for the dog, he or she didn't appear to be that old: maybe it was the puppy-like way the dog bounced and capered on the sand, or the way he tugged on the leash.

Maybe it's as simple as not being able to resist a man who loves dogs.

Not that Finn had any intention of getting any closer. With his family and friends, he felt confident and secure, but when it came to strangers, his shy nature got the better of him every time.

No, his Fantasy Man was better being viewed from afar—and brought to mind when Finn was alone in his bed.

Finn washed the last plate and placed it on the dish drainer.

Did no one ever think of installing a dishwasher in this place? Then he reconsidered. The kitchen was tiny, and everything that *could* have been put in it had been squeezed in, including the washer at the end of the narrow room. It was the first time Finn had encountered a washer in a kitchen, but he figured that was because the place was a rental, with no space elsewhere for it. And the lack of a dishwasher wasn't much of an irritation. Thankfully, Finn had grown up in a house where the kids did the chores, so washing the dishes was nothing new.

His phone buzzed as he poured himself another coffee, and Finn smiled when he saw the name on the screen. "Hey."

"Am I calling at a bad time?" Levi inquired.

"Not at all. I've eaten, I've washed the dishes, so now I'm all yours. What's up?"

"It's about those rocking chairs you made for Teresa and Ry. They're beautiful. So I was *wondering*…"

Finn chuckled. "Aren't you a bit young for a rocking chair?"

"Dork. Okay, yes, I *am* asking if you can make a chair, but it's not for me. It's Grammy's seventieth birthday in June. I thought I'd plan a party for her, and invite as many people from her Christmas card list as I can. She would *love* one of your rocking chairs."

"June? That's doable. Any requests as to which timber I use, or are you going to leave that up to me?"

"I'll defer to your skill and judgement. And I take it you'll be coming to the party."

"Just you try and stop me." Levi's Grammy had been a part of Finn's childhood. She'd brought Levi up since he was a baby, and she'd made Finn welcome every time he visited. Finn had lost count of how many times he'd stayed over at Levi's place when they were growing up.

"It was good to see the whole gang at the wedding. I'm guessing the next time might be the party, depending on who can make it. Seb will be there, because school will have finished for the summer. As for Ben, we'll have to see. He's job-hunting at the moment."

"I thought he had a job?" Finn hadn't heard anything from Ben for a while, and during their catchup he hadn't talked about his work situation.

"Oh, he does, but I don't think he's happy there. Right now he's just looking. But better to look when you already have a job then when you don't." Levi paused. "Can I ask you something?"

Finn stilled. Levi usually came right out with it. "Ask away."

"That remark of yours at the reception… that I'm not the marrying kind. Is that how I come across? Because I *would* marry, in a heartbeat."

"But he'd have to be pretty special," Finn surmised.

"Yeah." Another pause. "How did you know?"

"Well, you're either really secretive about your dates, or you're really picky, because I can't name one guy you've dated." Even in high school, Levi had never spoken of crushes.

"It's just not very high on my list of priorities right now."

"So you haven't got anything going on with Noah?" Finn teased. "I mean, I didn't know about the bowling. Sounds… cute." Not that Finn believed that for a second. Noah was another one who gave little away. Finn picked up his coffee and wandered into the living room where he stood by the window gazing out at the street.

"*No one's* got anything going on with Noah." Levi laughed. "And getting him away from his trains is a miracle, believe me."

"Is he still doing that?" Noah's parents had let him use the space above the garage for his train track when he was a kid. Except Noah had had bigger ideas. He'd decided to build a small town, with a railway looping around and through it.

"He keeps adding stuff. There's a railway station

now, a fair, and the town keeps growing. It makes it really easy to buy him presents for Christmas and his birthday. I just find out what he needs for the model. But now and then, I drag him away from it and we go bowling or to a movie. He comes here sometimes too. Grammy loves it when he stays over."

"At least he's still around." Noah and Levi were the only ones who had stayed in Wells. The rest had all moved away.

"Yeah." Levi chuckled. "And speaking of Noah… Want to know what he said the other day?"

"I don't know why you ask, because you're gonna tell me anyway."

"He said, 'I guess Finn finally caved and joined a gym, like so many other gay men.'"

Finn snorted. "Who needs a gym, when you have to carry planks and boards around a site? And that 'so many other gay men' part…" He had to admit, Noah was an enigma. They'd been friends for years, but Finn still had no clue what made him tick.

Noah didn't give *anything* away.

"Aw, he was just making a joke."

Finn smiled to himself. *Levi the Peacemaker.*

"What about Teresa, putting us all on the same table at the reception?" Levi chuckled. "Because I'm sure it was her idea."

"It wasn't that surprising. We were all pretty tight in high school." Originally, it had been Finn, Levi, and Seb who'd been friends, and as time went by their number had increased. "Do you ever think about how we all got together?"

"Sure. I still say some of us had an invisible sign on our foreheads that said *gay*, that only another gay guy could see."

Whatever had drawn them to each other, Finn thanked God for it. He'd gained two friends who really *got* him, who didn't think he was a weirdo or depraved for liking guys. There had been few students who'd felt like *that*, but knowing Levi and Seb had his back had been a godsend. And Seb didn't give a shit if *everyone* knew he liked dick.

"There was safety in numbers back then," Finn added. He caught something out of the corner of his eye, and froze as his fantasy man walked right by his house, his chocolate lab straining at the leash.

Has he walked by here before? Finn didn't think so. He was certain he would have noticed.

"Finn? You still there?"

"Still here." Finn watched as the tall guy with salt-and-pepper hair turned down Belvidere Avenue, heading for the shore. That was the closest Finn had gotten to him, and he liked what he saw. Fantasy man had to be in his forties or late thirties at a push. And now that Finn had seen him up close, he wasn't about to move from this position in case he missed him coming back.

"You sure about that?"

Finn dragged his gaze away from the window. He knew from experience that Fantasy Man would be at least half an hour on the beach. "So what's with all the reminiscing?"

"I guess I was thinking about high school. Maybe it was seeing you guys. Remember when Aaron started dating that girl—what was her name? Daisy or something?"

Finn laughed. "I remember she didn't last long." When Daisy had found out who Aaron's friends were, she'd dumped him. "You think maybe she felt like we'd infect him or something? That our gay vibes would rub off on him?"

"Who cares what she thought? His next girlfriend was *so* much nicer. Vicky. She was a sweetheart. I think she hung around with Teresa, which makes sense. Teresa didn't give a damn that we were gay either." Levi let out another wry chuckle. "God, you remember that camping trip Aaron organized when we were seventeen? Ry swore it was an orgy."

Finn cackled. "Well, obviously. Eight guys going away for a weekend, in cars stuffed with camping gear… That says orgy to me. That was my first camping trip, and I have to say it was really useful."

"Why useful?"

"It taught me I can't stand camping! The mosquitoes alone… I've avoided it ever since."

Levi laughed. "Once bitten, eh?"

Finn cackled. "I see what you did there. Quick, very quick."

"Have we changed much, do you think?"

Finn glanced toward the window, just in case, but there was no sign. "I think so. I mean, Shaun's quiet, but he always did keep to himself. We just brought him out of his shell a little. Dylan… I still don't know about Dylan."

"What do you mean?"

"I know he dates girls—I think he dated all the girls in our graduating class—but sometimes… I don't know. I mean, we all knew Aaron was straight, but that didn't mean he was always asking questions. Far from it—Aaron acted as if none of it was his business. Dylan, on the other hand…" Dylan had asked a *lot* of questions.

"I just thought he was curious."

"Like Ben was?" It was only in the last four or so years that Ben had come out. Not that any of them had been surprised by his announcement.

Finn chuckled. "Ben was still figuring things out when he joined us."

"He didn't so much join us as we rescued him."

Ben seemed to attract the bullies. Even in junior high, Finn remembered watching Ben fleeing from aggressors during every recess. They seemed to take one look at that baby face, and yearn to punch it. In high school, Big Steve, the janitor, had found Ben cowering in the room that served as Steve's office. He'd told Levi, who had taken Ben under his wing.

"Did you ever wonder about Big Steve?" Finn had. It had felt like an odd thing for Steve to do, to bring Ben to Levi's attention, rather than tell a teacher.

We were better for Ben than any teacher could have been.

"Not then, but years later Seb told me he ran across him in the gay bar in Ogunquit. Apparently, Big Steve's boyfriend was a tiny little thing."

"Wow. Then Steve was looking out for Ben too." Finn smiled to himself. "Why am I not surprised Seb was the one who just *happened* to be in the gay bar? Of all of us, I think he ranks as the one who was always the most out-and-proud." He laughed. "Remember that day we found out he had gay magazines in his gym bag? I still don't know how he had the nerve to bring them to school."

"What I want to know is, how did he get them? He never did say." Finn heard a muted voice in the background. "I'll be right there, Grammy," Levi called out. "Sorry, Finn, gotta go. Let me know how much it will cost for the wood—and your time, of course—for Grammy's chair."

"I'll keep the receipt for the wood, but you are *not* paying me for making it. This is for Grammy, after all."

"Aw, thanks. We'll talk soon, okay?"

"Sure. Go take care of Grammy." Finn disconnected. He stared out of the window at the darkening sky.

So what are you gonna do—stand here all night on the off-chance he comes back?

Finn's inner voice of reason won out, and he reached for the TV remote.

Anything to distract him from the pull of that window.

I wonder what his voice is like?

It wasn't the first time Finn had lain in bed and contemplated the guy on the beach. Finn figured it would be deep, a rich, velvety voice that he could listen to for hours.

I wonder if he talks while he fucks?

And just like that, his thoughts veered off in a more carnal direction that had him reaching for the lube so he could rub one out. It wasn't as if he was ever going to get up enough nerve to talk to the guy, right? This was way safer. Finn could say whatever he wanted, and there was no risk of the guy rejecting him, disappointing him…

"Nice place you've got here." Fantasy Man peered at the living room. *"Quaint."*

Finn snorted. "Is that another way of saying small? And you didn't really come here to talk about the decor, did you?"

"Why do you think I left the dog at home?" His eyes gleamed. "I didn't want there to be any distractions." He smiled broadly. "So... want to show me where your bed is?"

Finn grabbed his hand and led him through the house to his bedroom. Once inside, all the air was punched from his lungs as Fantasy Man propelled him backward onto the bed, where Finn bounced before the guy pinned him to the mattress. His face was above Finn's, those eyes locked on his, his lips so goddamn inviting...

"Kiss me," Finn demanded, pushing up with his hips.

"Just kiss?" His eyes glittered.

Finn grinned. "For starters. We've got all night, right?" Then he moaned as the guy grabbed his wrists and pinned them to the pillow above his head.

"We've got all the time we want."

Finn stroked his cock, lost in his fantasy, trying his damnedest to make it last, to hold onto the dream, because that was all the guy would ever be—an unattainable dream.

Chapter Four

Joel had no sooner finished his call to his client than his phone buzzed again. This time, however, it was Carrie. "Hi there," he said as the call connected, closing the folder on the table in front of him.

"I know you're probably working, so if it isn't a good time to talk, let me know."

"Your timing is good. I just finished a call. What can I do for you?" He knew Carrie hadn't called to indulge in idle chitchat. That wasn't her style.

"It's about Nate's birthday present."

"Don't tell me he's crashed it already." Joel and Carrie had bought Nate his first car. It was three or four years old, in good condition, and perfect for getting him around.

"No, he hasn't, but… I kind of persuaded him it would be good if he visited you."

Joel's stomach clenched. "Look, if he doesn't want to come, don't force him. And I'm not sure I'm happy about him driving all the way from Augusta on his own." It would be a trip just shy of two hours, traffic permitting, but that was a lot of driving for a young man who was used to much shorter distances.

"Neither was I, which is why I suggested that for this first trip, I come with him, and Laura too."

"How did that go down?"

"Put it this way. What are you doing Saturday afternoon?"

Joel froze. "He said yes?"

"He liked the idea of having me along, but I think that's because he's a little nervous about the drive. Laura is dying to see the house, not to mention Bramble. She wants to see you too."

That was enough to make Joel's day. Then her words sank in. "I notice you don't say *Nate* wants to see me."

"I'd be lying if I said he jumped at the chance, but he agreed it was time you all got together. So… I was thinking of us driving down on Saturday, maybe taking Bramble for a walk on the beach, having dinner together, and then if Nate isn't happy about driving in the dark, I can take over and get us home."

"Plus, you like the idea of showing them we still get along, even though the divorce is finalized." Not that they'd ever argued *before* the divorce. It had been a bloodless separation.

"I thought it would be easier if I were there." She paused. "What do you think?"

Joel sighed. "I *think* it's a start. I *think* it's better than nothing. Any suggestions for what to cook? Something they both like?"

"Stick to your famous lasagna and I don't think you can go wrong. Do you want me to bring anything?"

"You're already bringing the kids. That's more than enough." His throat tightened. "Is Nate still unhappy about the divorce? Does he even *talk* about it?"

"Nate isn't saying much about anything, but he has lots of friends whose parents are divorced. He'll get used to the idea. Just like *I'm* getting used to the idea that just when I think one of my chicks has fled the nest, he pops back in again."

Nate had started college in the fall, and had been living in student housing. But when Joel and Carrie had told them about the divorce, and Joel moved out, Nate had made the decision to move back home. It wasn't much of a commute to get to classes, and he clearly preferred it this way. Joel had the impression Nate felt he had to be there for his mom, now she was on her own.

He's a good kid.

"Okay, I'll let you get back to work. I'll text you when we leave home, so you have an idea when to expect us." She chuckled. "You'll know how the trip went if I get there and I'm shaking."

"You'll be fine," Joel said confidently. "Nate's a good driver."

"He should be. He practiced enough with you, outside of his lessons, and you were always a careful driver."

Joel laughed. "Though maybe not as fast as he would have liked sometimes." He had vivid memories of driving along the highway with little Nate behind him in the back seat, yelling, *"Go faster, Daddy!"*

"If our plans change, I'll let you know."

Joel thanked her and then disconnected. Bramble obviously took the sudden silence to mean one thing. He got up off his bed and trotted over to where Joel was working. Bramble sat beside Joel's chair, his tail thumping on the floor.

Joel gave up any idea of work. "Okay, fine, I get it."

Bramble had decided it was time for a walk.

Ten minutes later, Bramble decided they were going to take the route past the fire station, and Joel wasn't about to argue. There was less of a chill in the air, but Joel was still grateful for the thick scarf around his neck. His mind wasn't on the route, but on Nate. Joel was sure Carrie was right, in that Nate and Laura would come around eventually, but he hated the barrier that had grown between him and the kids since they'd announced they were getting divorced. He supposed all kids went through this, and although he knew there had been no fights or disagreements between him and Carrie, his own sense of guilt told him it was right that Nate blamed Joel for the divorce.

He turned left onto Kings Highway, and instead of birds chirping away in the trees, there was the sound of hammer on wood, accompanied by laughter and chatter. The sign next to the sidewalk proclaimed the imminent arrival of a hotel, and if the artist's rendition was accurate, it would fit among the houses that lined the road, facing the ocean.

Joel glanced up at the building. The bare bones of the place were there, a myriad of posts and beams rising from the basement floor. As yet there were no walls, and Joel pitied the men working all day in the fresh ocean air. Then he smiled to himself when he caught sight of one guy who was wearing shorts.

There's always one…

Bramble tugged him toward the beach, and Joel had to pull tight on the leash before they crossed the road. Kings Highway wasn't busy as a rule, although he was sure it would be a different story when summer came. Once they had taken one of the many small paths through the rocks and were on the sand, Joel let out Bramble's leash as far as it would go, and the dog went to sniff along the shoreline. Joel walked at a steady pace toward the northern end of the beach, smiling when he found a piece of driftwood. He picked it up, and that was all it took to bring Bramble pelting back to him. They spent half an hour there, Joel throwing the chunky stick and Bramble chasing it, bringing it back to drop it at Joel's feet. Thirty minutes was about as much as Joel could stand of the bracing air.

"Time to go back."

He swore Bramble's tail drooped with dismay. Joel shortened the leash, and headed for one of the paths that led to the road. He gave the hotel another glance, and discovered he was the object of scrutiny. One of the workmen stood watching him. On impulse, Joel raised his hand and waved. He was close enough to see the guy's smile. When the man waved back, loud voices broke out from the site.

Maybe they're yelling at him because he stopped working.

Joel didn't want to be the cause of the guy getting into trouble. He walked toward Belvidere Avenue, Bramble pulling ahead as usual.

Time to head back to work. He had at least three hours of calls ahead of him. By then, Bramble would be ready for another walk.

Will they still be working at that time? That brief wave had been Joel's first contact with another human being for a few days. The only person he spoke to on a regular basis was the nice lady in the village store.

Maybe it's time I got out and started mixing with people again.

Joel didn't think he was cut out for a solitary life.

By the time Joel heard a car pull up outside, his heart was hammering. He had no idea what to expect. It would have been different if Nate had *wanted* to visit, but Joel got the idea Carrie had twisted his arm. He gave Bramble a warning glance. "Stay." Then Joel opened the door, leaving the screen shut.

Laura was already out of the car and running toward the house, her long wavy hair loose beneath the floppy, wide-brimmed brown hat she wore.

God, she looks like Carrie. Laura had Carrie's coloring, whereas Nate took after Joel. Laura beamed when she saw him. "Dad!" Her gaze went to the foot of the door, as though she expected to see Bramble.

Joel chuckled. "He's inside. If I open the door, he'll be out like a shot." Behind her, Nate and Carrie walked more sedately toward them. Nate's closed expression did nothing to ease Joel's apprehension. Joel waited until the three of them were at the screen door before opening it and standing to one side, ready to catch Bramble if he made a run for it.

As soon as Laura was inside the house, Bramble's self-control disappeared, and he launched himself at her. Laura sank to her knees and giggled as Bramble licked her face. "That tickles." She put her arms around him, a wriggling mass of legs and chocolate fur. "Dad, he's great. Can we take him for a—"

"Don't say the W-word," Joel and Carrie shouted in unison.

Laura laughed. "Don't be silly. He won't know what it means."

"Aw, bless her." Carrie grinned. "It's easy to see we've never had a dog, right?"

Joel coughed. "Don't *I* get a hug, or are they all for

Bramble?"

Laura's eyes widened, and she released Bramble instantly to get up off the floor and hurry over to where Joel stood. She flung her arms around him and hugged him "Hi, Dad."

He laughed. "Hey, sweetheart. You can take the hat off now."

Carrie chuckled. "You'll be lucky. I think it's now part of her head, she wears it so often." Then Laura let go of Joel and went back to fussing over Bramble.

Nate gazed at the interior of the cottage, and the lack of greeting pierced Joel as sharply as a lance. "It's good to see you, son."

Nate flashed him a smile that was gone as quickly as it came. "This place isn't that big, is it?"

"It's big enough for your dad," Carrie assured him. "And there's somewhere for you two to sleep if you want to stay over."

Laura jerked her head to stare at them. "We get to stay?" Her eyes gleamed.

"Not today, but sure, one weekend you can stay over." Joel pointed to the futons. "They open out into beds."

Laura rolled her eyes. "Great. I get to sleep near my brother."

Nate didn't look enthusiastic about the idea. "There's only one bedroom?"

Joel pointed toward the loft. "On the other side of that wall is my bed."

Laura was off the floor in a heartbeat, running toward the stairs. "Can I go look?"

"As if I could stop you," Joel said with a smile. He was thankful Laura hadn't morphed into a sullen teenager, but had retained her natural exuberance and love of life.

Nate on the other hand…

"This is so cool," Laura called out from above their heads before thumping back down the stairs.

"Is there a backyard?" Nate asked.

"Yes, not that there's much to see. There's just a lawn, surrounded by trees. There's also a deck, but if you go out there, be careful. I only do that when Bramble needs to go, and I don't venture far from the back door. Some of those boards look a little dicey to me." Joel looked to Carrie for help, and she gave him a compassionate glance.

"Do you have any hot chocolate?" she asked.

Great idea. Joel nodded. "And coffee for those who want it."

"I'll have coffee," Nate piped up. When Joel blinked, he gave a shrug. "I'm drinking coffee now."

"Only because he thinks he's a *grown up*," Laura interjected. "Well, *I* want hot chocolate." She glared at Nate. "Aren't you gonna say hello to Bramble?"

His chest tight, Joel left them to it. He went into the kitchen and opened the refrigerator to remove the milk. Carrie joined him, her gaze warm.

It'll be okay, she mouthed.

Joel wasn't so sure.

"He's so quiet," Joel commented, staring at Nate's back as he and Laura walked ahead of them with Bramble on the beach. Nate had said barely a word since his arrival. Laura, on the other hand, was obviously making up for lost time.

"That's because Laura hasn't let him get a word in," Carrie observed. She smiled as they strolled. "He loves Bramble, though."

"You'd have to have a heart of stone not to love Bramble." Joel paused, his hands deep in his pockets. "How did the drive go?"

"It went well. Nate used his phone to navigate, and he didn't seem all that nervous."

"He always was a confident kid." Not that Nate was a kid any longer. They resumed their sedate pace. "How's he doing in school?"

"Okay, I think. He's loving his classes. And he seems to be making friends. He's mentioned a few names, mostly girls," she added with a smile.

Joel chuckled. "I don't envy you."

"What does that mean?"

"You get to deal with him when some girl breaks his heart." Although part of him hoped that if such a situation ever arose, Nate would talk to him too.

"Well, I hope he waits a while before he goes and falls in love." Ahead of them Laura and Nate had reached the end of the beach, and had turned around heading back in their direction. Joel and Carrie did a one-eighty, and walked back the way they'd come. Carrie gave a nod toward the hotel. "They seem to be making progress."

"Be thankful you're here on the weekend," Joel told her. "I was out here one day when a woman walked past them. Let's just say they lived up to every conceivable stereotype about builders."

Carrie chuckled. "Has anyone whistled at you yet?"

Joel guffawed. "A gay builder? I think his coworkers

would hang him by his balls from the nearest beam. I did get a wave, however." Behind them, Laura's giggles grew louder, and the sound lifted his spirits. "I'm glad you all came."

Carrie tucked her arm through his. "Maybe next time, the kids will come on their own, if Nate feels up to that."

"He might feel up to the drive. I don't think *that* would be the issue." As to whether Nate would *want* to visit, Joel had no clue.

He shivered, and Carrie leaned in. "How about we all go back to the house, and Laura can help you make the lasagna."

Joel smiled. "Is she getting into cooking now?"

"She baked cookies last week. Okay, so they came out of the box, but she was *so* proud. I figure we should encourage her. As long as she doesn't cut herself. Maybe she can help stir, and *you* do the chopping."

"I like the sound of that." Nate and Laura caught up with them, and Joel gave them a warm smile. "We're gonna head home so we can start work on dinner." Laura let out a gleeful yell. As Nate put distance between them, Joel caught his muttered words as they drifted back to him on the breeze, and they froze his aching heart.

"It's *not* home."

Finn had put off cleaning his truck for as long as possible, but some wiseass writing the words *clean me* in the dirt had been the last straw. It had taken two buckets of soapy water to rid the truck of its layer of grime. He connected the hose to the outside tap, and rinsed off what remained of the suds. As he turned off the water he heard voices approaching. When a chocolate Labrador came into view, his heart beat faster, but then it sank at the sight of the four figures behind the dog.

Well fuck. I guess that answers that *question.*

Fantasy Man had a family.

As the couple and their two children walked past Finn's house, the man glanced in his direction, and Finn gave an internal sigh. *Dear Lord, that is a fine sight.* Short, neat hair, blue eyes, strong jaw line… Finn hadn't said as much to Max, but damn, Fantasy Man was *exactly* his type.

At least I didn't embarrass myself by coming on to him. Oh well. Yeah, like that would *ever* have happened.

It didn't mean Finn would stop looking out for him, however. In a village as small as Goose Rocks Beach, he needed all the eye candy he could find. And he had to admit, there was an illicit thrill in fantasizing about kissing a straight guy.

A straight guy with a great dog.

Maybe it's time I got a dog of my own.

At least he could still have the guy in his fantasies. It was better than nothing.

But only just.

Chapter Five

May

Finn's phone rang as he picked up the boxes of nails. He stacked them precariously before glancing at the screen with a frown. He clicked on *Accept*. "Christ, Ted, I've only been gone a half-hour. Missing me already? I've got the nails, okay? I'll be as fast as I can." The five boxes rested against his chest.

"I was calling to find out how many boxes you were picking up, and to remind you to keep the receipt."

"Well duh. This dumb ole boy would never have thought that. And I've got five. That should keep us going till the next delivery." In the background, he caught Lewis's yelp, followed by "Jesus fucking *Christ!*"

Finn chuckled. "What's he done now? Hit his thumb again?"

"For fuck's sake, dude—another one?" Ted groaned. "He's gone and busted his hammer again."

"Unbelievable. Put him on." Finn scanned the aisles and walked carefully toward the hammers, doing his best not to drop the nails.

"Hey, Finn? Seeing as you're already at the hardware store, can you get me a new claw hammer?" Lewis asked.

"Sure, I'll get you a new one. But can I give you

some advice? Pay the money for a decent one. If you keep buying these POS hammers that cost less than five dollars you've gotta expect them to keep breaking. For God's sake, pay for an Estwing or a Vaughan. Something that will last."

Lewis huffed. "Fine. Just pick one and get your ass back here. I'll be using my dick to drive in the nails till you get here."

For a second Finn was lost for a witty comeback, but then it came to him. "Oh, I'm sorry. I didn't realize we were using teeny tiny nails for this job. I'd better exchange these." He grinned. "You're using your dick? Well, they'll probably go in straighter than when you use a hammer. At least when you bend them, you can pull them out with your asshole. I'll be back as soon as I can." He disconnected, cutting off a spluttering Lewis. He scanned the shelf and picked out a suitable hammer, then headed for the check out. Thank God the hardware store in Kennebunk was only fifteen or so minutes away from the site. And the only reason he'd had to make the trip was because whoever had put together the supplies delivery that morning had forgotten the nails. *Someone* was gonna get their ass kicked when the boss got to hear of it.

He drove down Dyke Road and turned left onto Kings Highway, heading for the spot where he'd parked the truck earlier. It was still empty. As he switched off the engine, he caught sight of a familiar figure crossing the road in front of him, and a familiar dog pulling him along.

Finn's fantasy guy, closer than he'd ever been.

Say something. Be friendly. It didn't matter that the logical part of his brain was screaming *but he's straight.* Then all such thoughts fled his mind as the dog lurched forward sharply, pulling the leash from Fantasy Guy's hand. The dog charged up the beach, heading for the two retrievers playing with their owner at the far end.

"Bramble!" The lab's owner went running after it. "Bramble, get back here."

Finn dove out of the truck and hurried after him. "Don't run after him. Stop. *Stop*."

Fantasy Guy turned to stare at him with obvious incredulity. "But he's running away."

Finn nodded. "And if you chase him, he'll think it's a game. Lie down on the sand."

The guy widened his eyes. "Excuse me?"

"Lie on the sand, face down. Trust me. He'll think you're hurt, and he'll come back to investigate."

Fantasy Guy stared at the far end of the beach where his dog showed no signs of returning, and was barking at the two retrievers. "Fine," he muttered. He lowered himself to his knees, then lay on the sand, his head resting on his arms.

Within seconds, the lab had noticed, and came racing back. He sniffed at him, nudging Fantasy Guy's arm with his nose. Finn took advantage of the dog's focus, and walked around to grab his collar. His owner knelt up and did the same, their hands meeting at the dog's neck.

The owner grabbed the end of the leash. "Okay, I've got him." Then he got to his feet and brushed the sand from his jeans and coat. He gave Finn a grateful glance. "Thank you. I wouldn't have thought of that. You're obviously used to dogs."

"We always had dogs when I was growing up." Finn nodded toward the dog. "He's usually better behaved than this." When the owner blinked, Finn gave a sheepish smile. "You walk him by my house. I live on

Wildwood."

Fantasy Guy gave him a speculative glance. "Weren't you the one who waved to me the other day? From up there?" He pointed to the hotel.

Shit. Busted. "Oh. Yeah. That was me."

From behind him came Max's loud bellow. "Finn. Are you making the nails yourself?"

The dog's owner smiled. "So you're Finn. Thanks again, Finn. And this is Bramble."

Finn couldn't resist. "Does Bramble's owner have a name?"

He laughed. "Oops. I'm Joel." When another cry erupted, calling for Finn, Joel grinned. "Obviously a guy in demand. Well, next time you see me, wave. I'll know who it is." He held out his hand, and Finn shook it. Joel had a firm grip. "And now I'll get back to walking Bramble, but this time, I'll keep a tighter hold on the leash." His eyes sparkled with humor.

Damn, he was sexy as fuck.

Hoots from across the road cut short Finn's observations, and he hurried back to the truck to collect the nails and the hammer. As he crossed the road, Lewis stood there with his arms folded. "Please, don't let us stop you if you have something important to do, like flirting."

"I was *not* flirting. I was helping him."

Lewis's sole response was a quirk of his eyebrows. Then he gave a mock glare. "Hey. We need to talk. Don't ever diss the dick, okay?"

Finn pouted. "Aw. Did I hurt its feelings? I guess that's not so hard to do, given that it's already dealing with a massive inferiority complex." He handed over the hammer and the receipt. "Give that to Jon the next time he stops by. He can add it to my paycheck. He might insist you pay for your own hammer though."

Lewis gave it an experimental swing, smacking the head against his palm. "Hey, not bad. I guess you really do get what you pay for."

Finn glanced at the beach where Joel was strolling along, throwing a ball for Bramble, the leash extended as far as it would go.

"Talk about a gift horse. You couldn't have planned that better if you'd tried. So now you've seen him up-close-and-personal, is he as gorgeous as you thought he'd be?" Lewis asked quietly.

Finn didn't glance at him, but kept his gaze fixed on Joel. "He's even better. Unfortunately, he's spoken for."

"How do you know?"

"Because on Saturday, he walked by my house with his wife and kids."

"Well fuck. Better luck next time."

Finn watched as Joel bent down to stroke Bramble. A fantastic dog, and a very sexy owner, who was definitely *not* available. Lewis had nailed it.

Well fuck.

Joel closed the front door behind him before unfastening Bramble's leash. "You had to go running off, didn't you? You had to go talk to your doggy pals." Bramble gazed at him with those liquid brown eyes, his tail thumping on the floor, and Joel realized he was fighting a losing battle. He could never stay mad at this dog for long. He rubbed Bramble's ears. "Just don't do it again, okay?"

Bramble's soft *woof* might have been *Okay*, but Joel would lay even money it was more a case of *hey, why are you complaining? You got to meet a hot guy, didn't you?*

There was no denying it—Finn *was* hot, from the sweep of his hair off his brow, to those gunmetal eyes, the color of the ocean during a storm, to that scruffy beard and barely-there mustache. And then there was his build: the heavy coat might have hidden his frame, but it was obvious Finn was not a slight man, capable of being blown away by a stiff breeze.

It was no surprise to Joel that the word *stiff* came to mind. And now that he knew where Finn lived, Joel would keep an eye out for him when he took Bramble for a walk.

Down boy. You don't know anything about him—except that he's hot.

Joel went into the kitchen and set up the coffee pot. His work was already on the table, awaiting him. As the coffee dripped he gazed at his surroundings. After almost a month, the cottage was starting to feel like home. *Pity it's a rental.* The apartment he'd moved into in Augusta back in January had felt like a stopgap, a bridging place till he found somewhere more permanent. Joel knew deep down he couldn't live in a city again. The lure of the coast was too great. He wasn't concerned about winter in Maine—they'd moved to Augusta when Nate was two—so he knew what to expect from the climate. Of course, when the snow lay eighteen inches thick he might change his mind, but Joel didn't think so.

I could live here. Joel liked the village and the beach. Any stores he needed were within easy reach, and if they weren't, there was always Portland or Kennebunk. He'd taken on the cottage because he liked the area, and it hadn't taken long to acclimatize. Granted, the cottage wasn't perfect. The decor was a mishmash of styles, the furniture an eclectic mix, and there were parts that needed a severe upgrade or fix. But it served its purpose. It had given him a taste of life on the coast, to the point where he felt he didn't want to look any further.

Maybe I need to check if any properties around here are for sale.

His musings came to a halt when Bramble walked to the back door and sat there, whining.

Joel shook his head. "You were supposed to do that on the beach." He opened the door, and Bramble went tearing outside. It wasn't as if he could run off, as the yard was fenced in. Beyond it was nothing but trees. Joel stood on the deck, waiting while Bramble did his business. He glanced along the back wall of the cottage, and a flutter of movement caught his attention. There was some kind of moth on the wall, its wings spread wide. From his position, Joel couldn't see what kind it was, but its markings piqued his interest. He took a step toward it to see how close he could get, but the wood shattered, and his foot disappeared through the deck.

"Christ." There had been a brief flash of pain, but thankfully the deck was not too high, and he'd only gone through it to a depth of a few feet. Careful to avoid splinters, Joel pulled free of the broken wood. Bramble trotted over and sniffed at it, and Joel grabbed his collar. "That's it. You're not coming out here anymore. You'll end up getting splinters in your nose or paws, or maybe your butt." He led Bramble inside and shut the door.

Joel gave his ankle a rub, but the ache had already subsided. He walked over to the table, picked up his phone, and scrolled through his contacts till he found Mr. Reed, the landlord. When Mr. Reed answered, Joel related what had happened.

Mr. Reed sighed. "Sounds as if I need to add a new deck to the list. I am *so* tired of this."

"I'm sorry, but this is not my fault," Joel remonstrated.

"Oh, I'm not saying it is. It's just that the list of things to be done to that place is never-ending. For one thing, I have to keep replacing furniture. You know that armchair, the one with the sailboats? I got it from Goodwill. One set of tenants spilled red wine over the last one. Since I took on the property, it's been a never-ending search for cheap, second-hand furniture, because buying new just isn't feasible. People don't seem to look after anything these days."

Joel wanted to argue that he wasn't one of those people, but Mr. Reed continued.

"I know the place needs an upgrade. I was intending to do that over the winter, but family matters meant I had to put that on the back burner. And the way I'm feeling right now? I'm seriously thinking of getting out of the property rental business." He chuckled. "I'm sorry. I think this comes under the heading of too much information. You don't need to hear about my problems."

Joel's heart hammered. "If you're serious, I'll buy the cottage from you."

There was silence for a moment. "Excuse me?"

Joel didn't stop to think too much about it. "Well, it sounds as though you've had enough of the place. So… I'll buy it. Of course, the price would have to reflect its present state, and how much I'd have to lay out for the work that needs doing." *And I can't believe I'm even contemplating this.* All he knew was that he *wanted* this.

When Mr. Reed didn't come back with a declaration that he certainly *didn't* intend selling, Joel was heartened. If anything, there was definite interest in Mr. Reed's voice. "You thinking of going into the rental business then?"

Joel gazed at the interior of the cute cottage. "No, I want to live in it. What do you say?" He couldn't recall ever acting so quickly on an impulse, but it felt *right*.

"You haven't been talking to my wife, have you?" Before Joel could inquire what *that* meant, Mr. Reed chuckled. "She was only saying last week that I should get rid of it. How weird is that?"

"Then you'll consider it?"

Another pause. "Let me crunch the numbers, and I'll get back to you. If we can agree on a price, you've got a deal. The wife will be tickled pink." He cackled. "As long as she don't get ideas about going on a cruise with the proceeds. I've got a few ideas of my own."

Oh my God. There was a lightness in Joel's chest, and he wore a grin that only Bramble could see. "I look forward to hearing from you." Joel thanked him and disconnected. He sat on a chair at the kitchen table, and Bramble came over to rest his nose on Joel's knee. Joel stroked his silky head. "Hey boy," he said softly. "We might make this a home after all."

A home Nate and Laura feel happy to visit anytime.

It was an exhilarating feeling, this conviction that all the pieces of Joel's life were clicking into place, that he could finally live the way he'd dreamed of, back when he was seventeen and trying to keep secret the fact that he had a boyfriend.

And that was the final piece—someone to share his life with.

Someone to love.

Chapter Six

Joel was halfway along Dyke Road when he realized he had to tell someone about the morning's events. It had taken Mr. Reed two days to come back to him, but the result had more than made up for the waiting. Joel had been buzzing ever since his call early that morning, and there was only one person who could understand and share in his excitement. He pulled up Carrie's number and clicked *Call*.

"Hey. How are you doing?" She paused. "Are you outside? I can hear the wind."

"I'm walking to the store. I ran out of bread. Listen, I have news. I'm buying a house." Arranging the mortgage had taken up the second half of his morning, and the paperwork would be in the mail.

"Really?" Carrie sounded delighted. "That's awesome. Where is it?"

"Mills Road. A little place called Periwinkle."

Silence. "How can you buy it? I thought it was a rental."

"It is, but the landlord has decided to sell it, and I want to buy it."

"Have you thought this through?"

Joel chuckled. "Trust me, I've thought of little else for the past three days. He came up with a good price, I did the math, and I can afford the mortgage payments.

I really do like the place, Carrie. It feels good. And we agreed I could buy it as is, so at least I'll have furniture. That's one less headache."

"What brought all this on? I thought you were going to stay there for a while, and check out other places."

"So did I, until I put my foot through the deck out back."

"You did what? Are you okay?"

Warmth filled him at the concern in her voice. "I'm fine. Not even scratched. But talking to the landlord got me thinking. I arranged the mortgage this morning. And although it's premature, because I don't own the place yet, the first thing I need to do is sort out some repairs. Starting with that deck."

"If you're *really* buying the place, then don't repair it. Why not have an all-new-and-improved deck? Tear down the old one, and build a new one from scratch."

Joel liked that idea. "In that case, I'd better start looking for help." He stopped outside the store. "I'll call you when I have more news."

"Joel? I'm really happy for you. I'm glad you're putting down roots."

"Me too. I just didn't expect to be doing it so soon." They disconnected, and he went into the store.

The lady who was usually behind the cash register was stacking cans on the shelves. She smiled as he entered. "Hello there. Where's that gorgeous dog of yours?"

"At home. And you're going to be seeing more of us." That buzz hadn't abated in the slightest. "I'm buying a house."

She beamed at him. "Congratulations."

He thanked her, and went over to the bakery section, peering at the loaves. On the wall between the shelves was a noticeboard, covered in leaflets, notices, rewards offered for info about lost cats, and business cards. He stood in front of it, noting there were cards offering the services of a plumber, an electrician, a pool cleaner—and a card depicting someone sawing a piece of wood.

Aha. Joel looked closer. At the bottom of the card in white lettering were the words *Finn Anderson, Carpenter,* followed by a phone number. *Finn?* It had to be the same guy. Joel got out his phone and took a photo of the card. He paid for his bread, left the store, and hurried back home. Once inside, he pulled up the photo and made a note of the number. When he called it, the voice that answered was obviously the same man who had helped him on the beach. And now that Joel thought about it, Finn's voice was as sexy as his appearance.

"Finn Anderson here."

Joel cleared his throat. "Hi. This is Joel Hall. We met on the beach a few days ago, when you helped me—"

"Oh. Okay, I remember you. But... how did you get my number?"

"I saw it on your business card in the village store. That's why I'm calling. I'm buying a property and there are a number of jobs that need doing. And seeing as we've already met..." Joel paused. "That is, if you think you can fit me into your work schedule. The hotel site must keep you busy."

Finn laughed. "That's what evenings and weekends are for. Would you like me to come take a look, so I can see what I'd be undertaking?"

Joel smiled to himself. "That would be great. I live at 350 Mills Road. When could you stop by?"

"I could come over after work today. I usually finish

by about four. Would that be okay?"

"Any time after four o'clock would be good." Finn needed to see the place in daylight. "I'll see you then." Joel disconnected and put down his phone, his pulse quickening. *This is really happening.* He already knew Finn was a good guy. *Let's see if he's a good carpenter too.* Then he reasoned. *He's helping build a hotel. The man has to have some skills.*

Joel knew his rapid pulse was nothing to do with the prospect of a new deck, and *everything* to do with the attractive man who was coming to assess the work required.

Finn pulled off the road and up the driveway that led to Joel's house, and switched off the engine. Mills Road was lined with trees, with houses tucked in here and there. Joel's place was quaint, but one glance at the front porch told him it needed some TLC. He grabbed his notepad from the passenger seat, checked his pocket for a pen, and got out of the truck. Before he'd reached the front door, it opened, and Joel stood behind the screen.

"If you grew up with dogs, then I take it you have no problems with dog drool."

Finn chuckled. "Aw, he's just a puppy. And a little drool never killed anyone." Joel opened the screen door, and Finn stepped inside quickly. Bramble was there in an instant, tail wagging, his eyes bright, and everything about him saying *Pet me.* Finn bent down and stroked him, admiring the glossy coat. "He's gorgeous."

"He's my first dog. I think I lucked out."

Finn straightened, then glanced around at the interior. "Have you already bought this place?"

"At the moment I'm renting it, but the mortgage is going through as we speak."

Finn arched his eyebrows. "I obviously missed this one when I rented mine. Yours is way better."

"You rent too?"

"It's the best way. I go where the work is, but the last few years I've worked mainly on the coast, building houses mostly." He liked Joel's place. The windows let in more light than in Finn's rental, which had a dark, claustrophobic feel to it.

"Ever thought of building your own house?" Finn stared at him, and Joel frowned. "Did I say the wrong thing?"

"No, not at all. It's just… that's been my dream for as long as I've been a carpenter. To put by as much as I can, and either buy a plot, or a house I can tear down to build another in its place."

"What kind of house?"

Finn smiled. "One with lots of glass, to bring the light in. To be able to see the ocean. To hear the waves."

"*Now* you're talking." Joel's eyes sparkled. "That sounds like my idea of heaven."

Finn was already gazing at *his* idea of heaven, and the view was improving by the second.

Mind on the job, dude. Get your mind on the job.

"Yeah, it sounds wonderful, right? Except land like that doesn't come cheap. I might have enough by the time I retire." Finn grinned. "Only another forty-one years and…" He counted on his fingers. "Four months to go. Having said that, I can't see me still doing this when I'm in my sixties."

"It must be a very physical job," Joel observed. He looked Finn up and down. "But obviously one that keeps you fit."

Finn fought the urge to gape. *Did Mr. Married Straight Man just check me out?* He pushed the thought aside, dismissing it as nothing more than bedtime fantasies intruding into real time. *Mind on the job, remember?* He glanced around again, nodding. "This is a nice place. I like it." He smirked. "Show me this deck you made a mess of."

Joel beckoned with his finger. "This way." He led him toward the back door, pausing at the threshold. Joel smiled. "No, Bramble, you are *not* going out there. You just peed anyhow."

Finn loved how Bramble lay down, his head resting on his front legs, seeming for all the world as though he was sulking. Finn followed Joel through the screen door and out onto a deck. Finn saw instantly where Joel had gone through: he'd covered it with cardboard. The deck wasn't all that big, with space for a couple of small chairs, and at one corner was a single steep step that led down to the yard.

Finn stepped off the deck and walked to the rear fence. He turned and gazed back at the house, trying to envision how it could appear. "So… Am I fixing the deck? Or making a new one?" He already knew which way he wanted to go.

Joel joined him, chuckling. "You sound like my ex-wife. She thinks I should build a new one." He'd put on a thick coat.

His ex-*wife?* Finn was dying to ask if that was the

woman who'd been with him the other day, but it was none of his beeswax. "I agree with your ex." He opened his notepad, removed his pen from his pocket, and sketched quickly. "Right now the deck is lower than the threshold, but you could raise it. A deck shouldn't be more than two inches below the bottom of the door used to access it. And you've got enough space out here to make it bigger."

"How big?" Joel asked.

"Big enough for a table and four chairs. You could have dinner out here on summer evenings. I'd put a railing around it and steps leading down to the yard. If you want to go all out, you could have a pergola covering half of it." His pen flew over the paper.

"Really?"

Finn paused. "I don't know if you're into gardening, but you could grow fragrant flowers like honeysuckle and jasmine that would climb up the posts and cover the beams. It would be beautiful out here in the summertime. Plus, you can hang strings of little lights over it." He could see it in his head. "Maybe something like this?" He showed Joel the sketch.

Joel glanced at the notepad. "That looks amazing."

Finn smiled. "Thank you. I find it helps the client to visualize what I'm describing. *But…*"

Joel chuckled. "I figured there had to be a *but* in there somewhere. I was assuming that would be the price."

Finn laughed. "I'll get to that in a minute. I was *going* to say…I could have everything I just described done by the summer, but to do that, I'd need you to help, if you can. If you can't, I'll find someone who can."

"What kind of help? What are we talking about here?"

"I'm not suggesting you help with the installation. But before I start work…" He gave Joel a speculative glance. "This all assumes I get the job."

Joel laughed. "Keep going. You're doing fine. Put it this way, I don't think I'll be calling anyone else, unless you come up with a price that makes my head spin and my wallet weep."

Finn resisted the urge to do a fist pump. "Okay then… Before I start, the old deck will need to be disassembled, the debris and the supporting poles removed, the ground leveled—and dig holes for new posts." He flashed Joel a quick grin. "And *those* tasks would be down to you."

Joel didn't appear fazed by the idea. "I can dig."

Finn locked eyes with him. "We're talking holes that go down deep, maybe three feet, because they gotta be below the frost line. Then we fill them with concrete to support the new posts. I don't know if your job allows you any time to do this, which is why I'm saying I can find more help if I need to." He knew some of the guys at work would lend a hand.

Joel's confident smile gave Finn his answer before he'd uttered a word. "I'm a financial adviser. My office is in Augusta, and I spend one or two days a week there at the most. The rest of the time, I work from home, or I drive to meet with clients. So yes, I can help. Not sure how good I'll be at digging…"

"I'll measure up for you, and show you where the posts should go. Once the concrete is in, I'll do the rest." Bramble appeared at the back screen door, and Finn smiled. "He could keep me company while I work," he joked.

"I'm not sure that's a good idea. He can be a distraction."

Not as much of a distraction as you'd *be.* Finn was torn between hoping Joel wouldn't be around while he worked, and wanting to see more of him.

"About the disassembling part..." Finn grinned. "Do you want the easy way or the hard way?"

"Tell me both."

Finn cocked his head to one side. "Ever wielded a chainsaw?"

"No." Joel widened his eyes.

"I ask because that's one way to go really fast—chop, chop, chop, and it's gone. But some folks get nervous around a chainsaw. The second way is to use a Sawzall—that's a reciprocating saw to you laymen—or a Skil saw. You cut the deck into sections, then cut it into manageable pieces for transporting to the transfer station. And the third way? You get yourself a screwdriver and remove it screw by screw, board by board."

Joel gaped at him. "Hell no. Taking it down screw by screw? Forget that. I'm not happy about the chainsaw idea, but I could probably handle a Sawzall... except I don't have one."

"I have two," Finn told him. "I can loan you one. Just make sure you've got safety goggles and gloves." He closed the notepad. "So... you're happy with the plans?"

Joel beamed. "Perfectly happy. Of course, I'm saying this before I know how much it's all going to cost. I take it you've built decks before?"

Finn nodded. "I know what I'm doing."

"I don't doubt it. You strike me as very capable." There was that up-and-down glance again, only now Finn was certain—he was being checked out.

There was that voice again. *But he's straight, remember?*

A wife, kids?

An *ex*-wife. *Don't forget that part.*

Such thoughts were getting him nowhere.

Finn cleared his throat. "Okay. If you were to build it yourself, the *average* cost would be around twenty-five dollars per square foot, but that's just the materials. The final price would depend on the materials used, the size, the installation…"

"How big were you thinking?"

Finn rubbed his chin. "Maybe a twelve-by-twelve deck? You don't want it much bigger than that, and in this space, it wouldn't overpower the yard. Or, it could go along the entire back of the house, and not come out as far. So you could also have furniture out here—a sofa, chairs, an ottoman…" He grinned. "What they call a Patio Conversation Set nowadays." When Joel's eyes widened, Finn knew he'd hit the mark.

"What are the choices for materials?"

"You can have pressure-treated wood, hardwood, composite…"

Joel stared at the house, and Finn could almost hear the cogs clicking. "So if you had to put a price on it? I'm asking what your idea would be of the maximum I'd have to spend. Just so I know how much to budget for it."

Finn did some swift mental calculation. "Seven thousand, tops." He knew some companies out there would charge ten to fifteen grand for such an installation, but he wasn't greedy. He also knew he'd do a stellar job that Joel would be happy with.

Joel didn't even wince. "Deal."

Finn beamed. "When would you want me to start?"

Joel grinned. "Seeing as you won't be starting anything until I've done the groundwork, should it be more of a question of when *I* can start?"

Finn laughed. "Good point." Yeah, he really liked this guy. Decisive, funny, clearly intelligent... and the perfect age. *Damn.*

"When I've signed all the papers, we can talk again. But I like the idea of having this done in time for the summer."

"And you're sure you're okay preparing the site? I'd do it, but we're only talking evenings and weekends when I'd be available. It'll save time in the long run."

Joel nodded. "I might rope in my kids one weekend." His face tightened for a moment, and something flashed across those blue eyes. Something that looked an awful lot like pain.

What's hurting you, Joel?

As quickly as the thought flitted through his mind, another was hot on its heels. *Don't get involved. It's none of your business.*

Finn replaced his pen in his pocket. "About using the Sawzall..."

"I know I've never handled one, but how difficult could it be?"

Finn bit his lip. *Out of the mouths of babes...* "I'll show you how to use it when I bring it over. But if you do get your kids to help out, keep it out of their reach?" He smiled. "They look like they're sensible kids."

Joel blinked, his brow furrowing. "But how—" Then his forehead smoothed out, and his eyes twinkled. "You saw them, when we walked past. That day you were cleaning your truck."

The fact that Joel remembered only added more fuel to the fire.

Seems as though I wasn't the only one looking.

"I won't keep you any longer," Joel said suddenly.

"You must want to get home for your dinner. I'll call when things are settled." He extended his hand, and Finn shook it. "Thanks for coming over. You've gotten me excited about the prospect. I can't wait to get started."

Neither could Finn, but for very different reasons.

Joel walked him through the gate that led to the side of the house, and up to his truck. He stood in the driveway while Finn backed out onto the road, checking his mirrors for traffic. He gave Joel a final wave, then pulled away.

Joel was a mystery, one that Finn was dying to unravel, no matter what his head told him.

I want to learn more about him.

Once he started installing Joel's new deck, Finn might have the chance to do just that.

Chapter Seven

Joel poured himself a glass of whiskey and sat in the rocking chair. From his bed, Bramble raised his head and peered in his direction, then lowered it and closed his eyes. Joel gazed at the living room, mentally placing his possessions around it. He'd put a lot of things into storage when he'd first moved out, and now that he finally had a home it was time to think about reclaiming them. Carrie had his vinyl collection, not to mention the turntable that had belonged to his dad. There was no way Joel could ever think of parting with it: his dad had given it to him when Joel had left for college. Nate had teased him about it, offering to convert all his vinyl records into a digital format. Joel accepted his offer, knowing when Nate was done, he would still listen to his favorite music in its original form.

There were prints too, that he'd acquired over the years. Right then they were wrapped in sheets and standing in Carrie's garage. Joel assessed how much wall space he'd have. Enough for a few of them.

He picked up his phone from the top of the bookcase and scrolled through to Carrie's number. "Hey. Okay to talk?"

"Definitely. Your daughter is driving me nuts."

"I notice she's always *my* daughter when she's being problematic, but *yours* when she gets amazing grades at school," he teased. "What's she doing now?"

"She wanted help with her science homework. You know, the stuff I was never any good at, so I always steered her in your direction?" Carrie let out a sigh. "Is it okay to say I miss you right now?"

"I missed you too this morning," he confessed.

"You did?"

"Yeah. You always could cook eggs better than me."

She laughed. "Thanks for that. What can I do for you?"

"I've been thinking about retrieving some of my stuff from storage, now I have a roof to call my own." Not that he'd had it all that long—one week, in fact—but he was itching to put his mark on the place.

"Ooh, I like the sound of this. Especially if it means I get more space around here. I'll bring you a carload this weekend."

"Hey, not so fast," he said, laughing. "Can I at least give the place a lick of paint before you do that?"

"I suppose," Carrie said with obvious feigned reluctance. "Let me know what you want."

"Actually, a visit this weekend might be a good idea. I'm taking the old deck apart, and I wondered if the kids would like to help out."

"Want me to ask them?"

"Sure." He sipped his whiskey while he waited, aware of the muted rumble of voices. He was pretty sure Laura would be on board—Nate was another matter. Joel had expected some reaction to the news he was buying the place, but there had been none.

It's as if he doesn't care anymore what I do. The thought stung him. There was little Joel could think of doing that would alter the situation. The only solution was to bide his time and hope Nate came around.

"Okay. Laura squealed and is now bouncing off the walls, so thank you for that. Nate said he'll come."

Joel didn't have the heart to ask what Nate's exact words had been.

"Can you send your gardening gloves with them? If they're going to be handling the old decking, I don't want them getting splinters."

"I'll search out three pairs."

"Three?"

"Of course. I'll need a pair too." She paused. "That's if you don't mind me tagging along."

"Yeah right, as if I'd mind. If you're sure…"

"I'll sweeten the deal. You and the kids work on pulling the deck apart, and I'll bring food. I'll whip up a casserole that you can shove in the oven. How's that?"

"You're awesome." His chest tightened. "I'm sorry."

"For what?"

"I should have been honest with you from the start." He didn't deserve her.

In the silence that followed, Joel caught the murmur of his kids' voices: Laura's laughter, Nate's deeper rumble…

"Sweetheart." Carrie's soft sigh filled his ears. "I was glad when you finally told me everything. It helped me see the situation from a different perspective. I do understand why you asked me on a date all those years ago. You couldn't be yourself, so you had to create a persona that would fit in. And while I'm sorry we didn't have the kind of marriage I'd hoped for, I will *never* forget that it brought us the two wonderful human beings who are currently arguing about whose turn it is to load the dishwasher."

He chuckled. "They *are* wonderful. And I can't wait to see them Saturday. If you time it right, you might get to meet Finn. He's the guy who's going to transform my yard—when he's not working on that new hotel, of course."

"He's one of those guys? Why am I suddenly picturing a heavyset guy with his jeans halfway down his ass, a belch that would frighten small children, and sausage fingers?"

Joel laughed. "I'm happy to report that description doesn't fit him in the slightest. He's coming over Saturday to loan me some of his tools—and make sure I can use them without risking any limbs."

"Good luck with that."

"What does that mean?"

"*One* of us is mechanically inclined, and it isn't you."

"Hey!" he said in mock indignation.

"Tell me I'm wrong."

"I'm ending this call right now."

Carrie let out a hoot. "See? You know I'm right." They both laughed at that. "Okay, I'd better go see if Laura has gotten her head around the basics of DNA. When she told me what they were studying, she said she'd thought it would be easy, because she already knew all about it, having seen *Jurassic Park*."

Joel groaned. "To quote you—good luck with that." They said goodbye, and he disconnected. Joel shook his head. "'*Jurassic Park*'." He smiled. If Finn was around when Carrie arrived, she'd see just how wrong her assumptions had been.

Then he had another thought. Now Carrie had Eric, she might decide Finn was exactly what Joel needed.

Please, Carrie, don't try your hand at matchmaking. Because he had no idea if Finn was into guys, and if he wasn't, Joel would die of embarrassment.

Finn was reaching for a lump of cheese in the deli section of the Goose Rocks General Store when his phone buzzed. He smiled when he saw it was Seb. "Hey. Why aren't you busy grading papers?"

Seb snorted. "Because it's six o'clock and I just got in from school. Staff meeting. Long-ass day. Where are you?"

"Shopping for groceries." Finn dropped the cheese into his basket. The chocolate muffins caught his eye. "And debating whether or not to buy one chocolate muffin or two."

"Go with two. The way *you* burn off calories?"

Finn laughed. "Jealous much?" Seb was forever keeping an eye on his figure. He picked up two and added them to the basket. "Okay, why are you calling?"

"Do I need a reason?"

Finn laughed so loud, the customers in the store all looked in his direction. "You always have a reason. Spit it out."

"Hey, I just wanted to catch up, that's all. You know, find out what's new in your life…"

"You must be bored. Either that, or you're putting off doing something you *really* don't wanna do."

There was a pause. "Man, you know me far too well."

"After all these years? You know it. Come on, what's up?"

"I have to prepare for tomorrow. I'm being observed."

Finn's heart went out to him. "I forgot. You're working toward Professional certification now, aren't you? How's it going?"

"I did *not* call you to talk about teaching. Let's talk about something else. You getting any yet?"

Finn came to a halt in the middle of the produce section. "Did you miss the part where I said I'm at the store?"

"You getting all dainty on me? You work construction—I bet the air turns blue when you and your work buddies shoot the breeze."

"Sure—when there's no one around to listen in." Finn went to the cash register, deposited his basket, and helped the lady load everything into paper bags. "Can you wait just one minute till I get to my truck?"

"I can do that. It's not like I have something better to do."

"Yeah, you do—lesson planning, remember? I'll call you back." Finn pocketed his phone, paid for his groceries, and carried his bags out to the truck that was parked in front of the cedar shakes-covered building. He dumped them on the passenger seat, got behind the wheel, and hit *Call*. "Okay—*now* we can talk. Not that I have anything to share, but I didn't want the whole store knowing my sex life is a wasteland."

"Still? Jesus, you are *way* too picky."

"I'm not," Finn protested. "You know how it is. I'm always nervous about taking that first step."

Seb went quiet for a moment, and Finn glanced at his screen to check they were still connected. Finally Seb let out a gentle sigh. "You know your problem?"

"Enlighten me. Because I *know* you're dying to."

"You give your heart too easily. You meet a guy, you go on a date, you fuck, and suddenly he's your boyfriend. You give it a hundred and fifty percent. Only thing is, the guys you pick don't want that. *They* get a few weeks, maybe even a month, of great sex, and then they wanna move on. You part ways, they go on to the next guy, and *you* spend a while nursing a bruised heart. It knocks you down, and it takes you forever to work up enough courage to put yourself out there again, because for all your talk when you're among friends, you're a shy guy. And when you *do* make a move again? Boom. Instant replay."

Finn swallowed. "I guess you really know *me* well too." It pained him Seb saw so much, but then again, it was good to know.

"Only because we talk about every goddamn thing in our lives. How many boyfriends have there been since that first guy you met at Millbury when you were doing your training? Two?"

"Three."

"Mm-hmm. So that's three boyfriends in what, eight years? And none of them were long-term, were they?"

"No. But before you say another word... I'm not you, Seb. I don't do one-night stands. I can't be that casual about it." Finn didn't want just sex, he wanted the whole package.

"Has it ever occurred to you," Seb said in a voice so low that it sounded nothing like him, "that I do one-night stands because that's all I can get? It might surprise you to learn we're a lot more alike than you think."

In that moment, Finn truly *saw* him, and his chest tightened. "I'm sorry."

"I know how you all see me. The happy-go-lucky guy who doesn't give a fuck, the slut, the—"

"I have *never* thought of you like that, and I don't

think any of the others feel that way either," Finn said, his voice rising. "I know I joke about you making your way through the entire gay population of Maine, but that's all it is, a joke. *And* it's based entirely on shit you come out with, so can you blame me?"

Seb sighed. "Fair point. Okay, now you know. It's an act. And for what it's worth, I hope you find someone deserving to give your heart to. Because they'll be getting a great guy."

"Thanks." Finn made a promise to himself right there to never again tease Seb about his sex life.

"So there's really nothing new in your life?"

Finn paused, staring at the gray walls of the store. "Well…"

"There *is* something. Spill."

"There's this guy…"

Seb hooted. "Isn't there always? Who is he? How'd you meet him?"

"Whoa, not so fast." Finn related how he'd watched Joel from afar, and how they'd finally met, not forgetting the part where he could have sworn Joel was checking him out while they discussed the deck.

"So he's divorced?"

"Sounds like it. It doesn't appear to have been a bad break-up, judging by how they looked when they walked by the house. They seemed… happy. Relaxed. And it's not as if I'm gonna make a move on a straight guy, so I don't even know why I'm telling you about him."

"You're *telling* me because you're interested in him, and there's nothing wrong with that." Seb chuckled. "It gives you something to think about on those long, cold nights, right?"

Finn laughed. "Yeah, you know me *way* too well."

"Did you ever stop to think he might be bi? That might account for him checking you out—*if* that's what he was doing."

In the days since, Finn had come to the conclusion he'd imagined those glances. "You know what? I'm not gonna think about this. Why torture myself? I'm just gonna go there, get the job done, and leave."

"Wait—you're going there?"

Finn let out a noise of exasperation. "Did you *miss* the part where I said I'm going to build him a new deck? I'm going over there Saturday to show him how to use the saw, so he can break up the old deck."

"Okay, so you're going to build his deck. And in the meantime, you get to work in his yard, play with his dog, watch him up close…" Seb cackled. "Just don't get a boner while you're doing it."

"Okay, we're done. Get your lesson plan ready, Mr. Teacher. No more procrastination."

"You can be real evil, you know that?"

"Yup. But you know I love ya."

Seb went quiet for a second. "Love you too, man. You and the rest of our little gang. Are you going to Grammy's birthday party? I told Levi I'll be there. School finishes for the summer the week before."

"I'll be there. But I think we need to plan a get-together just for us. One where we can catch up."

"I'm up for that. You can all stay at my place. Of course, some of you will end up sleeping on the floor, unless we camp out in the backyard." He chuckled. "Because I *know* how much you love camping."

"Dork."

"Wow, such restraint. I thought that would at least merit a *Bitch*."

Finn laughed. "You have work to do. Talk soon?"

"You know it. Have fun with Joel Saturday." He disconnected before Finn could respond.

Finn wasn't sure how much fun he could expect from a quick session on how to use power tools, but hey, at least he'd get to be around the guy for a while.

And Bramble. Don't forget Bramble. That dog was adorable. Then he sighed. *Who am I kidding? They both are.*

Joel was funny, gorgeous—and unattainable. Talk about torture…

Chapter Eight

Joel took one final look around the place to make sure everything was as it should be. Carrie was due any minute, and Joel's heart was pounding. The last five months had been hard on him. He knew what he wanted—for the kids to feel comfortable enough to visit whenever they felt like it—but that would rely on Nate's willingness to make the trip.

I think we're still a way off that.

He knew what Carrie feared—that he was skating a thin line by not telling them everything. 'Wait too long,' she'd said, 'and they'll believe you don't trust them enough.' Nate wasn't coping with the divorce. Surely learning Joel was gay would only aggravate the situation.

Bramble got up from his bed and ran to the door, his tail wagging. He pawed at it with a soft whine.

"Are they here, boy?" Joel peered through the window. Sure enough, Nate's car was in the driveway, and Laura was already heading toward them. No sooner had Joel let her in, than she bolted toward the back of the house, Bramble dashing after her.

Joel laughed. "Going someplace? Don't I even get a Hi, Dad?"

"You'll be lucky," Carrie said as she came through the door, Nate behind her. "All she's been talking about the whole trip is attacking that deck. I had no idea we'd raised such a destructive daughter." She kissed Joel on the cheek.

Nate gave him a nod. "Hey, Dad."

Joel opened his mouth to ask how the drive had been, but Laura's plaintive cry cut him off. "I want to see what I'm demolishing."

"Hey, you're not demolishing anything," Joel told her. "*Your* task is to move stuff out of the way, and make sure your dad always has something to drink." He pointed to a clear plastic water bottle sitting on the kitchen table. "See that? If you see it getting empty, refill it. And if you're moving pieces of wood, always wear gloves."

Laura rolled her eyes. "You're as bad as Mom." She peered at the table. "Hey, what's this?" She picked up Finn's sketch of the proposed deck. Joel had left it there to show them.

"*That* is what is going to be built out there."

"Can I see?" Carrie walked over, her hand outstretched. Laura gave it to her.

"This is what Finn came up with."

Carrie nodded approvingly. "I think it will be beautiful. I can't wait to see it." She peered over her shoulder to where Nate still stood in the living room. "Come look at this. You'll find it interesting."

That had been Joel's hope too. But before Nate could see it, Laura got in first. "*Now* can we go out into the yard?"

Joel laughed. "Fine." He led them to the back door and unlocked it. Bramble was through the gap in a heartbeat, and Laura chased him, chuckling. Nate walked out onto the deck and glanced at the hole.

"Is that where your foot went through?"

Joel nodded. "The boards are a bit rotten. I think there's a leak from the gutter above. The rain poured through and rotted the wood." He cocked his head at the sound of a car engine. "That'll be Finn." Joel stepped off the deck and went around the side of the house to the gate.

Finn was walking toward the rear of his truck. "Hey, nice timing." He opened the flap and lifted out two large toolboxes. "You can help me carry them through." He peered at Nate's car. "Hey, is this a bad time? Only, your text said whenever."

"Carrie—that's my ex—and the kids are here. Come and meet them." Joel picked up one of the toolboxes and winced. "What have you got in here?"

Finn chuckled. "You haven't spent much time around power tools, have you? Lead the way. I'll come back for the rest."

"You mean there's more?" Joel exclaimed, feigning shock.

Finn merely grinned. He followed Joel through the gate, carrying the other toolbox. Joel did the introductions, and after putting down his tool chest, Finn shook hands with Carrie.

She glanced at the toolboxes and smirked. "So you're the one who's going to show Joel how to use a reciprocating saw?" Her eyes glittered. "Be afraid. Be very afraid."

Joel flashed her a mock glare.

Nate gazed with obvious interest at the toolboxes. "Do you use a lot of tools?"

"Anything to make life easier," Finn told him. "Back when I was training to be a carpenter, we had one teacher who told us the complete history of carpentry, going back as far as Egypt and ancient Greece, with a brief stop in the middle ages and the industrial revolution. He told us he used to measure using string and a tape. Nowadays, of course, it's all lasers and GPS." Finn squatted beside the toolbox and patted it. "Power tools are our friends."

Nate's eyes sparkled. "I want to be an architect."

Finn beamed at him. "Yeah? That's good. You at college?"

Nate's chest swelled. "I'm studying architecture at UMA."

Finn's eyes widened. "Way to go. Your portfolio must've impressed them."

"I guess." Nate gave a shy smile. "Did you always want to be a carpenter?"

"I hope you don't mind all the questions," Joel said quickly. Not that Finn appeared to mind, but Joel didn't know him all that well.

"Not at all," Finn assured him. "An interest in power tools? That's in our DNA, isn't it?"

Carrie laughed. "It might be in *my* DNA, but I'm not sure it's in Joel's." She gave him a sweet smile. "I think the correct term is mechanically challenged."

Nate chuckled at that.

Joel gave an exaggerated sigh. "Fine. Rub it in." He couldn't deny it.

Finn got to his feet. "Well, I'm here to show him how to use the tools." His eyes twinkled as he gazed at Carrie. "Maybe I should be showing *you*."

Nate let out a louder chuckle.

Carrie smiled. "Hey, he might have improved with age."

Joel coughed. "I'm right here, you know. How about you let Finn do what he came here for?"

"I think that's my cue to make the coffee," Carrie

said diplomatically. She glanced at the kids. "Guys? How about you bring Bramble inside? I don't think Dad wants him out here because there are going to be nails and stuff." Laura grabbed Bramble by the collar and tugged him toward the door, Bramble doing his best to resist. Carrie held the door for her, then closed it behind them, giving Joel a sympathetic smile.

"Can't I help?" Nate asked.

Joel narrowed his gaze. "What you *really* mean is, can I stay so I can watch Dad make an ass of himself?"

Nate laughed. "Hey, you said it, not me."

Finn reached into one of the toolboxes and pulled out a crowbar. "Here. Have at it. And if it's okay with your dad, I'll let you do some chopping too."

Nate beamed. "Great." He glanced at Joel. "That would be okay, wouldn't it?"

As if Joel was about to kill the mood. "Sure. Just let me get the hang of it first?"

Finn cleared his throat. "Can I have your full attention, please?" He opened the other toolbox and removed its contents. "Okay, this is a Sawzall. It can cut through just about anything. I've chosen this blade because it'll go through wood and nails." He tapped it with his fingertip. "Quick rule of thumb. The fewer the teeth per inch, the faster and rougher the cuts."

"If my dad is doing it, it'll be rough," Nate called out.

Joel gave him a mock glare. "I've changed my mind. Don't you have a puppy to pet, or something?"

Nate grinned. "This is much more fun."

"Give it up, *Dad*," Finn said with a chuckle. "I need all your attention."

Joel peered at the saw. "Don't you have to plug it in?"

Finn bit his lip. "Er, Joel? It's cordless." He tapped the squat base beneath the handle. "This is a heavy-duty battery." He held the saw out to Joel. "Wanna hold it?"

"Not really."

Finn laughed. "Okay, one hand on the handle, the other around here." He indicated the molded black section behind the blade.

Joel took it from him. "It's heavier than I thought."

"And it has some kick. You need to hold tight with both hands, and use some pressure to keep in control." Finn pointed to the railings around the deck. "You're going to cut through the base of that railing. Use the shoe—that's this guard here—to steady it. That'll cut back on the vibration."

Joel turned the power tool onto its side, laying the blade flat against the deck, the shoe snug up against the edge. Finn nodded approvingly. "Okay, you're ready. Go for it."

The second he turned it on, Joel understood what Finn had meant by vibration. He slid the blade across the base of the railing, and it went through like butter. Joel grinned. "Hey, I did it."

"Yes you did. Easy, right? And now I'll show you how to make a plunge cut." Finn glanced at Joel's body. "I'm just checking you're not wearing anything loose. You don't wanna get your clothing caught up in this." He pointed to the middle of the deck. "You're going to aim the tip of the blade here, at an angle. Just be careful when you cut through, because there's no guard on this thing. Don't pull it toward your body."

"I think I know what I'm doing." Well, he had an idea, but with Nate standing there, Joel wasn't about to admit the tool intimidated him.

"Good, but I think I'll stick around a while longer

and watch you in action," Finn told him. "At least until I feel you're comfortable with it."

Joel said nothing, but secretly he was pleased. He didn't want to take up too much of Finn's afternoon, but he hoped Finn would stay.

"Come on, Dad," Laura yelled. "Finn has run out of things to cut up."

Joel had no idea how it had happened, but chopping up the deck had somehow become a race. His job was to cut through the boards with the Sawzall, Finn would chop them into smaller pieces with the Skil saw, and the kids carried them to Finn's truck.

The only problem was Finn was working a hell of a lot faster than Joel.

"Yeah, Joel," Finn said with a grin. "Give me something else to chop up."

Joel speared him with a look. "You weren't even supposed to be here. Not that I mind, but doesn't this defeat the purpose? I mean, I was supposed to be doing this so that you could start work? And yet here you are…"

Finn laughed. "Okay, so I'm spending a little longer than I intended."

Carrie laughed. "You've been here for three hours. Dinner will be ready in about forty minutes." She glanced at Joel. "There's plenty of food to go around. I figured everyone would be hungry after all this activity, so I made a lot."

Joel knew what she wanted him to ask. "Why don't you stay for dinner?" he suggested.

Finn stilled. "Hey, I wouldn't wanna impose."

"You won't be, and like Carrie says, she's made a lot."

"Yeah, but a lot of what?"

"Beef casserole," Joel told him.

"Okay, but is she a good cook?" Finn asked in a stage whisper. Carrie gave a mock gasp.

"Mom is a *great* cook," Nate said. "This is one of our favorites."

"Look, if you have some place to be, we understand." Not that Joel wanted him to go. It had been an enjoyable afternoon. The kids had gotten into the spirit of the task, Carrie had made sure they had plenty to drink, and the deck was virtually gone. Nate and Carrie had worked on the removal of the supporting poles. All that was left was to remove the last bit of the deck, and level the ground. They'd accomplished a lot.

Finn rubbed his chin. "I have Chicken Ding back home waiting for me."

Joel frowned. "What the hell is chicken ding?"

Finn grinned. "I stick a knife through the plastic, I shove it in the microwave, and when it goes *ding*, it's done."

Joel laughed. "Well, if you prefer that over Carrie's beef casserole…"

Finn rolled his eyes. "I think you already know the answer to that."

"But there are only four chairs," Laura pointed out.

"There's a stool that I keep in the bathroom," Joel told her. "Someone can have that."

"Could you tell me about some of the jobs you've

worked on?" Nate asked Finn. "I'd love to hear about them."

"Hey, if you want to walk Bramble after dinner," Joel told him, "and if you can persuade Finn to go along, he can show you where he's working right now. He's building that hotel facing the shore."

Nate's eyes were huge. "A hotel?"

Finn laughed. "I'm not building it on my own, but yeah, you might find it interesting."

"That place on the road? Yeah I'd love to know more about it."

At least Nate had talked more during this visit, although most of the time it had been to Finn. Joel's stomach clenched.

I wish you'd talk to me, son.

Finn wiped his lips with a napkin and pushed his empty plate away from him. "My compliments to the chef. That was delicious." Carrie hadn't been kidding. She'd made enough for a small army. Joel was going to be living on leftovers for a few days yet.

"Glad you liked it." Carrie peered into the dish. "There's more, if you want."

"Two portions already have my belt straining." It had been a pleasant meal. Nate had asked lots of questions, and Finn had been more than happy to answer them. Joel had seemed a little quiet, but that was because Laura and Nate had done most of the talking.

What Finn couldn't get his head around was the

relationship between Carrie and Joel. They got along like a house on fire. They joked with each other the way Finn did with his friends, at ease with each other.

Well, of course *they're at ease. They were married for how long? These guys know each other really well.*

Finn watched them, rubbing his chin and scratching his cheek. His parents had divorced when he was seven, and Finn recalled the atmosphere, the tension…

In a burst of clarity, it came to him. *That's what's confusing me. They don't act like a divorced couple.* Okay, so not all divorces were alike, but… He couldn't help wondering what on earth had prompted the split.

As for Joel's glances the previous visit, there was no sign of them.

I was right. I imagined the whole thing. Well fuck.

Seb was right about one thing. At least Finn could have Joel in his dreams. Because that was about as close as Finn was going to get.

Chapter Nine

Finn slung his bag into the back of his truck. He was ready for a hot shower and a cold beer. Hell, he'd been ready three hours ago.

"Almost there," Ted said as he unlocked his car, which was parked behind Finn's.

"Almost where?"

Ted grinned. "The weekend, of course."

Finn shook his head. "Today is Wednesday, in case you hadn't noticed. You know, hump day?"

"No harm in looking forward to it, right? You got anything planned?"

Finn rolled his eyes. "Yeah. Laundry, groceries, cleaning…"

Ted bit his lip. "Wow. You sure know how to live." He climbed behind the wheel and gave Finn a wave as he pulled away from the curb.

Finn got into the truck and stared out at the ocean.

I wonder how he's getting along?

Joel hadn't been far from his thoughts since Finn had loaned him the manual post-hole digger on Saturday. He'd given instructions on how to use it, said goodbye to Carrie and the kids, and wished Joel luck.

The look Joel had given him as he'd gotten into his truck made Finn think he was going to need it.

Maybe I should check on his progress…

It was an excuse, and he knew it. It wasn't going to stop him from dropping by, however… *That's if he's even there.*

Finn got out his phone and composed a brief text. *You home?*

A minute later Joel's response came through. *Just got home.*

Well, that answered one question. *Okay for me to come over?*

Sure.

In less than five minutes, Finn was pulling into Joel's driveway. As he switched off the engine, the door opened, and Joel stepped out onto the front porch. "I haven't even had time to change," he complained. "I didn't think you'd be that fast."

Hoo boy. Joel in a suit was *all* kinds of delicious. Who was he kidding? Finn would lay even money Joel could wear a *sack* and he'd still look edible. He did his best not to stare as he got out of the truck and walked toward the house. "You're my pit-stop on the way to a much-needed shower, so I wouldn't get too close if I were you."

"You can't stay away, can you? Or is it just that you don't trust me to do what I'm supposed to?" Joel smiled. "I'm a trustworthy guy."

Finn grinned. "Okay, Mr. Trustworthy, let's see what you've gotten done so far."

Joel's smile faltered. "Yeah, about that… It was tougher than I thought. I've been on the road more than usual this last week."

Finn held up one hand to stop Joel mid flow. "How about you show me what you've accomplished?"

Joel pointed to the side gate. "Go on through. I'll

meet you at the back door."

Finn walked through the gate at the side of the house, turned the corner—and stopped. *I guess it really was tougher.*

One hole had been dug.

Joel appeared at the door. "I know, it looks bad." He'd placed a sturdy box below the door sill to use as a step.

Finn scrubbed a hand over his face. "Are you going to be able to get the other eight done by the time I'm ready to start work?" He glanced at the manual post-hole digger that lay on the ground beside the hole. "Did you get the hang of this?"

"I did what you said. I threw it into the ground like I was spearfishing. There *was* one thing you didn't tell me, however."

"And what was that?"

"This is a shit job. It didn't help that the dirt is dry and powdery, not to mention compacted. That made it difficult to cut through. Why couldn't I have wet dirt? Plus, to make matter worse, I had less time the last couple days." Joel grimaced. "Listen to me. I'm full of excuses."

Finn hastened to reassure him. "Okay, look… We've got a week-and-a-half before I'm due to start work. How about I stop by again Saturday and see how you're doing? The supplies will be delivered during the following week."

"Okay, that's a deadline. I can work to a deadline."

"Then I'll leave you to it." Finn gave him a hopefully reassuring smile. "Hey, at least you made a start. Think how embarrassing it would have been if I'd turned up and you'd done nothing."

Joel rolled his eyes. "One hole."

"That's one more hole than you had on Saturday. And look how much we got done *that* day." Finn indicated the dirt at his feet. "There was a deck here, remember?"

Joel bit his lip. "Are you *always* a little ray of sunshine?"

Finn grinned. "It works for me." He said goodbye and headed back to his truck. As he got behind the wheel, Finn pulled his phone from his pocket. He scrolled through his contacts.

"Arnie? There's something of yours I'd like to borrow, if that's okay."

Finn had a feeling Joel was going to need a little help.

"So what did you get done the last two days?" Finn asked as Joel opened the side gate for him. No suit this time, only a pair of faded jeans that clung to Joel's thighs like a second skin. He wore a black tee under his open red plaid shirt, looking every inch a Mainer.

"Don't ask." As they rounded the corner, he pointed. "It's not *all* bad. Where there was one hole, now there are two."

Finn stared at the ground. "You're not gonna get this done by next weekend, are you?" He wasn't concerned, not now he'd brought along his secret weapon.

"Hey, it's not like I have a choice. I'm not going to have you turn up, and find we're not ready. I'll get it done."

Joel's tone was earnest, but Finn knew that even with the best will in the world, it was unlikely he would have the remaining seven holes dug. He beckoned with his finger. "Come with me." He led Joel through the side gate, and over to where his truck stood. "I've brought something to help speed up the process."

Joel stared at the auger. "What is that? It looks like a giant drill."

"*That* is an auger, and it will take both of us to get it to the back of the house, *and* use it." Finn reached into his breast pocket and removed the orange ear protection. "You'll need these. This thing is *not* quiet." He handed a pair to Joel, who shoved them into his jeans pocket.

Between them, they lifted the auger out of the truck, and carried it through the gate to the yard. "How does it work?" Joel asked.

"It runs on gas," Finn told him. "You'll need gloves."

"Carrie left a pair here for me."

He laughed. "Your ex is awesome." They laid the auger on the ground, where Finn had marked out the positions of the nine posts. "Okay. This baby will have those holes cut in no time, even with the wrong kind of dirt."

His teasing tone sailed right over Joel's head. He frowned. "This isn't right."

Finn rubbed the back of his neck. "What isn't right?"

"This wasn't part of the deal. You did all that work Saturday, now you're here helping me again… I feel like I'm taking advantage of you."

Finn couldn't tell him what *he* was getting out of it—

the chance to be around Joel some more. "Look, normally you'd have to pay to rent one of these. I have a buddy who was more than happy to loan me his. It's faster than the manual type, but it needs two guys to use it." He grinned. "Trust me on that. I was on a site once, where a new guy tried to use it on his own. He sort of leaned over the middle and fired it up. Only thing was, it spun him around like a top before it threw him off completely."

"So how do we do this?"

Finn shrugged off his jacket and his shirt. "Let me go get my gloves from the truck. You grab the ones Carrie left."

"Here." Joel held out a hand for his outer layers. "I'll put them inside."

Finn handed them over, then headed for the truck. He picked up his gloves from where he'd tossed them onto the passenger seat. By the time he got back to the yard, Joel had removed his shirt, leaving just his tee. When Finn bit his lip, Joel gave him an adorably sheepish grin. "Well, seeing as you did it first… I kind of got the impression this is going to raise a sweat."

"And then some." Between them, they picked up the auger and stood, facing each other. Finn gripped the handles. "Okay. This is how it's gonna be. I'll fire it up, then we place the tip in the middle of where we want our hole to be. But once it bites, you have to keep the pressure on, pushing downward. If you don't, it'll just turn. And you'd better hope we don't hit a brick or something."

"Why? What happens then?"

Finn cackled. "It'll throw us off in two different directions." He met Joel's gaze. "You ready?"

"As ready as I'll ever be." He grabbed hold of the

handles.

"Wait. You got your ear protection?"

Joel shoved his hand into his pocket and pulled out the orange plugs. "Hang on." He placed them carefully into his ears, while Finn did the same.

Finn pulled the cord, and the hundred-decibel auger burst into life. He gave Joel a nod, and they placed the auger into its position. Joel kept his gaze locked on Finn's arms, mimicking his movement, and the spinning drill went about six inches into the ground.

Joel grinned, and that look of pride warmed Finn's heart. They repeated the action, pushing down hard on the handles, and with each pass the drill went lower, until Finn judged they'd gone deep enough. It took them about eight minutes to dig the first hole, but Joel showed no signs of wanting to stop.

What a guy. Finn loved his attitude.

Despite the temperature being in the low-to-mid fifties, probably the warmest day so far for May, Finn's T-shirt clung to him, the sweat soaking through the cotton. Joel's shirt was in the same state, and Finn had to work hard not to stare. *Lord, if it was white, it'd be see-through by now.*

Now *there* was a luscious thought.

Joel's nipples poked against the fabric, and the tightness of the shirt made it obvious Joel was a lean guy. Finn couldn't help admiring the curve of his biceps, his firm shoulders, the way his abs tautened as he strained to keep the auger under control.

An hour later, they had seven holes, each about three feet deep, and Finn's shirt was wringing wet. He switched off the auger, and they laid it on the ground.

Joel expelled a breath. "Woo. Who needs a gym? That just gave my arms a thorough workout." He glanced at Finn. "No wonder yours are in such good shape."

Finn flexed for him, grinning. Then it struck him. *Now I know for sure I'm not the only one who's looking.* "Help me put it back in the truck."

They carried the auger to the truck, and Joel stretched after laying it in the back. "I don't know about you, but I just worked up an appetite."

Finn's stomach gave a rumble, and Finn laughed. "Gotta replace all those calories you just burned off, right?"

"I was going to make chicken sandwiches. There's plenty, if you want to join me. Seems like the least I can do, after all you did today."

"Hey, *we* dug those holes," Finn reminded him. "And as much as I love the idea of a chicken sandwich right now, there is no way I'm gonna sit in your kitchen like this." He gestured to his sweat-soaked T-shirt.

Joel rolled his eyes. "I *do* have a shower, you know. *And* you have a shirt to put on after, remember? As if I'm going to begrudge you using my shower. If it weren't for you, I'd still have seven holes to dig."

"You sure?" Not that Finn minded the prospect of more time with Joel, but he didn't want to appear *too* eager.

"Let me grab a quick shower first, then it's all yours. There's plenty of hot water."

Finn gazed at the newly dug holes. "I tell you what. Go take your shower, and while you're doing that, I'll make a start on moving some of the dirt we displaced."

Joel grinned. "Do you ever sit still?" He went into the house.

Finn grabbed the shovel that was leaning against the wall, and began removing the loose dirt. By the time

Joel's shout of "Your turn!" reached him, the ground was level, and nine neat holes stood ready to be filled with concrete. Finn replaced the shovel against the wall, and used the box to step into the house. He toed off his boots immediately, leaving them beside Joel's on the mat.

Joel came out of the bathroom, his hair still damp, and wearing a clean T-shirt. "I've put out fresh towels for you, there's a new bar of soap, and feel free to use my shampoo."

Finn caught a whiff of it, and the scent went straight to his dick. *Gotta love the smell of a clean guy.* Not that he minded a little sweat, in the right circumstances. He hurried into the bathroom, not wanting Joel to get an eyeful. Once under the stream of hot water, Finn cleaned himself with all speed. This was no time for a leisurely shower. As he stepped out of the tub, he noticed Joel had hung his shirt on the hook behind the door.

"Lunch is ready," Joel hollered.

Finn dressed as fast as he could, and walked out of the bathroom to be greeted by the sight of two plates of substantial sandwiches, a bowl of chips, and two tall glasses of juice. Joel was already seated, and Finn joined him. "Thank you. This looks great."

"It's the least I can do. This morning, just one look out there was enough to depress me. I honestly thought I'd struggle to get it all done." Joel smiled. "Bringing the auger was inspired. I think we made a great team."

"You were right, though, what you said on Wednesday."

Joel frowned. "Which part?"

Finn chuckled. "It *is* a shit job." They laughed. Finn attacked his lunch with gusto, all talking forgotten for a while. Joel lapsed into silence while he devoured his sandwich. Bramble took an interest in their lunch, until Joel told him in a firm voice to go to his bed. Bramble's look of dejection tugged at Finn's heart.

"Don't fall for it."

Finn frowned. "Excuse me?"

Joel inclined his head toward the living room. "It's all an act. That dog is spoiled rotten."

Finn smiled. "He's really good at it though."

"Hmm. I think he practices in front of a mirror."

Finn's hunger having abated, he took a moment to study the man sitting opposite him. It was only then he realized Joel was doing the same thing.

"Sorry. I was staring. That was rude."

Finn smiled. "Do I have something on my face?" That would be one explanation.

Joel chuckled. "Actually? Yeah. A little mayo…" He reached over and rubbed his thumb over the corner of Finn's mouth, then wiped it on a napkin. "There. All gone." Finn stared at him, and Joel flushed. "Couldn't have you walking around with mayo on your face."

The simple intimate gesture sent a pleasurable shiver down Finn's spine. Joel was confusing the fuck out of him. Finn couldn't keep a lid on his curiosity a minute longer.

"Can I ask you something personal?"

Joel stilled. "O-*kay.*"

"It's about you and Carrie."

Joel blinked. "What about us?"

Finn's heart raced. "I just don't get it. I mean, I watched the pair of you last weekend, and…" He swallowed. "You seem to really get along so well. What the hell happened? How come you guys divorced?"

Joel lifted his chin. "It just wasn't meant to be, that's

all."

Finn looked him in the eye. "How long were you married?"

"Twenty years."

That accounted for their ease with each other, but something still didn't add up. "And how long ago did you split up?"

Joel put down his napkin with a sigh. "We agreed to a divorce last December. I moved out January, and it became final last month."

Now it made even *less* sense.

It wasn't like Finn to be this bold, but he'd been thinking about little else since he'd met Carrie and seen their interactions. "Okay, if I'm overstepping the mark here, you can tell me to take a swan dive off the poop deck, but…"

Joel's eyes twinkled briefly, but then all trace of humor fled, and his gaze grew a little pained. "You're going to be around here for a while, working on the deck. And you've already proved yourself to be a great guy. So I guess I can tell you the truth."

One glance into those blue eyes told Finn whatever truth Joel was about to share, he was scared shitless at the thought of it.

How bad could it be?

Chapter Ten

Where the hell do I start?

"Carrie was the one who asked for a divorce," Joel admitted. "Not that it was much of a shock. I mean, we both knew it was coming."

"Had things been that bad between you?"

"Not at all. There was no acrimony. She just sat me down, and said it was obvious—to her at least—that we'd grown apart. We were more like roommates than a married couple. And she was right." The relief that had accompanied that conversation… It had felt so wrong to experience the lightness that had suffused him on hearing her words, but Joel had quickly realized Carrie had felt it too.

"I think it's great you both felt comfortable enough to be honest with each other." Finn's voice was warm. "Listening to the way you and Carrie chat and joke around reminds me of how I am with my friends. We're talking about the people I'm closest to in the whole world."

Joel envied him that. He had few friends, and certainly none that he could say the same thing of. *Thank God for Carrie.* "This is why I count myself lucky. I lost a wife but gained a friend. Having said that, it could have gone very differently." *And isn't that the truth?*

"What do you mean?"

Joel studied him. He liked Finn, but then again what was there not to like? *How much do I tell him?*

There was only one answer to that, if he was to gain Finn's trust and friendship. And Lord knew, he wanted that.

"You want some more juice?" Without waiting to hear Finn's reply, Joel got to his feet and went to the refrigerator, his pulse quickening. He knew he was delaying the moment, but fighting his nerves was proving more difficult than he'd anticipated.

"I'm good, thanks."

Joel poured himself another glass of juice, then rejoined Finn. He took a deep breath. "You know there's more to come, right?"

Finn bit back a smile. "I kinda got that."

"For me, agreeing to the divorce was the starting point." Joel smiled. "I guess that sounds a little odd. Divorce is an end, right? But Carrie being so honest with me about how she felt, encouraged me to show her the same honesty. There was no need for me to hide the truth any longer." He shivered, recalling the fear that had consumed him, right up to the moment when Carrie had burst into tears. Not tears of sadness, but relief that he'd finally felt able to share.

Finn was so still. "The truth?"

"I think telling her the truth was in some way responsible for our relationship today. *Now* we have no secrets, yet from the moment we met, there was one huge secret—and it was mine."

Finn said nothing, but stared at him.

"Carrie said we grew apart, but I know deep down why that was. I knew it was my fault." She'd denied that, of course, but Joel would never be convinced otherwise.

"It can't have been *that* horrendous," Finn remonstrated. "I don't think you'd be as close as you are, if you'd shared something awful, something bad enough to break you up."

Joel had gone around Robin Hood's barn long enough. "Coming out to her was the hardest thing I've ever done." His heart pounded.

Finn swallowed. "When you say coming out…?"

Joel nodded. He lifted his chin to meet Finn's questioning gaze head on. "I've always known I was gay." He waited for some reaction—a gasp, a wide-eyed stare, anything—but Finn didn't as much as flinch. Joel raised both hands, his palms toward Finn. "I know there are probably a lot of people who'd say I'm bi, not gay. And technically? They'd be right. Yes, I did sleep with Carrie. But she's the *only* woman I've ever slept with. The thing is, I never thought of myself as bi. For as long as I can remember, I was more interested in guys than girls. I mean, we're talking since elementary school here."

Finn's breathing hitched, but he said nothing. His lack of disgust encouraged Joel to continue.

"When I was younger…" Joel's cheeks were on fire at the recollection of his early exploits. "Did you have sleepovers when you were younger?" Finn nodded. "Me too. Only thing was, we didn't just read comics or watch TV. I was always spending my time trying to get the other guy—or guys—to fool around." He smiled. "It worked sometimes too."

Finn widened his eyes. "Oh my God. I bet you were a handful when you were growing up."

Joel stared at him. "If *one word* of what I'd gotten up to had found its way back to my parents… I grew up in a very conservative state."

"That explains it." When Joel gave Finn a puzzled glance, he smiled. "You don't sound like you're a born-and-bred Mainer."

Joel laughed. "Lord no. I was raised in Idaho. Carrie and I moved to Maine when Nate was little. My family was extremely conservative, but by that I don't mean religious. All through my childhood, through my teenage years, we were fed the line of 'get married, have kids.' You have *no* idea of the pressure. There I was at age seventeen, in the mid-90s, desperately wanting to be myself, in a place where most people thought being gay was synonymous with having HIV." He sighed. "And trying just as desperately to keep secret the fact that all through high school, I had a boyfriend."

Finn took a drink from his glass. "Wow. That must've taken some doing."

Joel nodded. "We went through college together too. His name was David. We spent most of our time together. But there was no way we could come out."

"Why not? Look, I don't begin to understand what you must've gone through. But surely… once you got to college…"

"That didn't matter. David and I knew coming out wasn't an option. We'd have lost our friends and our family. The only way to live as openly gay would have been to move out of state. And for both of us that wasn't an option either. So… we came to a decision."

Finn exhaled slowly. "You dated girls."

"We both did. The first girl I dated was Carrie. We'd been together three months when she suddenly asked me to marry her."

Finn smiled at that. "Carrie doesn't mess about, does she?"

Joel chuckled. "Not when she sees something she wants. I hope this isn't TMI, but at that point, we hadn't had sex yet. This is *probably* where I should say David and I had stopped having sex too, as soon as I made the decision to date girls. I didn't like the idea of carrying on a relationship with someone and effectively cheating on them. David wasn't so keen on the idea, but he accepted my decision. So… Carrie proposed, I said yes, and three months later we were married. Neither of us saw any reason to wait."

"And you started to live a lie."

Joel nodded. "It wasn't a complete lie. I used to read gay fiction whenever I got the chance. I watched gay porn too, but yeah, for the most part I kept a huge part of myself hidden."

Finn sucked in a breath. "Now I'm not surprised you divorced. That must have put one hell of a strain on your relationship."

Joel shrugged. "I did what so many gay guys did. We stayed in the closet, we got married, and we had kids, because that was what was expected of us. Coming out was too big a risk, so we didn't."

"How did Carrie take it?"

"Better than I deserved. It brought us together somehow." Joel's stomach clenched at the memory. "She said I have her blessing to go out and find someone."

Finn stilled. "Hey… if you're out now… you and David could—"

"No, we *couldn't*," Joel said in a firm voice. "He got married too." He paused. "Although, he also got divorced."

Finn grinned. "Sounds like an opportunity."

The remark sent heat radiating through Joel's chest.

He'd hoped Finn would be okay with his revelations, but this level of acceptance blew him away. "And perhaps it would be—in fiction. However, in real life? David got divorced because his wife found out he was cheating on her with a guy."

"But you never did that," Finn said, looking Joel in the eye.

"No sir, I did not. I took my vows seriously."

Finn cocked his head to one side. "Do the kids know? That you're gay, I mean?"

Joel shook his head. "When we told them about the divorce, Nate reacted badly. I don't mean that he grew argumentative or sullen. He just… withdrew into himself. He doesn't talk about it. He doesn't *talk*, period." He smiled. "I think *you* got more out of him last weekend than I've gotten in six months."

"And Laura?"

"Laura is an amazing kid. Part of me feels that if I tell her, she'll be okay with it. But I'm not sure I'm ready to take that big a risk." He swallowed. "Nate blames me for the divorce."

Finn's eyes narrowed. "Has he *said* that?"

"No, but I think he's gotten this idea in his head that Carrie is somehow covering up for me, and that I did something that split us apart. Now, if I come out and say 'Hey, guess what? I'm gay,' I think that will just exacerbate the situation."

"You can't keep it quiet." Finn didn't break eye contact. "You're probably right, you know. Keeping this huge secret eroded your marriage from the inside. But when I see you and Carrie, I think… You were right to tell her. And maybe telling the kids won't go as badly as you think."

Joel pushed back his chair, got up from the table,

and walked to the back door. He stared out at the trees beyond the glass, their branches swaying slightly in the breeze. "I was so tired of hiding my true self. Here, I get to be the person I feel I was *meant* to be—an out gay man. But I'm not there yet. Maybe when I'm comfortable in my own skin, *then* I'll tell them." In the silence that followed, Joel turned to look at Finn, unable to miss his furrowed brow. "You think I'm wrong. You think I should tell them."

Finn drew in a deep breath. "No good ever comes of hiding stuff. And I say that from experience. My parents went through a messy divorce, but they didn't hide any of it from me. They always stressed that telling the truth was the way to go. Some of my friends weren't so lucky." He held up his hands. "But it's your life, Joel. You have to live it the way you think best." His face glowed. "I think you're awesome, not to mention incredibly brave."

Joel breathed a little easier. "Thank you."

"For what? The compliments? I meant every word."

"No, for sitting here and listening. For not judging."

Finn bit his lip. "I'm in no position to do that. You wanna know *why* I think you've been immensely brave? You just revealed something intensely personal to someone you've known for so little time."

Joel came back to the table and retook his seat. "I trust you," he said simply. "I know we haven't known each other all that long, but there's something about you…"

Finn smiled. "Like calls to like, don't they say?"

Joel stared at him. "I don't understand."

"Okay, let's try another. It takes one to know one."

Joel's heartbeat raced, and something fluttered deep in his belly. *No way.*

Finn gazed at him, those storm-colored eyes locked on his. "One of my friends says family is not always the one you're born into, but the one you choose. The people you *choose* to surround yourself with. The people you invite into your life, who accept you, support you, love you." His eyes sparkled. "To put it another way, in the words of Sister Sledge… 'We are family.'" He bit his lip. "With my apologies for the fact that I really can't carry a tune."

Holy fuck. "You're gay."

Finn nodded. "Welcome to the family."

Chapter Eleven

Finn's head was spinning. *What are the odds?* Then a thought struck him. *Okay, so maybe he* was *checking me out after all.* He smiled to himself. *I didn't imagine it.* Then he pushed that assumption aside. *And maybe I'm too full of myself.* Thinking Joel would be interested in him smacked of arrogance.

Joel seemed to have been shocked into silence by Finn's revelation. Either that, or he'd run out of words.

"Thank you for trusting me," Finn said at last. "That means a lot. And hearing your story… I think I had it easier growing up than you did."

"Nowadays, coming out isn't such a huge deal—or at least, that's how it seems to me," Joel mused. "Every time I switch on the TV or check my phone, someone in the public eye is coming out, and no one bats an eyelid." He leaned forward, his elbows on the table, clasping his glass in both hands. "I guess our stories must be very different."

"Not so much as you might think." Finn grinned. "Except for the sleepover part. Although… Now I come to think about it…"

"What do you mean?"

"You got me thinking about one of my friends, Seb. You know, I haven't thought about it before, but…"

He chuckled. "That sneaky little fucker." *How come I missed that?*

"Are you going to tell me *what* you haven't thought about before?" Joel asked with a smile.

"When I was thirteen or fourteen, I had a couple of friends who used to sleep over regularly. Seb was one of them. I was a gentleman—I always let one of them have my bed, and everyone else slept on the floor in sleeping bags. Well, there was this one time when Seb turned up without his sleeping bag, and asked if he could share mine. And of course I said yes."

Joel grinned. "I take it Seb turned out to be gay?" He cocked his head to one side. "Did he try anything?"

"I think I'd have noticed if he had," Finn said with a chuckle. "Although… Okay, it wasn't a big sleeping bag so we were a bit squashed, but… I woke up with his arm around me. I didn't think anything of it at the time."

"I must meet him sometime. He sounds as if he's as devious as I was." Joel sipped his juice. "So you had a gay friend? Safety in numbers, right?"

"Actually, back in high school there were three of us. We thought of ourselves as the three gay Musketeers. As I said, like calls to like. We found each other, and we stayed friends."

"That's amazing. Are these the friends you were talking about?"

Finn nodded. "Levi and Seb were the original two. Then Noah, Ben, Shaun, Dylan, and Aaron sort of latched onto us." He smiled. "My family."

Joel blinked. "They're not *all* gay, surely. The odds of eight gay teens becoming friends must be astronomical."

"I'd agree. I'd say four of us are gay, but don't quote

me on that." He wasn't so sure about Dylan and Shaun, not that either of them had been vocal about their preferences. "And one of the four has only recently come out. He says it took him longer to figure stuff out."

"I envy you. I never had any close friends growing up."

Finn's heart went out to him. "I can understand that. You had to hide. To watch everything you said. But things are different now. It's like you said… now you can live the way *you* want. You're free to meet guys, make friends…" He grinned. "Hell, you met me, right?"

Joel's eyes shone. "Are you going to be my friend?" He rolled his eyes. "That makes me sound like I'm six years old."

Finn laughed. "I can see us becoming friends for sure. I know I'll be working for you, but I think we're past the employer/employee stage, don't you?"

Joel's smile was bright. "Yes, I do." Happy was a good look on him. "Thanks again for what you did today."

Finn smiled. "Bringing the auger?"

"That, and the conversation. You have *no* idea how important this was."

The idea that he'd brought Joel a measure of happiness made Finn feel like a million dollars. "You have a whole new life ahead of you. That must be pretty exciting."

"Exciting—and scary as hell."

Finn knew he was thinking about his kids. And although he could happily have spent the rest of the day talking to Joel, there were jobs awaiting him at home, not to mention the auger sitting out there in his truck.

"Thanks for lunch, but I really need to take the auger back. Its owner is building his own house right now."

"That's your dream too."

Finn smiled. "You remembered. Yeah. One day, maybe. But then I do have a few chores to fill the rest of my weekend. *Next* weekend, you get to watch me pour concrete."

Joel's eyes twinkled. "Be still my beating heart. I'm not sure it can stand that much excitement." He pointed to Finn's T-shirt that he'd placed over the back of one of the chairs. "Don't forget to take your laundry with you."

"Thanks again for the use of your shower."

"Don't mention it. Oh, and by the way? The other day when you told me not to get too close?" Joel grinned. "I didn't mind the way you smelled at all."

There was no mistaking that glint in Joel's eyes.

Why, Mr. Hall. You're flirting with me.

Finn coughed. "I'd better be going." He grabbed his jacket and T-shirt, and Joel walked him to the door. Bramble got up from his bed and trotted over. Finn reached down to pat him. "Good boy." That earned him a tail wag.

"I'll be sure to look for you, next time I'm walking Bramble on the beach. Have a good week."

They said their goodbyes, then Finn headed for his truck. He switched on the engine and pulled out of the driveway, casting one last glance at Joel in the rear-view mirror.

Well, what do you know about that?

Finn wasn't about to make a move on him—that wouldn't have been professional—but he couldn't deny something had changed.

I can always hope, right?

Joel smiled when he saw Carrie's name on his screen. "Hey," he said as soon as the call connected. "I have holes."

Carrie chuckled. "Do you want maybe to rephrase that? Or at least supply more information."

Joel laughed. "Finn stopped by today, and he brought a very useful tool with him. All the holes are dug, ready for the concrete."

"He did them all?"

"No, *he* didn't—*we* did. He couldn't have done it without me." He knew that sounded smug, but Joel didn't give a shit.

"I can see it now. Kevin O'Connor will be asking you do to a guest spot on *This Old House*."

"You may mock, but you should've seen me."

She laughed. "So Saturday is concrete day?"

"Yes. Finn says he'll leave it to cure, and then it'll be full speed ahead."

There was a pause. "Nate and Laura want to visit next weekend—on their own."

Joel's heartbeat slipped into a higher gear. "Seriously? Nate feels okay about that?"

"Yeah, he's happy about the drive. But I'll only let them come if you're sure they won't be in the way."

Joel chuckled. "They won't be in my way. Finn is the one doing the work."

"There is one thing though. Laura asked if they

could stay over."

His chest tightened. "Was Nate okay with that too?"

"He says so." Another pause. "What's more important is, are *you* okay with that?"

"Why wouldn't I be? It'll be great. I'll make sure to get in some popcorn and sodas, and we can watch a movie." Then he realized a shopping trip was on the cards. He'd need more bedding.

"Hey, go easy on the soda. Laura is hyperactive as it is. You don't want her bouncing off the walls."

He laughed. "Laura doesn't need soda to bounce."

"True." Carrie cleared her throat. "So… Finn… Definitely *not* how I pictured him."

Joel recalled her description. "He sure isn't."

"In fact, I'd say he's really cute." Her tone grew teasing. "Are you interested? Is *he* interested?"

Oh fuck.

"Now you stop that. You don't know anything about him. You hear me trying to set *you* up with guys?"

Silence fell at the other end of the phone. "What are you not telling me?"

Dammit. "What makes you think I'm not telling you something?"

"Because I *know* you."

Having someone know him the way she did was both a blessing and a curse. "We did a lot of talking today. He asked some questions about us. He wanted to know why we get along so well, despite the divorce. And… I told him about my past."

"Wow, that must have taken some courage. Is he the first person you've told since we talked?"

"Yeah." Joel still couldn't believe he'd found the nerve to do it.

"I'm proud of you. And?"

"And what?"

"How did he react?"

There was no getting around it. "It turns out… Finn is gay."

A delighted cackle filled his ears. "Okay. I like the way this is going."

"Hey, it's not *going* anywhere. So he's gay." Joel raised his eyes heavenward. *I knew she'd do this.*

"Yes, he's gay. He's also cute and funny, not to mention sexy as hell."

Isn't he though? Not that he'd say as much to her.

"Is he available, or does he have a boyfriend tucked away somewhere?"

"I don't know. He didn't say, and I didn't ask."

"But why on earth not? If it had been *me* in those circumstances…"

Joel's pulse quickened. "Hey. So what if he's gay? That doesn't mean he'd be interested in me."

"Oh, but he is." He could hear the smile in her voice.

"Is what?"

"Interested."

"And what are you basing that on? Female intuition?"

"No, on something *much* more tangible. I watched him when you were having your lesson on how to use a saw."

"I thought you were making coffee at the time." A*nd what the fuck did she see to make her think he's interested?*

"Okay, so I multitask. Trust me, he likes you."

"I like him too. He's a nice guy."

"You know what I mean."

Something fluttered in Joel's belly. "No. No. I am *not* going down this road. If I start to think like that, I'll be reading too much into everything he says, every look, every action."

"How does the saying go? 'Hope springs eternal'? Okay then, I'm gonna hope, and you can't stop me doing that."

"Fine. You hope. In the meantime, *I'll* live in the real world."

"Joel." Carrie's voice softened. "There's nothing wrong with admitting you like him, okay? Or that you'd like something to come of this. I get it, you're nervous. God knows, I understand exactly how you feel." She gave a wry chuckle. "Listen to us. We've regressed to being teenagers again."

"Things still okay with Eric?"

"Things are more than okay. He's… he's asked me to go away with him next weekend."

Joel laughed. "*Now* I understand why the kids are staying over. I'm the sitter."

"No, you are *not*. As a matter of fact, Laura had already asked me before Eric brought up the subject."

"Mm-hmm."

"No, really."

"And are you? Going away, I mean?"

"Yes. I have no idea where he's taking me, and it's only for one night. Is it okay for me to admit I'm nervous?"

Joel chuckled. "Join the club. Just go out this week and buy yourself some new lingerie. Something to wow the socks right off of him."

"I'll do that, but only if *you* promise not to give up on the idea of asking Finn on a date. And before you tell me he's not interested, let me tell *you* something. The way he looked at you, when you sawed through that first post? *That* was freaking adorable."

Joel wished he'd seen it too.

"Hey, Joel? Maybe *you'd* better go shopping for some new sexy underwear. You know, just in case…"

"Will you stop that?" As if he hadn't known she'd go down that path. "Tell the kids I'm looking forward to them staying over. And have a great weekend." They said their goodbyes, and Joel disconnected.

Is she right about Finn?

Despite his fervent protestations that he wasn't going to make a move, Joel knew Carrie was right about hope.

She'd just lit the fire under his.

Finn lay in bed, his laced fingers cradling the back of his head as he stared at the ceiling.

Joel is gay.

That added a whole new dimension to Finn's imaginings.

Sounds like it's been twenty years since he was with a guy. But sex was like riding a bike, right? Still, the thought of Joel rediscovering the joys of fucking brought with it delicious images. At least now Finn had some concept of what the hot body that lurked beneath Joel's clothes looked like.

He slid his hand down his belly and gave his stiff cock a leisurely rub, his eyes closed. As an afterthought, Finn grabbed the lube from the nightstand, and the small towel hanging from the drawer knob.

He was going to need them.

"What do you want to do?"

Joel's breathing hitched. "Everything?"

Finn rolled out a lazy chuckle as he stroked a single finger down Joel's torso, noting the tremor that rippled through him when Finn reached his dick. "How about we narrow the field a bit? Where do you want to start?"

Joel's lips parted and his pupils dilated. "With your cock in my ass?"

Finn could work with that. "Roll over."

Joel flipped onto his stomach, his hips tilted up, and Finn slid his hands under him to unzip Joel's jeans. He grasped them firmly and taking his time, eased them lower to reveal that gorgeous ass.

Joel twisted his head to gaze at him. "Don't make me wait. It's been too long."

The hint of a plaintive whine in his voice went straight to Finn's dick. He tugged Joel's jeans until they were off completely, then knelt between his legs, spreading Joel wide with his knees.

"Fuck, yes," Joel whispered.

Finn took one look at that furry crack and dove right in, pulling Joel's cheeks apart as he teased that tight little hole with his tongue. Joel tilted his ass higher, and Finn went to work, kissing, licking and probing Joel's hole until Joel was in constant motion, and Finn's cock was leaking pre-cum in a steady stream.

"Ready for me?"

Joel turned his head, his face flushed. "Put it in me."

Finn palmed his dick with slicked fingers, then brought the head to kiss Joel's pucker. "Breathe, baby." He gave a gentle push, groaning as Joel's body gave way and he was finally inside him. "Fuck, so tight."

Joel gasped. "What did you expect? You're the first guy in there for a couple of decades." Then a moan fell from his lips as Finn slid farther into him. "Oh God, so fucking deep."

Finn rocked his hips, sliding his cock against the

cotton sheets, gaining momentum as in his head, Joel pushed back to meet his thrusts. The friction was goddamn perfect, and too soon Finn felt his orgasm approach. He stiffened as he came, the towel hastily shoved beneath him to catch the first shot. Finn held his shaft around its base and trembled as he emptied himself. When he was done, he wiped himself clean, shuddering as the towel passed over the sensitized head.

He flopped onto his back, his dick limp against his thigh.

Whoa. That had to be the hottest fantasy yet. He felt a twinge of guilt at the idea of jerking off to thoughts of Joel. *He wants a friend, remember?*

Finn could be a friend.

The only thing was, he wanted to be so much more than that.

Chapter Twelve

For about the third time that morning, Finn gazed at the beach, scanning it for any sign of Joel. He'd tried not to be obvious about it, but a couple of the guys had noticed, with much resultant teasing. Finn had fired back that *they* stared often enough at people passing by, so why the hell shouldn't he? Not that their teasing got under his skin—it was more a case that he regretted handing them ammunition.

Then Joel came into view, and just like that, Finn's day got a whole lot better. Joel wore a brown leather jacket and jeans, his scarf tucked under his chin. Bramble appeared to be in a hurry to get his morning run: he was pulling hard on the leash, but Joel had a tight grip on it. Once Joel was on the sand, he let it out and Bramble was off, dashing to the waves that lapped the shore and sniffing everything in sight.

What I'd give to be down there, walking with him…

At that moment Joel looked up at the hotel, shading his eyes. Finn knew the moment Joel laid eyes on him—he raised a hand and waved. Finn waved back, realizing too late his greeting hadn't gone unnoticed.

"*Oh*. We're *waving* now, are we?" Tim said in obvious delight.

Finn forced as much nonchalance into his reply as

he could. "Fuck off."

Not enough, apparently.

"We hit a nerve, guys. Let me see." Max picked his way over the boards to the edge, peering down into the road. "That him? The guy on the beach?" Finn didn't respond, but that wasn't going to stop Max. "So, what's he like in bed?"

Finn grinned. "Why—you thinking of adding him to your To Be Fucked list? I'll ask him if he can slip you in this week."

Max returned his grin. "And has he *slipped* into you yet?"

Finn gave him the finger. "I'm just doing some work for him."

Ted cackled. "Is *that* what they're calling it these days? That reminds me. The hot little piece I met on the weekend... I'd better call that number she gave me and see if she wants any 'work' done." He hooked his fingers in the air and the others hooted.

"That the guy you borrowed my auger for?" Arnie asked. He grinned. "I bet *he* sure got a drilling."

Finn simply waved his hand and went back to work. He knew it wouldn't be long before they found another topic to occupy their grubby little minds. Sure enough, they got talking about Max's latest conquest, and Finn switched off. He didn't want to hear about Max's supposed sexual prowess. When break time arrived, he sat on his tool chest as usual and poured himself a coffee from his thermos.

Lewis came over and hunkered down next to him. "Is that right, you're working for him? Mr. Dog Lover?"

"Yup. I'm building his new deck. And his name's Joel."

Lewis's eyes lit up. "Joel, huh? Sounds kinda cozy. But hey, working for him must open up a lot of possibilities. Maybe you can lure him to the dark side. You know, convince him that batting for the other team ain't so bad. *You'd* be a hell of a lot less maintenance than some woman."

Finn glanced over his shoulder, making sure the others were nowhere in earshot. "He already bats for my team," he said in a low voice.

Lewis's eyes widened. "No shit. Really?" He got to his feet and looked out at the shore. "He's still there, you know." He gave Finn an evil grin. "You could always invite him over here. You know, to share your coffee."

Finn was sure most of Goose Rocks Beach heard his snort. "Yeah right."

"Aw, why not? I'm sure the others would *love* to meet him." He peered at the beach. "Don't look now, but he's watching us." That evil grin was still evident. "Should I give you a smooch? To make him jealous?"

Finn snorted. "You're not my type. And sorry to disappoint you, but there's nothing going on."

Lewis leaned in close. "Yet. Nothing going on *yet*. But give it time." He patted Finn's shoulder, then went to join the others.

Finn took a drink, his gaze locked on the lean form, strolling along the beach, Bramble doing his running-in-circles thing.

God, he wanted Lewis to be right.

Finn had just finished his dinner when the phone buzzed. He smiled when he saw Seb's name. "Are you calling me from school, or did they let you out?"

"Yeah, I'm laughing my ass off. I don't *live* there, y'know." He chuckled. "It just feels like it sometimes." A sigh filled Finn's ears. "Roll on summer."

"I guess for you, it must feel like when we were kids, when school is out. The prospect of all those weeks of freedom."

"You know it. But I'm not calling about my plans for a hot summer—because trust me, it's gonna be. I want to know how it went with Mr. Divorcee. That is, if he *is* divorced."

Finn laughed. "And why would you want to know about him?" As if he didn't know.

"Duh. I wanna know if there's a chance you and him are gonna end up between the sheets. Because if ever a guy was crying out to get laid, it's you. And so what if he's straight? That don't mean he ain't curious." Seb let out an evil chuckle. "Been there, sweetheart. There was this one—"

"Before you launch into some dirty action replay, I need to bring you up to speed." Finn paused. "He's not straight."

"He's—holy *fuck*." Seb let out a whoop of obvious delight. "Sounds like your birthday present came early this year—and I'm betting it's not gonna be the *only* thing coming early. After all this time, you'll go off like a rocket."

Finn had long passed the point of being shocked by what poured out of Seb's unfiltered mouth. But before he could say a word, Seb pressed ahead.

"You like him, don't ya?"

"It doesn't matter if I like him. He's not looking for

anything more than friendship."

"Did he *say* that? And you didn't answer my question. Don't think I didn't notice that."

Finn scraped his fingers across his scalp. "No, he didn't say that, and of course I like him. He's a great guy."

"Mm-hmm. A great guy that *you* thought was checking you out."

Finn rolled his eyes. "Are you not listening? He's not interested."

"Then he's blind. Hell, you're not my type, but even *I* know you're hot AF." Seb paused. "Hey, this is *me* you're talking to. You can be honest, okay?"

Finn swallowed. "He *is* a great guy, all right? He's smart, sexy, funny…"

"Sexy, huh? *Now* we're getting somewhere."

"He's also been married for a couple of decades, and he's only just now living as a gay man. He's got this whole journey of discovery ahead of him."

"Sounds to me like he might need a guide." Another pause. "But joking apart… if you want this guy, for God's sake, *tell* him. Because you don't know if he could be more than a fantasy. And he is, right?"

"Sexiest fantasy ever," Finn confessed, his pulse quickening.

"Then go for it. He can only say no, and while a rejection stings like hell for a while, it won't kill ya." Seb chuckled. "Jesus, I sound like a teacher."

"A very *good* teacher." Finn sighed. "Thanks, Seb."

"For what?"

"Listening. Looking out for me."

"Always. See you at Grammy's party, unless I run into you beforehand."

They disconnected, and Finn put his phone on the

table. *Gotta love Seb.* When it buzzed once more, he grinned. *What's he forgotten to say?* Then he saw the name, and heat raced through him.

It was Joel.

Finn clicked on *Accept.* "And you say *I* can't stay away." The temptation to stop by Joel's place after work had been enormous, but Finn had resisted. He could have claimed to be checking the supplies delivery, but that had felt like a flimsy excuse.

"Am I disturbing you?"

Lord no. I'd listen to your voice for hours, given half a chance.

"No. I'm done eating. Did the delivery arrive?"

"Yes, this morning. I think I annoyed the driver."

Finn chuckled. "What did you do?"

"Hey, I did exactly what you said, and checked off everything on the list you left with me. He was just going to drop it all off and go, but I wouldn't sign for the delivery until I'd checked."

"Let him be pissed. You were in the right. I take it there was nothing missing?"

"No, it's all here. It's also in my front yard, which I'm not happy about. Anyone could stroll up and take whatever they wanted."

"Unless someone is on the lookout for some free decking and cement, I doubt it." Finn grinned. *And* there's *a potential bright spot to end my day.* "Look, if you're worried, I'll come over and move it all to the backyard."

"You don't have to do that," Joel protested, though not all that strenuously.

"It's no big deal. I was only gonna watch TV. Let me grab my gloves, and I'll be right over." He disconnected before Joel had the chance to protest again.

By the time he pulled onto Joel's driveway, Joel was already in the front yard, humping a sack of cement toward the side gate. "Hey!" Finn called out as he climbed out of the truck. "Stop. I'll help you."

Joel regarded him with arched eyebrows. "Are you implying I'm not strong enough to do this?" His lips twitched, however. "Way to go to make me feel emasculated."

"I'm implying nothing. I do this for a living, so I'm used to it. You might... pull something. And I'd hate for that to happen." Finn put on his gloves as he marched over to Joel. "At least open the gate first."

Joel opened it, then came back to the sack. "These things are heavy."

"No shit." Finn pointed to one end of it. "You take that end. But bend your knees when you lift, okay?"

Joel chuckled. "Yes, sir." Between them they wrestled the sacks through to the backyard, and then continued back-and-forth with the boards. Joel wiped his brow as they deposited the last board, and headed back to the still substantial pile of supplies. "I had no idea a deck would need all this."

Finn laughed. "It does if you want one that will last more than five minutes. But hey, you don't have to think about *any* of this. *Your* job will be to stand at the door, nodding and smiling while I work, and occasionally asking me if I want a coffee or something." *And provide me with something gorgeous to look at.*

"I can do that," Joel said confidently. His eyes twinkled. "Is that your way of saying 'Stay out of my way while I'm working'? Do you ever get clients who think they can do the job better than you?"

Finn snorted. "Hell yeah. God save me from do-it-yourselfers who wanna give me a lecture on how to use a saw because I'm not 'doing it right,'" he air-quoted.

Joel laughed. "I won't be one of those."

Once everything was out of sight behind Joel's fence, Finn removed his gloves. "There. Happy now?"

"Ecstatic." Joel inclined his head toward the house. "Want a coffee, or something stronger? Seems the least I can do."

Finn didn't need to consider the invitation for more than a nanosecond. "Sure, why not? Although I might have to say no to the stronger stuff. Driving, and all that."

Joel grinned. "I wasn't planning on getting you intoxicated. One beer. You could manage one beer, surely? And besides, *how* far away do you live from here?"

Finn could do with a beer right then. "Okay, you're on." He put his gloves back in the truck, then went into the house. Bramble was at his feet in a heartbeat, and Finn stroked his sleek head and soft ears. "Hey, boy."

Joel was already at the kitchen table where two beer bottles sat. "As it comes, or do you want a glass?"

He laughed. "Glasses are for daintier souls than me." He took the proffered bottle and peered at the label.

"Pale ale okay with you?" Joel asked. "If it isn't, I've got a milk stout or a Belgian-style wheat beer."

"Pale ale is fine, although I'm more of a lager man. I just don't recall seeing this label before."

Joel tapped the bottle with his index finger. "I get it from a microbrewery in Portland. Which reminds me… I'm running low. Must get some more next time I'm passing through."

Finn arched his eyebrows. "I have to say, this is a new experience. Usually I make do with a Bud."

"Well, there's nothing wrong with trying new things. Let me know what you think. I have a feeling you'll like it."

They went into the living room. Joel sat in the rocking chair and Finn in the armchair. Bramble followed them, choosing to sit at Finn's feet. He leaned forward and scritched behind Bramble's ears. "Your dog likes me."

"My dog likes anyone with a pulse who will pay him attention. Sorry." Joel raised his bottle. "Cheers."

Finn mimicked him, then took a long drink. He gave an appreciative nod. "I like it."

Joel's smile lit up his face. "See? Told you."

"Yes, you did." He stretched out his legs and relaxed into the chair.

"Hard day?" Joel inquired.

Finn chuckled. "No harder than any other day."

"It obviously keeps you fit."

The hopeful part of Finn's brain kicked in instantly. *Is he saying that because he likes what he sees?* He shoved the idea aside. He could *not* afford to think that way about Joel. Besides, it wasn't as if Joel was staring at him, or undressing him with his eyes, right?

And what a shame that *is.*

"Did you grow up around here?" Joel asked, rocking slowly.

"Not that far from here. I was born in Wells, about twelve miles that-away," he said, pointing due south. "Not that I haven't been out of state—I moved to Millbury, Massachusetts for four years while I did my training. Having said that, I was back home most weekends."

"Homebody, huh?"

Finn chuckled. "Not exactly. Most of the guys in my class spent their weekends getting hammered, and I wasn't a big drinker. Saw too much of that growing up."

Joel's eyes widened but he said nothing.

"There *was* one year when I did fewer trips back home."

"Let me guess. Something to do with a guy?"

Finn nodded. "Eli was my first boyfriend. We met in class, which made things a little awkward when we broke up. It wasn't a bad break-up. We were pretty hot 'n' heavy for about three months, until someone else caught his eye, so we agreed to call it a day. By the time I'd finished my training, he'd gone through men like I go through saw blades."

"Have you had many relationships?" Joel stilled. "Unless you don't want to talk about this. You *can* tell me to mind my own business, you know."

Finn waved his hand. "I'm okay with it. And there's not a lot to tell." He liked Joel, but there was no way Finn was going to share his failures.

"Tell me about these friends of yours."

Finn drank some of his beer. "What do you wanna know?"

"Well, from what you said the other day, it sounds like you've been friends with them for a long time. That part about sleepovers… you've known some of them since your early teens?"

"Oh, way before that. At least, Levi and me, we've been tight since the start of junior high. We met Seb in eighth grade. Then when we got to high school, the others sort of drifted our way."

"But you didn't know Levi and Seb were gay when you were in junior high, did you?"

Finn shook his head. "That came later." He snorted. "Discovering gay magazines in Seb's gym bag was a bit of a giveaway, but then, he never was subtle about liking guys."

Joel bit his lip. "Okay, you don't have to answer this, but… your gay friends… did you guys ever…?"

It didn't take a genius to work out where that question was going.

Finn burst out laughing. "Lord no. They're more like my brothers. Not that I ever felt attracted to any of them, you understand. Which doesn't mean they're ugly, because—"

Joel's eyes twinkled. "Quit digging that hole. I get it."

"There's nothing wrong with them," Finn continued. "It's just…"

"Just what?"

Finn shrugged. "They're not my type."

Joel's smile did things to Finn's insides. "So you do have a type?"

Lord yes, and I'm looking right at him.

Finn coughed. "I'm gonna plead the fifth."

Joel's breathing hitched. "I see." He took a drink from his bottle, and neither of them said anything for a couple of minutes.

I could've lied. I could've said I was interested in firefighters, doctors, any *kind of men. Anything to keep him from knowing I'm into older guys—well,* one *older guy in particular.*

Joel stopped rocking. "Oh. Something I forgot to mention. It won't just be me who'll be watching you from the back door this weekend. The kids are coming over, and they're staying here Saturday night."

Finn beamed. "That's great." He cocked his head when Joel didn't respond. "Isn't it?"

"I suppose. I'm happy Nate feels confident enough to make the trip without Carrie as support."

"You never know. Maybe not having Carrie around will mean he opens up a little." Finn could only guess at how much the situation hurt Joel.

"Maybe. We'll see." Joel nodded toward Finn's bottle as he drained the last of his beer. "Want another?"

"Better not." Finn glanced at the clock on the wall. "In fact, I'd better be going. I have to be up very early." He stood, and Joel got up too.

"Sure. Thanks again for coming over. I really didn't expect you to do that." He held out his hand for Finn's bottle, and as Finn handed it over, Joel's fingers brushed his. Joel's gaze met Finn's. "Thanks for sharing, too."

"You're welcome." Neither of them moved, until Bramble sat on Finn's foot, leaning against his leg. Finn glanced down at the dog and laughed. "Can I help you?"

Joel let out a soft chuckle. "He doesn't want you to leave." With that, he went into the kitchen with the bottles.

Finn knelt in front of Bramble and held the dog's head in his hands, gazing into liquid brown eyes. *That makes two of us.* Then he stood once more as Joel came back into the room. "I'll see you Saturday, bright and early."

"I'll look forward to it." Joel walked him to the door.

As Finn gave a final wave before pulling out into the road, his mind was wrestling with one question.

Is he looking forward to getting the job done—or seeing me?

Finn knew which one he wanted it to be.

Chapter Thirteen

Finn opened the side gate and walked through to the back yard. He'd awoken at sunrise like he usually did, but he'd waited a couple of hours before leaving the house. It wouldn't be good to wake up his new client by clattering around the back yard before seven-thirty.

He glanced at the roll of landscape fabric. That would be the morning's first task. Then he turned his head toward the back door as it opened. Joel stood behind the screen, a cup of coffee in his hand. The aroma was almost as tantalizing as the view: Joel wore a pair of soft-looking gray sweatpants and a loose sweater.

Is there anything *that doesn't make him look good?*

"Good morning." Joel glanced down at his body. "Please excuse the clothing. I was about to get dressed when I heard your truck." Bramble nudged his head past Joel's leg and let out a soft *woof.* Joel glanced at him and reached down to stroke him. That was apparently all Bramble wanted. He disappeared from view.

Finn smiled. "Hey. I came straight on through. I wasn't sure if you'd still be sleeping. I wasn't gonna ring the doorbell at this hour."

"Don't worry. I'm an early riser." Joel cocked his head to one side. "Do you get up early because that's what you've gotten used to with the job, or is this just how you are?"

"The latter, I guess." Finn gestured to the landscape fabric. "I was mentally planning my tasks. When do the kids get here?"

Joel chuckled. "I have no idea, but I doubt it will be early. Let's just say when it comes to getting Nate out of bed, a crowbar comes in handy."

Finn laughed. "That reminds me of my friend Ben. He is *not* a morning person. We used to sit near him in the first class of the day, to nudge him when he fell asleep."

Joel held up his cup. "I was going to pour myself another. Want one?"

Finn bit his lip. "That isn't fair when I'm ready to start work."

"Sorry. I just didn't want to drink my coffee alone this morning."

As if Finn could refuse an offer like that. "In that case, I'll go around front, seeing as you'd need climbing gear to get in through the back door."

Joel rolled his eyes at Finn's joke. "Because of course, my back door is *so* high off the ground." He closed it. Finn walked through the side gate and around to the front porch. Joel had already opened the door, and as soon as Finn stepped inside, the mouthwatering aroma of coffee and bacon filled his nostrils.

"I like how your morning smells." He toed off his boots and walked across the hardwood floor in his socks.

Joel let out another chuckle. "Bacon kinda lingers. Help yourself to coffee. And while you're doing it, tell me what you expect from me in the way of beverages and snacks throughout the day."

Finn stared at him. "I don't expect you to feed me. I

have a Thermos of coffee and a couple of bottles of water, and I made sandwiches."

"Well, don't even think about eating those out there. The kids will want you to join us for lunch, I can tell you that now." Joel pointed upward. "I'm going to put some clothes on. You know where the coffee pot is." And with that, he headed up the staircase.

Finn walked into the kitchen and surveyed the clutter-free countertops. "Joel? Where do you keep your mugs?"

"Cabinet above the coffee pot," Joel called down. "There's creamer in the refrigerator. You don't take sugar, right?"

"You have a good memory." Finn opened the cabinet and grabbed a mug. Bramble appeared at his side, and Finn gave him a pat. "Good morning to you too, Bramble." The dog did his thing of sitting on Finn's foot and leaning, and Finn laughed. "You can't stay there. Go on, back to your bed. You can have cuddles in a minute." Bramble let out a small huff, then wandered back into the living room. "Hey, Joel? You do know the concrete is only gonna take me half the day, right? I might be done by the time you're ready for lunch."

Joel's chuckle reverberated around the cottage. "Lord, I love your optimism. You think you're going to keep at it when the kids get here? You don't think you might have a few *interruptions*?"

Finn laughed. "Okay, you may have a point. You ready for tonight? You must be happy about them spending the night. First time in the new place, and all."

"Happy—and nervous."

"Why nervous?"

"Because they haven't done this before. When I

moved out, they didn't come visit me—I went to them. So this is kind of a big deal."

Finn wasn't fooled by Joel's calm voice. "No—this sounds like a *huge* deal. What have you got planned for them?"

"There's pizza for dinner—because how can you go wrong with pizza?—and then I've got sodas and popcorn for later, while we watch a movie."

Finn stilled, his mug halfway to his lips. "Er… who's choosing the movie?"

Joel chuckled. "They are. I'll just put Netflix on and hand over the remote. Because God forbid I choose a movie they think is old, or boring, or… I am *so* out of touch with the jargon kids use nowadays."

"I think letting them choose is the safest option. Just be ready to veto it if you think it's inappropriate." Joel's kids didn't strike Finn as being the kind who'd want to watch slasher movies, but then again, what would he know? There might only be seven years between him and Nate, but a whole chasm of difference in their worlds.

Joel came into the kitchen, dressed in jeans and a T-shirt. "I'm also a little nervous because it'll be Nate's first time driving here without Carrie." On the kitchen table, Joel's phone buzzed, and he went to it. He smiled. "It's my sister. I'd better take this." He picked up the phone and went into the living room.

Finn walked over to the back door, his mug in his hand, and stared out at the yard, assessing how long the job would take. In theory, he could build the deck in three days, but that didn't allow for unforeseen circumstances. He also needed to make a start on Grammy's rocking chair, but that might be a task he did in his evenings—the next couple of weekends were all

Joel's.

I want it done for when June gets here. That was doable.

"No, you can't come over. I don't *care* if Lynne is dying to see the place, I have plans today." Joel's voice rose, a contrast to his usual quietly-spoken state.

Finn smiled to himself. *Looks as if Joel might have a houseful of people.*

"Megan… the kids will be here… I don't know… Plus, I'm having work done…" Joel sighed. "Yes, I *know* you're not that far from here… Okay, so you haven't seen them for ages, but… I don't *care* how fast you can whip up—did you say mac and cheese? Talk about playing dirty."

Finn stifled a chuckle. Maybe that saying about the way to a man's heart wasn't so far off the mark.

Joel heaved a sigh. "Fine. Make it one o'clock. I'm sure they'll be here by then… Sure… See you then."

Finn didn't move from his spot by the window. Joel soon joined him, another mug of coffee in his hand. "I'm guessing you caught most of that."

Finn bit back a smile. "Family, hmm?"

"My sister also lives in Maine. In fact, it's probably because of her that Carrie and I started thinking about a move here."

"She sounds like she's an older sister."

Joel arched his eyebrows. "Astute assumption. She's four years older. She lives in Portland with her partner Lynne."

Finn blinked. "I guess there *is* such a thing as a gay gene." He drank his coffee and placed the mug onto the countertop. "Well, if you're going to be invaded, I'd better get started and finish as much as I can before they pour through that door." And with that, he went over to the front door, put on his boots, and stepped outside.

He walked around the house, mentally trying to picture what Joel's sister might look like. All he came up with was a female version of Joel, just as tall, but with longer hair.

I can't wait to meet her. Judging by the way their phone conversation had gone, Megan sounded like she could be a lot of laughs, but a handful at the same time.

Lunch could be fun.

Joel opened the front door as Nate and Laura got out of the car. "How was the drive?" It was a little past twelve o'clock, and Joel had already called Carrie to find out what time they'd left home. When she said Nate hadn't gotten out of bed until nine-thirty, Joel had laughed. *No change there.*

"Okay," Nate said with a shrug. "Mom told me to take a different route, because of construction on 295, so we took the turnpike instead. Traffic wasn't too bad."

"Nate was swearing," Laura said with a grin.

Joel narrowed his gaze. "One, don't tattle on your brother, and two, Nate, don't swear in front of your sister." He stood aside to let them enter, and Laura immediately dropped her bag in the middle of the room in her rush to greet Bramble. Joel picked it up and set it down next to the futon.

Nate placed his bag beside hers and glanced at the living room. "You haven't done anything with the place yet."

Joel chuckled. "How long has it been since your last visit? Two weeks? Rome wasn't built in a day, isn't that what they say?"

Nate peered along the kitchen to the back door. "Someone's out there." He turned to face Joel. "Is Finn here?"

Joel nodded. "He's pouring the concrete today, so Bramble is definitely staying indoors. Otherwise, there'll be doggy paw prints in the post bases."

"Aw, Bramble just wants to leave his signature, you know, like at that theater in Hollywood." Laura stroked Bramble along his back.

"He can want all he likes, he's still not going out there." Joel glanced at the clock. "By the way, your Aunt Megan will be here soon. She's bringing lunch."

Laura's face brightened. "Is Aunt Lynne coming too?" When Joel nodded, she beamed. "Cool."

"Can I go talk to Finn?" Nate asked.

Joel's stomach clenched. "Sure. Just don't get in his way, okay?" Nate gave a nod and headed for the back door.

He can't even spend five minutes in my company? Joel pushed down hard on such thoughts. Nate was going to be with him until the following day, right? They had plenty of time to talk. *If he wants to, that is.* The signs were not good, however.

He gave Laura his full attention. "If you want, you can take Bramble for his walk after lunch."

She widened her eyes. "Really? Great. Maybe Aunt Megan and Aunt Lynne will come too."

Joel liked the sound of that. Anything to give them less time around Finn. When it came to matchmaking, Megan was *way* worse than Carrie, and nowhere near as subtle. She'd already tried setting Joel up with some of her friends, but he'd shot down her efforts pretty fast.

Finn, however? He'd be a sitting target, and Joel knew Megan wouldn't be able to resist.

"Hey."

Finn glanced over to where Nate stood. "Hey. Well hello there, Mr. Solo Driver. How'd it go?"

Nate gave an adorably shy smile. "It was okay." He peered at the ground. "What are all these tubes?"

"They're to help form the concrete. I half-fill 'em with cement, I use a piece of two-by-four to remove any air pockets, and then I fill the rest of the way." He only had two more posts to do.

"Can I help?"

Finn stilled. "You'd better ask your dad if that's okay."

Nate scowled. "Why? He won't mind. And it's not like he cares what I do."

Ouch. Finn let the remark ride. "Okay, pass me one of those J-bolts." He pointed to the two remaining bolts lying on the fabric.

Nate picked one up and handed it to him. "I guess they're called that because of their shape."

Finn grinned. "Go to the head of the class. You embed the anchor bolt in the concrete, leaving no more than an inch of thread showing—and making sure it lines up with the other bolts. That's what this string line is for."

Nate's eyes sparkled. "What happened to the lasers?"

Finn cackled. "Ooh, you're quick." He pushed the bolt into the concrete after lining it up with the others. "Hey, if you want a job, pick up that bag of gravel over there, and backfill around the concrete forms, like you see I've already done."

"I can do that." Nate picked up the bag and carefully poured the gravel into the gap between the dirt and the tube.

"Pack it down tight," Finn told him. He watched as Nate did as instructed, the question right there on the tip of his tongue. By the time Nate was done, Finn couldn't hold it in a second longer. "What makes you think your dad doesn't care?"

"If he gave a flying leap about us, he wouldn't have divorced Mom."

Finn straightened and moved his wheelbarrow to the final hole. There was more than enough concrete left to finish the job. "I do understand what you're going through," he said quietly.

Nate's eyes flashed. "Really? And why's that?" Then he stared. "Did your parents divorce too?"

Finn nodded. "And I know you might not believe me right now, but you're lucky. Far luckier than *I* was."

"How do you work that out?"

Finn began shoveling concrete into the hole. "I've seen your parents together. They get along pretty well, and they're good people."

Nate blinked. "How can you know that? You've known us for what, five minutes?"

Finn paused. "You ever meet someone, and right off the bat, you get a good feeling about them? Well, that's how it was when I met your parents." *Especially your dad.*

"Didn't stop them getting a divorce though, did it?" Nate looked Finn in the eye. "How were your parents after they divorced?"

Finn swallowed. "I was only seven when they split, but I still remember how it was, the tension, the sniping... When I was a little older, my mom explained *why* they'd gotten a divorce. She said... she couldn't cope any longer with my dad's drinking."

Nate winced. "Oh God."

Finn nodded slowly. "That's why I said you're lucky." He tamped down the concrete with the two-by-four.

Nate sat on Finn's toolbox. "At least you know *why* they split. All *I* get is some half-assed excuse about growing apart. And I know there *has* to be more to it than that."

"Why don't you talk to them about it?"

Nate's face tightened. "Talk to my dad? He's the one who walked out. He left us."

"Well, what about your mom?" The pain in Nate's voice tore at Finn's heart. *That poor kid...* Him and Joel just needed to sit down and *share*.

"I can't talk to Mom about this. She'd only get upset."

Finn gave him a speculative glance. "You sure about that? She doesn't seem as though she's not coping with the divorce."

"She's putting on a front, that's all." Nate set his jaw.

It was clear to Finn nothing he could say was going to change Nate's mind, but that didn't mean he wasn't going to have one last try.

"Look, maybe I've got this all wrong," he said in a gentle voice, "but... I still think you need to talk to them, when you think it's the right time. Because you have questions, and *they're* the only ones with the answers."

Right then the door opened, and Joel appeared. His gaze went from Finn to Nate, and Finn hated how Nate sat so stiffly.

"Your Aunt Megan is here, and it'll be lunchtime soon." When Nate didn't respond, Joel returned his attention to Finn. "You still staying for lunch?"

"Let me finish this post, and I'll be right there," Finn assured him.

Joel gave a nod and one final glance at Nate, then shut the door.

Finn drew in a deep breath. "You're here till tomorrow, and your dad has been looking forward to this so much. And you only have to look at him to know he does care about you, *both* of you. So please... try to cut him a little slack while you're here?" He sighed. "I've known my fair share of assholes, and trust me, your dad is *not* an asshole." When Nate's lips twitched, Finn groaned. "And do *not* repeat what I just said to him."

Nate let out a soft chuckle. "I won't, I promise. But it's not like I haven't heard the word before." He grinned. "It'll be our secret."

"Cool." Finn gestured to the final J-bolt. "Now pass me that, and we can go eat. My mouth's been watering all morning at the thought of mac and cheese."

Nate's face was suddenly alight. "Aunt *Megan*'s mac and cheese? Why didn't you say so?" He grabbed the bolt and thrust it at Finn. "Come on, stick it in, before we get in there and find out Laura's eaten it all."

"That little girl? She's as thin as a toothpick."

Nate snorted. "Yeah right. She can still eat more than double her body weight in pizza."

Finn laughed. "Then we'd better get inside." He finished off the last post. That would be it until the following weekend. *Unless I come over to check on how the concrete is curing.* Anything to see more of Joel.

As he and Nate walked around the house, Finn's mind was turning over the things Nate had said.

They really need to talk. All of them.

Then he put that aside. He was about to meet more of Joel's family, and it promised to be *very* entertaining.

Chapter Fourteen

Finn liked Megan from the moment she looked at him with blue eyes *so* like Joel's, and said. "Well, hel*lo* there." She held out her hand. "Megan Hall. That beautiful creature in the kitchen is my better half, Lynne." That got him a wave from Lynne and a *very* firm handshake from Megan. Finn liked that her smile went all the way to her eyes.

"Hi, Megan. I'm Finn Anderson."

Megan's eyes gleamed. "Oh, I know *all* about you. Funny how Joel didn't mention what a looker you are."

"Down, girl," Joel murmured as he brought a stool to the table. "Behave."

Megan fired him a glance. "Hush. Don't spoil my fun." She brought her attention back to Finn. "Now, I know what you're thinking. How come I got all the looks in the family? Just lucky, I guess. But I'm sure Joel makes up for that in other departments." That twinkle in her eyes was downright evil.

Joel coughed. "Remember who's listening?" He inclined his head toward the living room where Nate and Laura were making a fuss of Bramble, teasing him with his squeaky hamburger.

"Why do you think I'm talking in innuendos?" she replied, her eyebrows arched.

Finn chuckled. "I was right. You're a handful."

Megan beamed. "You got it."

Finn snuck a glance at Joel, who was rolling his eyes. "For the record?" he said quietly. "She doesn't have *all* the good looks."

Joel flushed. "You get another helping of mac and cheese for that. Which you'll probably burn off in two seconds flat."

Finn patted his belly, and Megan chuckled. "Do *I* get to do that, or is it only Joel's privilege?"

"Will you stop that?" Joel muttered. "I have *never* done that, and what makes you think Finn would even *let* me?" He gazed earnestly at Finn. "I didn't breathe a word about you being..." He mouthed *gay*.

"Why not?" Megan grinned. "Is it a secret? Because... really?" she muttered under her breath as Nate and Laura approached the table. "Everyone hungry? There's plenty."

"We need another chair," Lynne said as she deposited a covered dish on a mat in the middle of the table. She gave Finn a warm smile. "I think you've earned *your* lunch."

Finn liked Lynne too. She was shorter than Megan, with closely-cropped gray hair, gold-rimmed glasses, and a great smile.

"Admiring my Lynne?" Megan gave Lynne a peck on the cheek. "I don't know what she sees in me sometimes."

Lynne smiled. "You're adorable and you know it."

Finn thought they were both pretty adorable.

"Thanks for helping out my little brother," Megan added. "Although I still think he's crazy to buy this place. Too damn small."

"It's cozy." Finn glanced at Joel. "Nothing wrong with cozy."

"And we *still* need another chair," Lynne said with a touch of exasperation.

"It's okay," Finn said quickly. "I'll stand."

"You will *not*," Megan retorted. "I'm sure *someone* will let you sit on their lap." A smile played about her lips.

"Finn doesn't need to sit on anyone's lap," Joel said in a firm voice. "There's a folding chair in the closet under the stairs." He went to get it.

"This looks yummy," Laura said as she surveyed the table.

"Aunt Megan makes the *best* mac and cheese," Nate told Finn. That earned him a warm glance from Megan.

"Okay, *now* we're ready," Joel said as he unfolded the chair. It was a bit of a squash to get everyone around the table, but they managed it. Lynne dished out, and it wasn't long before everyone was eating with noises of appreciation.

Finn took one mouthful of food and groaned. "Oh my God."

"I know, right?" Nate's eyes shone.

"Did you put *bacon bits* in this? And that topping is delicious." Finn took another mouthful. He grinned at Joel. "That second helping you mentioned? I'll take it." Bramble wandered over to investigate, his brown nose twitching. Joel simply gave him a pointed stare, and the dog huffed and returned to his bed.

"You'll have to fight Laura for it," Nate murmured. That got him Laura's elbow in his ribs, and he winced. "What? It's true!"

"How's school?" Megan asked Laura. "You still at the head of your class?" She flashed Finn a glance. "This is one smart kid."

"Hey, who's a 'kid'? I'm fifteen," Laura retorted. Then her face softened. "That's okay. I guess *kid* is a germ of endearment."

Finn chuckled, and Nate rolled his eyes. "That's *term* of endearment, you dork."

Laura ignored him and helped herself to more mac and cheese. "I tell *all* my friends about you, Aunt Megan. And you too, Aunt Lynne."

"Why would your friends want to know about us?" Megan peered into the dish. "Does anybody else want some before Laura eats it all?"

Laura's eyes twinkled. "Are you kidding? It's really cool, having aunts who are lesbians. It's the in thing."

"So now I'm a 'thing'," Megan said with a grin.

"A couple of my professors are gay," Nate added.

"How do you know that?" Joel asked.

"They talk about themselves. There's one professor who's always telling funny stories about himself and his husband."

"And you don't have a problem with that?" Finn glanced at Joel as he posed the question.

"Why would I? So what if he's gay? He's a great teacher."

If Finn could have mouthed *See?* without being spotted, he would have done, but instead he merely arched his eyebrows. Joel narrowed his gaze and continued eating.

"So, Finn…"

He steeled himself. It hadn't taken Finn long to realize absolutely *anything* could come out of Megan's mouth. "Hmm?"

"You sound like you're a local boy."

Okay, that wasn't so bad. "Absolutely. I grew up in Wells."

Lynne smiled. "Really? I swap recipes on Facebook with someone who lives in Wells. She makes the *best* oatmeal raisin cookies. Linda Brown."

Finn gaped. "You're kidding."

Lynne widened her eyes. "You *know* her? No way."

"One of my best friends, Levi? She's his grandmother."

Lynne's face lit up. "She talks about him all the time."

"And you're right. She makes the best cookies." Then her words sank in. "Wait a sec—Grammy is on *Facebook*?" Finn wasn't sure why that should've surprised him: Grammy was a remarkable woman. She'd stepped up to the plate when Levi had needed her, *that* was for sure.

Lynne laughed. "She's amazing. Wait till the next time I'm on there—I'll tell her I met you."

Finn gave an exaggerated swallow. "Just don't mention apples, okay?"

"I get the feeling there's a story behind that," Megan said with a smile.

"Grammy once took a broom to my behind when she caught me stealing apples from her tree. I couldn't sit down for a whole day."

Everyone around the table laughed.

"Have you got much more to do out there?" Joel asked, inclining his head toward the back yard.

"Nope, I'm done. I'll just straighten up before I go. Nothing to do now until the concrete cures. Next weekend I can start putting the deck together."

"I think you're going to need a party when it's finished, Dad." Laura grinned. "Like when they launch a new ship? I saw it on TV once. Only, it'd be more like, 'God bless this deck and all who step on it.'"

Joel chuckled. "Any excuse for a party." He peered into the dish. "My God, Laura's left some. Quick, Finn, grab it before she notices." Laura gave him a mock glare as laughter rippled through them.

Finn looked at the people seated around the table. *Joel has a great family.* His gaze lingered on Nate, and Finn's stomach clenched.

Joel needs to tell Nate the truth.

Finn knew the divorce had nothing to do with Joel's sexuality, but maybe if Nate knew, he'd understand better why his parents had grown apart in the first place.

Joel stood by the window, watching as Finn packed up his tools and generally cleaned up the yard. As Finn bent over to pick up what remained of the roll of landscape fabric, Joel's gaze was drawn to his butt, the denim stretched tight over it.

Oh my.

"Now *that* is one gorgeous ass," Megan murmured from beside him.

Joel almost jumped out of his skin. "Christ, give a guy some warning before you sneak up on him."

Megan smirked. "If I gave you warning, it would hardly be sneaking, would it?"

Joel glared at her. "And what are *you* doing, ogling Finn's ass?" he said in a quiet voice.

Megan widened her eyes. "What am *I* doing? What about you? And why shouldn't I look at that gorgeous butt? I may be a lesbian, but I'm not dead." She leaned in. "Tell me you're at least going to make a move on him."

"No, I am *not*." Joel watched Finn moving around out there. "For one thing, it wouldn't be appropriate. I'm paying him to build a deck. That makes me a client. And for another, he's not interested in me." When Megan didn't react, he turned toward her. "What?"

Megan bit her lip. "Honey, he was checking you out."

"When?"

"While Lynne was getting the lunch ready." Her eyes sparkled. "You think I can't tell when someone is checking out my brother? We are talking *definite* interest there."

Joel checked over his shoulder to make sure the kids weren't in earshot. "I'm not saying you're seeing things… but it doesn't matter anyhow."

Megan put her arm around his shoulders. "Tell them? Please? Because maybe then Nate will get back to being the great kid he used to be, and *you* can find a little happiness. God knows you deserve it. You've denied yourself for so long. It's time to *live*, Joel." She nodded toward Finn. "And he could be a part of that new life."

Joel couldn't say a word. He'd had the same idea, but every time he thought about Nate and Laura, his stomach tied itself up in knots. He knew exactly what had gone through Finn's mind during lunch, when the kids had talked so casually.

He thinks they'll be okay with it, and maybe he's right.

But Finn wasn't the one who had to tell them, and Joel hadn't found enough courage to accomplish that task.

"I still say we should've watched *all* the *Toy Story* movies, instead of just number four," Laura complained as she helped Joel make up the futons.

Joel chuckled. "Do you have any idea how long that would've taken? Maybe if we'd started watching a bit earlier…" He looked at the bed. "You got enough pillows?"

She nodded before smiling at the comforter. "This is pretty." Red, vibrant poppies stood out against a white background.

"It's new. I bought it just for you."

Laura walked around the futon and seized Joel in a tight hug. "Love you, Dad."

Joel kissed the top of her head. "Love you too, munchkin."

She turned her face up toward his, her eyes shining. "You haven't called me that in ages." Then she gave him a mock glare. "Except munchkins are small, and I've grown a couple inches since last year." She tightened her arms around him and pressed her face to his chest.

"You okay, sweetheart?"

Laura nodded against him. Finally, she released him. "I love your house."

"I'm glad. I want you to feel good about visiting."

Nate came out of the bathroom, and Laura grabbed her pajamas. "My turn." She dashed across the floor, banging the door after her.

Joel gestured to the double futon. "This okay?

There's a space heater if you get cold during the night."

"Thanks. This looks okay."

Joel's heart ached. Nate hadn't said much during the movie, apart from telling Laura not to hog all the popcorn.

Am I right to wait?

Joel didn't know anymore.

Laura came out of the bathroom, and Joel smiled. "Those are cute." Her pajama pants were covered in dozing pandas, and the top bore a single panda with one eye open, and the words *Don't Disturb A Sleeping Panda.*

Laura rolled her eyes. "Cute?"

Joel laughed. "There is nothing wrong with cute." He made sure the door was bolted, then glanced at Bramble. "I don't need to guess where you'll be sleeping tonight." The dog had already jumped up onto Laura's bed.

"Is that okay?"

Joel kissed her cheek. "It's fine. Just watch out. He takes up a lot of room, and you might find yourself being pushed out of the bed." He looked over to where Nate stood. "Goodnight, son."

"Night, Dad."

Joel made his way up the stairs to his bed. Laura's laughter drifted up from below as Bramble licked her toes, and he smiled to himself. *It's great having them here.* He undressed and climbed into bed, switching off the lamp that cast a warm glow on the white painted sloping ceiling. The kids were obviously too excited to sleep, but Joel had expected that. His mind was still turning over Megan's words.

Is she right? Is Finn interested?

And if so, was Joel prepared to do anything about it?

Because he could no longer deny he was interested in Finn, but he wasn't about to make a move. He wasn't that confident.

"Why do you have to be such a grouch all the time around Dad?"

Joel stiffened. Laura had spoken quietly, but her voice carried.

"Shut up," Nate said with a sigh.

"No, I will *not* shut up. You need to be nicer to him."

"You're still a kid. You don't know anything."

"Oh yeah? I know enough to realize you being like this is hurting him."

Joel swallowed. *Is my pain that obvious?*

"And just because they got a divorce doesn't mean he's changed. God, when I was little, you used to rave about what a great guy he was." Laura sounded pissed.

"What do you mean, *was*? You're still little."

"And you're changing the subject. Go on, tell me I'm wrong. Tell me you didn't think he was the greatest dad."

"And there's that word again—'was'. Don't tell me he hasn't changed. He must have, okay? *Something* must've changed. Because they got divorced. And I'm not gonna talk about this. Go to sleep."

Joel waited for more, but there was nothing but silence.

It was a long time before sleep claimed him.

Chapter Fifteen

When Bramble whined for the third time in an hour, Joel knew a walk was imminent. It was already past five o'clock, and he was ready to call it a day. A walk on the beach before dinner sounded exactly what he needed after an afternoon stuck at the kitchen table, making phone calls.

"Come on then."

Bramble dashed to the front door where the leash hung from a hook, and took the end of it in his teeth, tugging it onto the floor. Joel laughed. "I guess I'm not the only one who needs to stretch his legs." He put on his leather jacket and boots, grabbed his scarf, and headed out of the door. "How about we walk through the village this time?"

As if Bramble cared which route they took, as long as it led to the beach.

Joel took a left onto Winter Harbor Road, enjoying the feel of the light breeze on his face, and the sound of birds singing in the trees that lined the road. There were five or six properties along it, each one set back and surrounded by trees. Then he took a right onto Beaver Pond Road, heading for Summer Breeze Lane and Skyline Drive. That was one of the things he loved about Goose Rocks Beach—the quaint street names.

It was a mile or so to the beach, and he was in no

hurry to get there. As he walked, there was only one thing on his mind—a certain carpenter. Finn hadn't been at the house since Saturday, not that there was anything for him to do there until the concrete set, and it hadn't taken Joel long to realize he missed having Finn around.

"You like Finn, don't you, boy?" he said to Bramble as they strolled. He wondered why Finn didn't have a boyfriend—he hadn't *said* as much, so Joel was making an assumption. *And you know what they say about assuming stuff…* Any guy in their right mind would want to date Finn. He was good-looking, sexy, funny, talented…

Joel would date him in a heartbeat, if Finn showed any inclination. Megan could say what she liked about Finn checking him out—that didn't make it true, more like Megan's wishful thinking.

My wishful thinking too, if it comes to that.

Joel sighed. "Look at me, boy. Too scared to ask a guy out, for fear he'll say no. I've been out of the game way too long."

They turned onto Wildwood Avenue, and Joel recalled something Finn had said the day they'd met. "Hey, boy. Finn lives somewhere around here." And he'd be home by then. All Joel had to go on was Finn's comment that Joel had walked the dog by his house, because Finn had seen him. There were five roads that led off of Wildwood in the direction of the beach, but Joel wasn't about to take one of them until he'd worked out where Finn lived.

So what are you going to do when you find his house? Knock on his door, unannounced? Not cool. That wasn't going to stop him from looking, however.

Joel scanned the driveways as he walked along, searching for Finn's truck: it was the only thing he had to go on. *And what if he's not home? What if he's gone shopping?* Joel was beginning to feel like a stalker.

As he approached the intersection with Belvidere Avenue, he came to a halt. Finn's truck was parked over on the right, in front of a single-story house covered in pink cedar shakes. To the left of the property was a wide grassy area shaded by trees.

Joel's heartbeat quickened. *He's home.* That was no excuse for dropping by, and he knew it. *Walk away. Take Bramble to the beach. Finn will never know I've been here.*

And then such thoughts became moot as the front door opened and Finn came out, walking over to his truck. Joel froze to the spot, not daring to move, until he reasoned that would appear pretty ridiculous. Bramble settled the matter by tugging on his leash, barking and straining to get to Finn.

"Bramble, calm down," Joel called out, forced to jog after him.

Finn jerked his head in their direction, and his smile lit up his face. "Hey. You taking a walk?"

Joel nodded. "Until you came out and Bramble spotted you. So I guess now I know where you live," he said with as much nonchalance as he could muster. *And I haven't been looking for your house, honest.*

Finn inclined his head toward the house. "You wanna come in? There's coffee. You'll have to excuse the state of my table though. I'm in the middle of something."

"Hey, if you're busy, we'll leave you to it."

Finn grinned. "Not too busy to take a break. Come on in."

There was no way Joel was going to refuse him again. "Is it okay if Bramble goes inside?"

"Sure. He's house-trained. It's not like he's gonna

pee on the rug, right?" Finn squatted and rubbed Bramble's head. "You wouldn't do that, would ya, boy?" He straightened. "I just came out here to get something from the truck." He opened the passenger door and pulled out a large brown packet. "Sandpaper," he said, waving it. Then he locked the truck and headed back to the house, where he paused at the door and peered at Joel, still wearing that cute grin. "Well? Do I have to drag you inside? Bramble, bring Daddy."

That was all the invitation Bramble needed. He followed Finn, his tail wagging. Finn opened the door and stood aside for them. "Welcome to *my* rental."

The first thing Joel noticed was the cramped living room. "Now *this* is what I call cozy." He smiled when he saw the coffee table, with its chess and backgammon boards carved into the surface, along with lines of holes between them for scoring. "Wow. This really *is* a holiday rental." Then he spied the fireplace. "Hey, at least you can keep warm while you play chess with yourself."

"Do you play?"

Joel nodded. "My granddad taught me."

Finn chuckled. "Levi *tried* to teach me. He gave up." He glanced at the interior. "What do you think?"

Joel looked at the pine-clad walls of the living room, then through to the equally pine-clad kitchen and dining room. "The guy who decorated this place either had a whole lot of timber that he needed to use to free up some space, or he *really* liked pine."

Finn laughed. "Either could be true. It's everywhere. And there *is* a third option. Pine is the cheapest wood, so that's what gets used most." He beckoned with his finger. "Take a look at what I'm working on."

Joel followed him into the tiny dining room, where

the table had been covered by a sheet. On it sat several pieces of shaped wood in different sizes. "What's this?"

"I'm making a rocking chair for Levi's grandmother. It's her seventieth birthday soon, and he commissioned me to make it." Finn smiled. "As if I'd say no."

Joel stroked one of the pieces. "I think you're very talented. I also think it's a great idea." He frowned. "This the same person Lynne was talking about? The one who makes cookies?"

Finn smiled. "That's Grammy. She's a very special lady. Not many people would do what she did."

Joel was intrigued. "What did she do?" Finn bit his lip, and Joel regretted his curiosity. "Look, if you don't want to tell me, that's okay. It's none of my business."

Finn sighed. "It's not a secret—I mean, all Levi's closest friends know, and so does most of Wells, if it comes to that, because you *know* how things get around—but Levi doesn't talk about it much." He pulled out a chair and gestured to the one facing it. "Please, have a seat." Joel did as instructed, Bramble beside him, his nose on Joel's knee. "The thing is... Levi's mom got into bad habits when she was younger. We're talking younger than Nate, by the way. Bad habits—and worse friends."

"What kind of habits are we talking about?" Joel asked cautiously. Not that he didn't already have an idea.

Finn's gaze met his. "You do know Maine has an enormous drug crisis going on, right? It's in the news often enough. It's been that way for years, but I think it's worse in inland areas."

Joel nodded. "I think drugs are becoming a bigger problem wherever you live in this country." He knew Nate was sensible, but Joel hoped to God his son didn't start along that particular road. *It has to be a temptation, right?* One he prayed Nate was strong enough and wise enough to resist.

"Anyway, when Levi's mom was eighteen, she left home. She made a whole lot of excuses about feeling trapped and having no freedom, and she was of age, so there wasn't a whole lot her parents could do. She got herself a job, moved away from Wells, and *sort* of stayed in touch."

"How do you know all this?"

Finn shrugged. "Levi told me. He shared it with all of us. He said Grammy was worried sick. And then the day came when his mom turned up on Grammy's doorstep, pregnant."

"Oh God."

"Yeah. She didn't know who the father was—or at least that's what she said—and she swore to Grammy she'd turn things around."

"Why do I get the idea that didn't happen?"

Finn met his gaze. "Because you've seen enough to know how these situations usually work out? And you're right, of course. It wasn't long before she slipped back into her old ways."

"But… she was *pregnant*." Joel couldn't understand how *any* woman could abuse their body with drugs when they knew there was a life growing inside them.

Finn nodded, his face somber. "Apparently, she stuck around for a while, then moved back to wherever she'd been living. Grammy was going out of her mind. So when they woke up one morning to find a baby on the doorstep, with a note saying he'd be better off with them, they weren't really surprised."

"Did they try to find her, to make sure she was okay?"

"Yeah. Grammy had social services working on it, and she even went so far as to hire a private detective. But the thing is, most social services are in the southern Maine/Portland areas. That's a very small part of a very large state. People living outside the area don't often have access to the help they need."

"Did they eventually find her?"

Finn shook his head. "No one in Wells has heard from her since she left Levi with Grammy. Levi doesn't know if his mom is alive or dead."

Joel's heart went out to Finn's friend. He'd burned his bridges with his own parents when he and Carrie had divorced, but at least Nate and Laura still had a relationship with their grandparents. "So Levi's grandmother raised him?"

Finn nodded. "She became the mom he needed. Which got tougher when his grandfather died, not long after Levi was born. Levi said it was his grandfather's heart condition that killed him. I'm not so sure."

"No wonder you hold her in such high regard. It sounds like you saw a lot of her when you were growing up."

Finn smiled. "I spent most of my time at Levi's house. I guess we're more like brothers than friends. Except... I'd never take my brother to a gay bar." He chuckled. "You should have seen us. Our first time... We were so nervous."

"It couldn't have been that long ago. How old are you now?"

"Twenty-five, almost twenty-six. And yeah, we waited until we were twenty-one."

"Does Grammy know? That Levi is gay, I mean."

Finn laughed. "Try keeping *anything* secret from Grammy. He came out to her when he was sixteen—

he'd known for much longer, but it took him that long to get up enough courage. Grammy just took it in stride, like she did with everything."

Joel stroked Bramble's head. "I envy him that. There was no way I could ever have shared that with *my* parents. Or even gone to a gay bar."

"But I bet you've made up for it since," Finn said with a smile.

"Actually? I've never been to one." He nodded when Finn gaped at him. "I would never have gone to one while I was married, and since I moved out, I just haven't found the time."

"Haven't found the—what you *really* mean is, you're nervous about it."

"You don't miss much, do you?"

Finn's eyes were warm. "I guess I'm getting to know you."

Joel liked the sound of that. "You're right, of course. It's been on my to-do list, but to be honest, I put all my efforts into finding a place to live, keeping up with my clients, finding new ones… I kind of pushed it onto the backburner."

Finn leaned back in his chair, his legs stretched out in front of him, his hands clasped on his stomach. "I have an idea," he said slowly.

Joel chuckled. "Ooh, why do I not like the sound of this?"

Finn's eyes gleamed. "There's a gay bar—except it's really a nightclub—in Ogunquit that I think you'll like. It's called MaineStreet."

Joel's heartbeat raced. "I've driven past it a few times." *Yeah, more like a dozen.*

"Then I think it's high time you went inside." That gleam was still evident. "What are you doing this

Saturday night? Are the kids coming over again?"

Joel shook his head. "Not this weekend."

Finn gave a satisfied smile. "In that case, how about you and I pay a visit to Ogunquit? It's only a half-hour drive along route one, give or take."

Joel's heartbeat quickened.

"It's one of a couple of gay bars in Ogunquit, but the other one is more of a restaurant. MaineStreet is where I go when I want to dance and have a good time." He cocked his head to one side. "Do you dance, Joel?"

Joel swallowed. "Not for years. And I'm not sure how I'd feel about getting down on a dance floor surrounded by a bunch of guys in their twenties."

Finn blinked. "How old are you? Forty-one, forty-two?"

Joel let out a wry chuckle. "I'm forty-two, but right now I feel like I'm eighteen all over again. And just as nervous."

Finn beamed. "Trust me, you'll see a whole range of guys at MaineStreet. Some are my age, true, but there are also guys your age."

There was a lightness in his chest that Joel hadn't experienced for a long time, not to mention a rush of adrenaline.

"I'm guessing you like the idea."

Joel chuckled. "That obvious, huh? Right now I'm torn between two emotions. There's an empty feeling in the pit of my stomach that I know is down to nerves. But there's also impatience to discover something I've waited so long for." Bramble let out a soft whine, and Joel rubbed his ears. "That was *you* saying, 'I thought we were going on a walk, Daddy.'"

Finn laughed. "So you like my plan?"

"I love it—that doesn't mean I'm not scared to death too."

Finn reached across the table and laid his hand on Joel's arm. "I'll take care of you. Trust me."

The sweet gesture almost undid him. "I believe you." Joel took a deep breath. "Okay. Saturday night." He shivered. "Jesus, I am *so* nervous. I don't have a clue what I'm going to wear."

"Don't worry about that," Finn told him. "I'm gonna be at the house Saturday, working on the deck. I'm pretty sure I can find five minutes to take a look at the contents of your closet. I'll have you looking like a million dollars."

"I don't want to look like a million dollars—I just don't want to look out of place." Could his heart beat any faster?

Finn locked gazes with him. "You'll be fine." Another whine from Bramble brought a smile to his lips. "You'd better walk that dog, before he does pee on the rug." He glanced at the pieces of wood. "And I can keep working on Grammy's chair."

Joel got his feet and grabbed the end of Bramble's leash. "I'll leave you to it. See you Saturday?"

"Bright and early."

Joel smiled. "I'll have the coffee ready."

Finn laughed. "You're gonna need more than coffee—you'll need gloves."

Joel blinked. "I thought you don't like it when clients butt in."

"I don't, but I *do* need someone to hold the wood while I do my thing. Now, that can either be you, or I'll call up some of my friends, see if they can help out."

Joel decided to ensure all his work was completed by Saturday. "I can do it. All I have to do is hold wood?"

"That's it," Finn said with a smile. "*You* hold, and I clamp, drill, or screw. I *could* do it alone, but it would take a damn sight longer. And seeing as I have you right there…"

You could have me wherever you want me. Christ, all he'd said was *screw*, and Joel's mind had gone straight there, like a horny teenager.

Bramble whined again, and Joel flushed with guilt. "I'd better go." Finn walked him to the door, and Joel stepped outside. He gave Finn one last smile. "Maybe we'll get as far as the coffee *next* time?"

Finn's eyes widened. "We were so busy talking. Okay, you got it. You walk by here again, and if I'm home, I'll make you a cup of coffee."

"Sounds good." Joel crossed the street, Bramble tugging again. He turned and waved to Finn, then waited until Finn had gone back inside.

"Come on, boy. There's a beach down here that's crying out for you to play on it."

As he walked along Belvidere Avenue, Joel's mind was full of the prospect of dancing with Finn. *But what kind of dancing? Slow dancing? So close that we're almost touching?*

He had a feeling he'd be thinking about it long into the night.

Chapter Sixteen

"Is it plumb?" Finn asked, his hammer poised to secure the post with a structural nail. He glanced at Joel who was kneeling on a mat beside him, holding the post.

"The little bubble is in the middle—on both of them," Joel added quickly.

"Okay. You hold it steady, and I'll hit it."

Joel chuckled. "Sounds like an old comedy routine. You know, where one guy ends up hammering the other guy's fingers."

Finn laughed. "As long as you keep your fingers out of the way, we'll be fine." He tapped the nail into position.

"Aren't these posts a little high?" When Finn peered at him, Joel flushed. "Oops. Sorry."

Finn chuckled as he got to his feet. "You can let go of it now." He went over to his tools and picked up his chalk line. "Now we measure all the posts so we can saw off the tops to get them to the right height." He beckoned to Joel. "I need you over here," he said, pointing to the rear wall of the house. Joel followed him, and Finn pointed to a mark he'd made on the wall. "I need you to hold *this* end of the chalk line on *that* mark, okay?"

"Okay."

"And don't move. This has to be accurate."

Joel rolled his eyes. "I think I can hold it steady."

Finn laughed and pulled out the line, walking to the farthest post. He clipped the little level onto the line and peered at it, adjusting the line a fraction. "Okay, hold it there." Finn snapped the line, leaving a blue chalk mark on the post. Then he proceeded to mark off the other posts.

"Now what?"

"Now, you hold the posts around the base while I cut off the tops with the Sawzall." Finn grinned. "Unless you wanna do the cutting?"

Joel snorted. "I think I'll leave that up to you."

Finn gave him a sweet smile. "I think that's best."

He'd never had this much fun working with someone else.

Joel came out of the bathroom to the sound of Finn singing in the yard, and he smiled.

Someone sounds happy.

They'd gotten a lot done that morning, and Joel had called a halt so he could make lunch, leaving Finn outside to cut a couple more beams to the correct lengths. Not that he'd even started on lunch yet—the bathroom had been his first stop. Joel walked over to the door and peered through the screen.

Finn was standing beside the base of the deck, his Sawzall in one hand, be-bopping away to whatever was playing through his ear buds, and lost to the world. Joel caught his breath as Finn rolled his hips before giving little thrusts of his pelvis.

Damn, he can move.

And then there was the way he wore that tool belt, slung low on his hips. Up to that moment, Joel had not been aware he had a thing for muscular guys with tools—in particular, guys whose muscles were the result of hard, physical work, rather than hours spent in the gym—but hey, he was learning something new every day.

Finn was singing again, and Joel had to bite back his laughter when Finn gave a sexy little wiggle as the words "Ooh, baby baby, baby baby…." fell from his lips.

Joel might not have been up-to-date with the latest music, but even *he* knew that one.

He opened the door, and Finn came to a dead stop, his cheeks flushed. "Hey." He put down the Sawzall and hurriedly reached for his phone.

Joel held up his hands. "Don't let *me* stop you. Not when you seem to be having such a good time." He grinned. "Although I wouldn't want you to *push it*."

Finn laughed and switched off the music. "Gotta love Salt-N-Pepa."

Joel folded his arms and leaned against the door frame. "Are you getting some practice in for tonight?"

Finn's eyes glittered. "Honey I don't *need* to practice. I got *all* the moves." He gave a swivel of his hips, then burst out laughing. "Okay, you caught me. I didn't think anyone was watching."

Joel smiled. "I thought it was cute."

Finn bit his lip. "Is cute good?"

"Cute is *very* good," Joel assured him. "And now I've disturbed you, can I drag you in here to eat?"

Finn's belly gave a growl, and he gave a sheepish grin. "I think that might be a good idea. Just let me finish this bit first."

Joel nodded toward the deck. "This is looking really good. I should think we'll have this finished by the end of the day." When Finn gazed at him with widened eyes, Joel hastened to correct himself. "The base, I mean. I think you'll have all the beams in place."

Finn wiped his brow and let out an exaggerated sigh. "Phew. You had me worried for a sec. There is *no* way I can finish the deck today, but yeah, I can have the base done—with your help, of course. That leaves tomorrow for the boards and posts. If I put in a lot of hours, I could have it done by Sunday night."

"Don't push it," Joel said. Then he snorted. "See what I did there?"

Finn laughed. "Once was funny. Twice might be seen as *pushing* it."

Joel held up his hands. "Okay, that's it. No more. I'll make lunch—*you* go back to your dancing—I mean, your sawing."

"You mean it's not ready yet?" Finn rolled his eyes. "I'm gonna complain to the management."

Joel snorted. "Yeah, good luck with that. I happen to know he's a hardass." And with that, he closed the door.

He went to the refrigerator to get the cheese for the sandwiches, and as he passed the window, he couldn't resist taking a peek at Finn. The ear buds were back in place, and Finn was in his element, shaking his hips, his arms high above his head.

I love the way he moves. Part of his anatomy clearly liked how Finn moved too. Joel glanced down at his crotch. *Don't go getting any ideas. That cute ass is out of bounds.*

Now all he had to do was get through the night without embarrassing himself.

Finn peered at the rack of shirts in Joel's closet. "Is this everything?" Not that there was anything wrong with Joel's shirts—he just wanted Joel to look great for his first visit to a gay club, and the shirts screamed accountant or financial adviser.

That's because he is *a financial adviser. Duh.*

"There are three drawers full of T-shirts, if you can't find anything suitable." Joel's face tightened. "Maybe we should rethink this."

Finn knew Joel's nerves were getting the better of him. "And maybe you should show me the T-shirts," he said quickly. "Besides, a T-shirt is a better idea." He grinned. "Have to show off that body, right?" When Joel blinked, Finn realized what he'd said. "Hey, if you've got it, flaunt it. You've got a great chest and good arms. I'll be wearing something that shows off *my* best feature."

"And what's that?"

Finn gave a wiggle. "My butt."

"Oh, I don't know. I think you have a lot of good features. Starting with your eyes." Then Joel stilled. He cleared his throat. "The T-shirts are over there." He pointed to the drawers in the corner of the closet.

For a moment, Finn was too stunned to speak. *He likes my eyes.* Then he remembered he had a job to do. He yanked open a drawer and pulled out a black tee.

Finn unfolded it and gazed at it. "Perfect."

Joel arched his eyebrows. "Okay, that was faster than I expected."

Finn chuckled. "You can't go wrong with black. And you won't look out of place, I guarantee it. Now all we have to do is put it with a pair of tight jeans."

Joel blinked. "Do they have to be tight?"

"What did I say about looking out of place? And I don't mean so tight that you can't move in them, just something that shows off your legs." Because *damn…*

"I think I have a pair that will fit the bill." Joel didn't sound all that convinced, however.

Finn sighed. "You're going to look amazing, okay? Don't sweat this."

Joel expelled a breath. "Okay. Just glad you're going to be there with me."

"I won't let you out of my sight, I promise. Unless you wanna visit the restroom. I figure you're big enough to do *that* all on your own." Finn closed the drawer.

Joel laid his hand on Finn's shoulder. "In case I forget to say this tonight? Thank you."

Finn took one look at Joel's earnest expression, and all he wanted to do was kiss him, hold him, and tell him everything would be all right.

Because that mouth was crying out to be kissed.

Finn smiled. "You're welcome. And now I'll go back to my place and get ready. I'll pick you up at eight-thirty, okay?"

"I'll be ready." Joel's eyes sparkled. "Nervous, but ready."

And there it was again, that urge to kiss those soft-looking lips.

Finn had to get out of there before he made a move

he might regret.

Finn switched off the engine and glanced at Joel. "Ready?"

Joel peered through the windshield at the sign. "Okay, so far so good. A rainbow flag and a cocktail glass." All the way there, his stomach had been in knots, and the situation hadn't improved now that they'd arrived.

Finn laughed. "You're gonna have a good time tonight. So how about we get in there?"

Joel took a deep breath. "Let's do it."

They got out of the truck and walked across to the door of the club. Out front was a patio packed with guys, talking, drinking, with music playing in the background. Above him was another deck, equally full.

"You should be here at the height of summer," Finn told him. "You can't move out on those decks."

Joel noted the abundance of T-shirts. "Aren't they cold?"

Finn laughed. "May days can be T-shirt-warm or windbreaker-cool. All depends which way the wind's coming from, especially on the upper deck. And tonight's not that bad." He paused at the door and held out his hand. "I gotcha, okay?" Joel took his hand and Finn squeezed it. Then he released it and led him into the bar. Inside was darker than Joel had thought it would be, but bright, vibrantly colored lights blinked to the beat. The space was filled with bodies, male *and* female, moving in time to the music or standing around and talking.

"I thought this was a gay bar," Joel said above the music.

Finn nodded. "A better description might be a gay-*friendly* bar." He grinned. "But no discrimination here. The only thing that'll get you thrown out on your ear? Acting like an asshole." He pointed to the bar that was lit up in a soft purple glow. "Want a drink?"

Joel had never needed a drink so badly.

They inched their way through the throng to the bar, and Finn turned to look at him. "What's it gonna be?"

"Can I be really boring and have a rum and coke?"

Finn grinned. "You can have whatever you want." He turned to attract the bartender's attention, and Joel took a good look around them. It didn't take long to see Finn had been right. There were men of all ages, all sizes and all shapes, and the realization was doing wonders for Joel's nerves. Lady Gaga's 'Bad Romance' filled the air, and Joel was relieved to hear something he knew.

"I don't listen to a lot of music," he admitted when Finn finished ordering. "And I wasn't sure what we'd be dancing to." He grinned. "Of course, if they play Salt-N-Pepa, *you're* okay."

Finn laughed. "They play a good mix here." The bartender placed the glasses on the bar and Finn handed one to Joel. He raised his own. "To your first time."

Joel chuckled. "I'll drink to that." He stared at the crowded floor. "Is it always this busy?"

"You should be here on nights when it's Dueling Drag Divas," Finn told him. "That's a lot of fun. This place has two dance floors and three bars, so there's plenty of room, but it still gets full. Wanna take a look around?"

"Sure."

As they moved away from the bar, a loud voice called out Finn's name. "Oh my God. You haven't been here in *forever*."

Finn's face lit up. "I might have known you'd be here." He turned to Joel. "This is my friend Seb. I think I've mentioned him."

Joel smiled. "Yes, you did."

Seb grinned. "All good, I hope?" He was tall, with a shock of wavy hair that came down over his eyes and stopped just below his ears. He had pale blue eyes that twinkled, and the same scruffy beard and mustache that reminded Joel of Finn's.

He's the teacher? Seb came across as someone who belonged on a board, riding the waves.

Joel grinned. "Let's just say, I got the impression you're quite a character."

Seb regarded Finn with raised eyebrows. "And just *what* have you been saying?"

"Nothing but the truth," Finn assured him.

Seb looked Joel up and down. "Whereas *you* are exactly as he described you. Good to meet you, Joel." Lady Gaga faded, and in its place was a dance track that Joel didn't recognize. Seb's eyes lit up. "We *gotta* dance to this one."

"Hey, we've got drinks," Finn remonstrated.

Seb rolled his eyes. "Jesus." He hollered to the bartender. "Pete? Take care of these drinks, will ya? They'll be back for them."

Pete grinned. "Sure, Seb."

Finn snorted. "What is this, *Cheers*, where everybody knows your name?"

"Hush. We gotta dance." Before Joel could refuse, Seb grabbed his hand and tugged him toward the dance floor, Finn following them.

The rhythm was relentless, and the lyrics blew Joel's mind. Seb was apparently in his element, swaying sinuously, and giving flirtatious glances at the guys dancing around them. Finn danced in front of Joel, never breaking eye contact, and Joel breathed easier. He allowed himself to relax, and let himself be lost in the music.

"I guess dancing is like riding a bike too," Finn said with a smile. "Because it looks like it's all coming back to you."

Joel had to admit, he was loving it: the bass pulsing through his feet; the movement all around him; the lights that flickered, and the guys who sang along to the song. Then he caught a snatch of the lyrics and stopped dead.

"Did she just say G-spot? I swear I heard that. *And* I thought I heard blindfold and hardcore in there somewhere. What *is* this song?"

Seb laughed. "It's 'Dirty Talk' by Wynter Gordon. Filthiest lyrics ever." He grinned. "It's the kind of song that will bring every gay out of the restroom and onto the dance floor."

"Speaking of restroom…" Finn gave Joel an apologetic glance. "I'll be right back, okay?"

Before Joel could respond, Seb patted Finn's arm. "I'll take real good care of him."

Finn merely raised his eyebrows before hurrying to the restroom.

Seb carried on dancing, and Joel relaxed once more. That cryptic remark had worried him a little. *What exactly does taking care of me involve?* But Seb seemed happy to dance, and that was fine by Joel. The song changed again, and Kylie's voice filled the air.

"I like this one," Joel said loudly with a smile.

"And I like *that* one." Seb was staring at a guy a few feet away. "Yum."

Joel followed his gaze. The object of Seb's attention was a guy maybe in his mid-to-late forties, with graying hair and dark eyes, who was dancing with a younger man. He returned his attention to Seb. "Ok*ay*."

Seb's eyes glittered. "Just my type."

Joel took a guess. "Older guys do it for you?"

"E-ve-ry time," Seb enunciated.

"Well, not *every* time," Joel corrected. "Because *I'm* obviously not your type, but I'm probably a bit younger than that guy."

Seb bit his lip. "Are you *kidding* me?" He pulled Joel through the crowd to the side of the room where there were fewer people dancing, then looked Joel up and down, a lingering glance that got Joel's pulse climbing. "Honey, I would climb you like a tree in a heartbeat, but that would be wrong."

"Why?" Not that Joel was unhappy about Seb's reluctance to make a move on him, but he was puzzled.

"Because I love Finn like a brother, and I wouldn't do that to him." When Joel frowned in confusion, Seb sighed. Gone was the flirtatious manner, replaced by a serious expression that made Joel's chest tighten. "You don't sow seed in another man's garden, okay?"

"Excuse me?"

That got him another sigh. "Finn likes you, so you're out of bounds."

Joel gaped at him. "But... me and Finn... we're... we're not together. He brought me here tonight because I've never been to a gay bar, and he thought I might need some support. That's all." His heart pounded.

Seb arched his eyebrows. "Okay, you go right on believing that."

And what the fuck does that *mean?*

Seb took a deep breath. "The only reason I'm talking to you like this, is because we have something in common."

"And what's that?"

He looked Joel in the eye. "Finn. Not that he means the same to both of us. Like I said, I love him like a brother, but I'm pretty damn sure *you* don't want to be his brother." Seb raised his eyes. "Well? Am I right?"

Warmth flooded through Joel, and his dry mouth was suddenly dry no longer. His breathing quickened and he shivered.

"I guess I have my answer. And just so you know?" Seb gave a slow smile. "I'm not the only one who prefers older guys."

Holy fuck.

"Am I interrupting something?"

Finn's voice broke through, startling him. Joel swallowed. "Not at all. Seb and I were just… talking."

Seb smiled. "And now *you're* back, I'm gonna try my luck with that daddy over there." He kissed Finn's cheek. "Have fun." For a moment, his gaze met Joel's. "You too." And with that, he danced his way into the middle of the crowded floor.

"Wanna dance some more?" Finn asked.

Joel nodded, his mind in a whirl. For the first time since he'd met Finn, he entertained the idea that something happening between them was not as unlikely as he'd thought. Then the music changed again, to a song with a good beat that was impossible not to dance to.

Finn shifted closer. "I don't bite, y'know."

Joel's heart rate climbed. "Is that a promise?" He seized his courage and closed the gap between them a little more, until they were dancing scant inches apart.

Finn widened his eyes. "Unless you happen to *like* biting, of course."

"Not my thing," Joel said with a grin. Rihanna was assuring the men dancing that she was the only one who understood how to make them feel like a man, and instead of letting the song wash over him, Joel *listened*. He moved as sensually as he knew how, in sync with Finn, the two of them locked into a fragile moment that felt as though it would shatter if they so much as *breathed* wrong.

Finn didn't look away, but focused on Joel, lip-syncing as they moved to the music. The beat was pumping and yet more heat surged through Joel's body when Finn sang, their gazes locked as he told him he could come inside.

Joel didn't break eye contact, his breathing erratic, his heart hammering.

And when Finn shifted closer still, inviting Joel to take him for a ride, Joel knew beyond a shadow of a doubt what kind of ride he had in mind.

Make it last all night, Finn mouthed, and *Lord*, Joel wanted that. He wanted to have Finn's body against his, to feel every motion, every undulation. And the more Rihanna sang, the more convinced Joel became that the song had nothing to do with being the only girl in the world, and *everything* to do with getting down and dirty.

Joel could *so* do down and dirty right then.

When Rihanna faded into a much slower song that Joel didn't recognize, his heart soared as Finn closed the gap between them.

"I don't know who this is," Joel confessed, aware that he was trembling. All around them, guys were swaying to the music, arms looped around necks or waists, cheeks pressed together, bodies moving in sinuous harmony.

"Kacey Musgraves," Finn told him. Joel had to strain to hear him. "This one's called 'Rainbow'." His gaze kept drifting to Joel's mouth, which only served to speed up Joel's heartbeat.

They were dancing *so fucking close*.

It could have been the sheer volume of guys pressing in around them, but it wasn't. At least, that was what Joel hoped. He wanted to put his hands on Finn's waist, or around his neck, but he didn't dare.

He wasn't *about* to dare, not until Finn spelled it out in words that even an idiot could understand. Because in that moment, that was how Joel felt—a hapless idiot, out of his depth, wanting something with every fiber of his being, but not possessing enough courage to reach out and take it.

Because it didn't matter what Carrie said, or Megan, or Seb…

What mattered was Finn—who was looking at him with widened eyes. And then Joel's heart almost burst with joy when Finn cupped Joel's nape, and pulled Joel to him to claim his lips in a kiss that left Joel in no doubt at all that Finn wanted him as much as he wanted Finn.

Chapter Seventeen

Joel crushed his lips against Finn's, tasting rum and coke and pure Finn. And when Finn slid his tongue inside, desire poured through him in a torrent. He grabbed Finn's hips, pulling him closer until the solid heat of Finn's crotch met his own.

Finn stopped the kiss with a gasp, and they parted. "Jesus."

Joel fought to catch his breath. "If you knew how much I've wanted to do that…"

Finn was a little breathless too. "I think I get the idea."

Then the music changed, and the spell was broken. Kacey Musgraves was gone, and in her place Shania Twain sang about feeling like a woman.

Joel grinned. "Can't say I feel the same right now." When Finn gave him a perplexed stare, he forced a laugh. "Feel like a woman. Actually, I feel like a complete horndog."

Finn expelled a breath. "You sure haven't forgotten how to kiss."

Joel strove to keep a lid on the urge to drag Finn to a dark corner so they could make out like teenagers. "It's been a while."

"Well, why don't we dance some more, and then I'll

take you home." Finn's eyes gleamed in the lights. "So you can show me what else you remember." When Joel caught his breath, Finn stilled. "That's if you want to."

A boldness Joel had never experienced before seized him, and he grabbed Finn's hand, dragging it to his crotch. "What does that tell you?"

Finn shuddered. "Fuck." Joel had to stifle a moan as Finn cupped his solid shaft and gave it a gentle squeeze.

"My thoughts exactly." Joel wasn't sure how long he could keep dancing when all he could think about was Finn naked in his bed, in his arms.

Finn appeared to feel the same way. "Okay, we have three options. One, we leave now."

Talk about being torn.

"We just got here." Joel glanced around them at the guys dancing together. "And while I do want to get you out of here, I want to enjoy this a little longer. Because so far I'm loving it." Not to mention part of him wanted to hold onto that fluttery feeling in his stomach, the tingling all over his body, the delicious sensations that accompanied anticipation. *I've waited this long. I can wait a little longer.*

Not *too* much longer though.

And then there was the exhilarating feeling of being in a crowd of gay men, of being accepted.

Of being *out*.

Christ, that was heady as fuck.

"I kinda feel the same." Finn took a deep breath. "Option two. I take you to the restroom and… relieve some of this pressure." Another gentle squeeze of his dick. "Although… it wouldn't be my first choice because while the restrooms here *are* clean and well-lit, they're also a little on the cramped side." His smile sent a tingle all the way to Joel's balls. "I'm all for a quickie when you positively can't wait a second longer, but gimme comfort any day."

Joel had *not* waited twenty years to get sucked off in a restroom. "So option three is we stay a while?"

Finn nodded. He grinned. "Think of it as extended foreplay."

Joel bit his lip. "Not *too much* foreplay, okay? I'm liable to cream my jeans if you touch me again."

Finn's lips parted, his tongue darting out to lick his lips. "We can't have that, right?" Then he laughed. "Don't turn around. Seb is grinning like a Cheshire cat and making obscene gestures with his hands."

Joel shifted a little closer, finally getting *his* hands where he wanted them, on Finn's waist. "He *might* have let slip that you're into older guys."

Finn locked his arms around Joel's neck. "Oh really? Then I *might* have to have words with him."

"Don't. He was looking out for you. And if he hadn't said that, I might never have found the courage to—"

Finn stopped his words with a kiss, and Joel went with it, holding Finn to him as they swayed to the music, their tongues coming into play. Joel lost himself in the moment, enjoying the feel of Finn's lips on his, the solidness of Finn's body, the smell of him…

Then a thought struck him, and he broke the kiss. He brought his lips to Finn's ear. "I don't have any condoms at home."

Finn's breath tickled his ear as he whispered. "And I don't have any on me, but that's not a problem."

Joel's heart hammered. "I… I can't—"

Finn stopped his words with a hand to Joel's lips. "In case you missed them? There's a big plexiglass canister in the lobby, and a smaller one at the end of the bar. They're covered in glossy notices about the Southern Maine AIDS Walk and 5K Run, and they're both half full of condoms, free for the taking, courtesy of the Franny Peabody Center. So stop worrying and keep on dancing. We've got it covered." He grinned. "Literally. So breathe, and let's dance while we can. When we get back to your place, we can carry on with a little horizontal dancing."

Joel leaned in close. "Thank you."

Finn frowned. "For what?"

He exhaled. "Keeping your head. Helping me hold onto mine. Not rushing this."

"You've waited this long. A few more hours won't kill ya." Finn gave a slow, sexy smile. "Hey, anticipation is important. Building up to something, enjoying the excitement…"

Joel gave a shaky laugh. "Oh, I'm excited, all right." The realization that Finn wanted this as much as he did was intoxicating.

The fact that Finn wasn't rushing into it made him feel lighter.

Joel came back into the house and locked the front door. "Okay. Bramble's business is taken care of." Finn was sitting in the armchair, his coat on the floor beside it, his boots kicked off, and the sight of him sent shivers through Joel. He came to a halt and stared at him, uncertain of his next move, his heart racing, the muscles in his stomach twitchy as fuck.

Finn rose and walked over to where Joel stood. He cupped Joel's nape and looked him in the eye. "It's okay." His voice was so soft. Then he leaned in and kissed Joel, a lingering tender brush of lips that was nothing like their heated, bruising first kiss. Joel sighed into it, his hand on Finn's neck, stroking him there as they deepened the kiss.

He broke it long enough to let one word fall from his lips. "Condoms?"

Finn smiled. "In my jeans pocket."

A pleasurable shudder coursed through him, and he took Finn's hand in his. "Then come with me." Joel led him to the foot of the stairs, then let go of him to climb them, Finn following. Once up there, Joel went over to the nightstand to switch on the lamp, allowing warm light to spill into the space, reflecting off the white sloping ceiling.

Joel took a deep breath. "Jesus, my heart."

Finn gently pushed him down until he was sitting on the edge of the bed. "Move back a little." When Joel did as instructed, Finn straddled his lap and their lips met once more. Joel slid his hands around to cup Finn's ass, and Finn sighed. "Wanna hear what *my* heart's doing?" He cupped Joel's head and pressed it to his chest, and Joel listened to the steady, comforting beat of Finn's heart, pounding away like Joel's.

He feels it too.

Joel grasped the hem of Finn's T-Shirt and pulled it upward, with Finn raising his arms to help him remove it. He stared at Finn's broad chest with its down of dark hair. "You look amazing." He leaned in and laid a gentle kiss on Finn's nipple, aware of the hitch in Finn's breathing. The lure of Finn's lips was too strong to ignore, however. Finn's hands were on Joel's head, holding him tenderly and reconnecting their lips as he settled into a slow rocking motion.

"Wanna see what you look like." Finn grabbed Joel's T-shirt and tugged it up and over Joel's head. He gazed at Joel's body, tracing a line from his navel up to his nipples, and Joel shivered. Finn's smile eased his hammering heartbeat, just a little. "I like what I see."

He grabbed Finn and lifted him, setting him on the bed and lying beside him. Joel leaned over him and they kissed, their hands employed in a ballet as they moved over flesh, stroking, teasing, caressing... Joel found the courage to reach lower, his fingertips brushing over the metal button on Finn's waistband. "Can I?"

Finn's breathing quickened. "Let me." He popped the button free, and Joel eased the zipper down a little, enough to see the dark fuzz of Finn's pubes.

"Oh fuck." His heart pounded even more.

Finn snuck a hand into one pocket and removed three condoms before repeating the action with the other. He dropped his stash onto the bed, and despite his nerves, Joel laughed. "Exactly how many do you think we're going to need?"

Finn grinned. "Hey, you've just been through a dry spell so big it could be a fucking *desert*. I had no idea how many times you'd want to drink before you were done." Then he lifted his hips off the bed and took his jeans off, his cock bouncing up and smacking against his belly.

Joel resisted the urge to touch the hard pink shaft, and instead covered Finn with his body, lying between Finn's legs, spread for him. Finn took a second to fumble with the button and zipper on Joel's jeans before cupping his head once more and pulling Joel down into a kiss that sent heat flooding through him.

He stroked his tongue in and out of Finn's mouth, and each time Finn's low moan sent his need spiraling that little bit higher.

When Finn reached into Joel's jeans and freed his dick, Joel had to fight not to come on the spot. Finn gave it a couple of leisurely tugs while they kissed, slow, drugging kisses that fed something deep in Joel's soul, a connection he didn't want to break. His cock swelled in Finn's hand, and Joel groaned. He hadn't thought it possible to be this hard.

"I want you inside me," Finn whispered between kisses.

Joel didn't hesitate. He knelt up and pushed his jeans and underwear to his knees, falling sideways as he tried to remove them gracefully. Finn didn't laugh, thank God, but helped him, tugging at the lower hems to free Joel's legs. When he was naked, Finn reached for him. Joel lay on top of Finn, his feet resting on Joel's butt as they kissed.

Joel had never done drugs of any kind, but for the first time in his life he knew the meaning of addiction. He slid his tongue into Finn's mouth, fucking it with slow strokes, his hunger rising to the point where he knew he couldn't wait any longer. He shifted farther down the bed until his face was an inch above Finn's dick, Finn's knees fallen to the sides, Finn's hands on his head.

That first taste of Finn's cock on his tongue... The sounds Finn made as Joel teased the underside of his dick... The way Finn rocked his hips...

Sweet Jesus.

Before Joel had a chance to savor it, Finn tugged Joel higher, wrapping his long legs around him again as he claimed Joel's mouth in a fervent kiss. Joel rolled his hips, sliding his cock over Finn's hot, hard shaft.

Then Finn broke the kiss and pushed him backward, shifting to lie on top of him, their mouths once more joined. Joel stroked Finn's hair, raking through it with his fingers, his body on fire.

Finn ceased kissing and looked into Joel's eyes. "My turn." He laid a trail of kisses down Joel's body from neck to groin before kissing and licking the swollen head of Joel's cock.

"Oh God." Joel closed his eyes as Finn wrapped one hand around his shaft and sucked on the head, taking a little more into his mouth with each downward motion. Then Joel realized he had to *see*. He opened his eyes and lifted his head from the bed to watch as Finn worshipped his shaft with lips and tongue, from the tip of his dick to Joel's sac before reversing direction and taking Joel into his mouth once more. No hurry, no frenzy, just a measured, deliberate worship of Joel's cock.

"Fuck, I want you," Joel blurted.

Finn stopped mid suck and smiled. "You've got me." He sat astride Joel's hips and rocked, his hips so fucking fluid and sensual.

Joel had reached breaking point.

He pointed to the nightstand drawer. "There's lube in there." Then he sat up against the headboard, pillows stuffed behind him, and grabbed one of the condoms, his heart racing.

Finn straddled him again, and handed him the bottle. "Get me ready?"

Joel drew in a couple of deep breaths. "I'm liable to go off like a rocket as soon as I get inside you."

Finn cupped his chin and pulled him into another leisurely kiss. "Then we get to do it all over again as soon as I get you hard. Okay?"

He forced a chuckle. "Do you always know *exactly* the right thing to say?"

Finn grinned. "It's a gift. Now… there's a tight little hole here that needs your fingers." He gripped Joel's chin. "Because it's been a while for me too, all right?" Before Joel could respond, their lips collided in a kiss that told Joel how much Finn needed this. When they parted, Finn locked gazes with him. "Now. Please."

Joel's hand shook as he squeezed lube onto his fingers. Finn knelt, cupping his cock and balls and drawing them upward to give Joel access. Joel reached back and his fingertips encountered a furry cleft. He slid a single finger through it, his own cock twitching as Finn moaned, spreading his legs wider. Joel brushed the pad of his fingers over Finn's pucker, and Finn shuddered. "Yes," he whispered.

Joel applied a little pressure, his breath hitching as he slowly sank a finger into Finn's warmth. Finn let go of his dick and it stood upright, jerking with each glide of Joel's finger as he teased Finn's hole with long, unhurried strokes. It wasn't long before Finn was riding it, his body writhing with a fluidity that held Joel spellbound.

"You can add another," Finn told him. "And a bit more lube."

Joel applied more, then leisurely pressed two fingers into Finn's body, while he stroked Finn's belly. He looked up at Finn, loving the shine in his eyes, the glisten of perspiration on his chest. "Let me know when."

Finn rode his fingers a little harder, his breathing erratic and harsh in the quiet bedroom. Joel stroked him on the inside, seeking Finn's prostate, unable to miss the exact second he found it. He kept up the sensual massage until Finn was writhing, his breathing rapid.

"When," Finn said abruptly, pumping his cock and smearing the pre-cum beading at the slit like dew.

That was all Joel needed.

He tore the condom wrapper with his teeth, removed the rolled latex, and squeezed the tip as he covered the head of his dick. "Been a while since I've needed one of these." When he was gloved, he wrapped his arms around Finn's waist and pulled him close. Finn bent lower and their foreheads met.

"I'm glad it's you," Joel whispered before taking Finn's mouth in a sweet kiss, his hands on Finn's back. Finn reached behind him to guide Joel's cock to his crease, then left it there as they continued kissing, Finn rocking as Joel's dick slid over his hole. Then Finn reached back to spread himself, Joel pushed—

And he was home.

Joel exulted in the sensation of being inside Finn. Their lips fused as they kissed, each feeding the other noises of pleasure and desire. Finn moved in slow motion, sinking lower and lower, until Joel was sheathed in his tight body. And still they kissed, Joel craving the feel of Finn's mouth on his.

Finn raised himself up, and Joel gasped as his body tightened around Joel's shaft. "Oh fuck," Joel said weakly. "That feels…"

Finn nodded, his gaze on Joel's face, his lips parted. "Amazing." He rocked, Joel's cock sliding out of him, only to sit back on it at that last second before complete withdrawal. "Fucking amazing."

Joel moaned. "No—amazing fucking." Except this was nothing like he'd imagined it would be. The pace was goddamn perfect, as was the feel of Finn in his arms, the taste of him on Joel's lips, the smell of him… All of it combined to create a sensuous spell that wove its way around them, connecting them.

Finn rode him harder, bouncing on Joel's dick, tossing his head back, his chest damp with sweat.

Joel knew he wasn't ready for it to end. "Get on all fours," he blurted.

Finn complied, twisting to gaze at Joel over his shoulder. "Put it back in me."

Joel covered Finn with his body, kissing his nape as he slid his cock deep inside once more, and Finn shuddered as Joel tugged him upright, his dick wedged in Finn's ass. He pressed his lips to Finn's back, laying a trail of kisses down his spine, and Finn turned his head, a silent yet obvious demand for Joel's kiss. Joel enfolded Finn in his arms, keeping him there as his cock tunneled into him, picking up speed, their bodies meeting with loud slaps. Then he came to a stop, Finn's body wrapped around his shaft as Joel kissed his neck and shoulders, Finn twisting to connect their lips, his hands covering Joel's, holding them to his chest.

Joel knew he couldn't last much longer.

He pulled free of Finn's body. "On your back, sweetheart." The endearment fell from his lips without a second's thought. Finn lay down, and Joel stuffed a pillow under his ass. Finn drew his knees toward his chest, Joel guided his dick to where it wanted to be, and *fuck yes*, he was inside Finn again.

Finn rested his calves on Joel's shoulders, his arms around Joel's neck, and they were kissing once more, Joel fucking Finn's mouth with his tongue, keeping to the rhythm of his cock as he drove it into Finn's ass. They broke the kiss, their damp foreheads meeting as

Joel rocked into him, their breathing harsh, both pushing out urgent sounds that told Joel how close Finn was to coming. Joel fucked him with short, quick strokes, his hips snapping at that first zap of electricity that went all the way to his balls.

"Fuck, I'm there," Joel moaned, unable to hold it back. He thrust deep, slamming into Finn's ass as he shot hard, his throbbing dick held tight within Finn's body. Joel kissed him with a fervor he hadn't known he possessed, Finn's arms locked around him, their mouths colliding as Joel's cock pulsed the last drops into the latex.

Finn let go of Joel to grab his own shaft, and seconds later he came, covering his belly. Joel eased his dick from Finn's hole and bent over him to lick up every drop, savoring the taste of another man's cum for the first time in so many years. Then he carefully removed the condom and tied it before dropping it to the floor.

They lay on the bed, arms around each other, legs entwined, their kisses as slow as molasses in winter. Joel lifted Finn's chin and looked into those storm-colored eyes.

"Stay?"

Finn's nod was the perfect end to a perfect day.

Chapter Eighteen

Finn opened his eyes. *So it wasn't a dream.* Joel's chest was pressed against his back, his leg hooked over Finn's. They'd fallen asleep with the lamp on, but that was daylight pouring in through the window above their heads.

Finn wasn't ready to greet the day, however. He wanted to burrow beneath the sheets and hold Joel in a soft cotton cocoon that diffused the light. To kiss some more, because *damn*, he couldn't get enough of Joel's kisses.

Who was he kidding? He couldn't get enough of Joel.

From below, a soft whine arose, and just like that, Finn's plans changed.

Aww, poor puppy. Snuggling would have to wait.

He gave Joel a careful nudge with his elbow. "Hey, sleepyhead." When Joel rolled over with the cutest snuffling noise, Finn came to a decision. He eased his way out of the bed, pulled on his jeans and T-shirt, and padded barefoot down the stairs to where Bramble was sitting by the front door, still whining.

"Sorry, boy. Daddy and I overslept." He put on his boots, grabbed the leash from its hook, attached it to Bramble's collar, and unlocked the door. He let out the leash and Bramble headed for the nearest tree.

Finn breathed in the brisk morning air. *Wow. That was some night.*

Not exactly the night he'd planned, but he wasn't complaining. That first kiss had taken his breath away. He smiled to himself. *We didn't stop kissing all night.* And Joel in bed was…

Finn couldn't quantify the experience.

He wasn't sure what he'd expected. Maybe a bout of frenzied fucking, given the length of time that had passed since Joel last had sex with a guy. Or perhaps a really short fuck, because Finn knew Joel had to be on the edge. But what he'd *gotten* had been exquisite. And *way* beyond anything Finn had experienced before.

After weeks of fantasizing about Joel, reality took everything his imagination had come up with, and kicked it out of the door. And Finn wanted more.

Then he realized Bramble was back at his side, gazing up at him.

Finn's stomach growled, and he was glad no one was around to hear it. He peered at the dog. "Breakfast?"

Bramble wagged his tail with more vigor.

Finn laughed. "Let's feed you, and then I'll feed your daddy." He headed back to the house, unable to stop smiling.

I don't know which appetite I want to deal with first.

Because the thought of going back to the man lying in that warm bed was *so* tempting.

Finn closed the door and went into the kitchen, in search of something for Bramble. He found a sack of dry dog food in the cabinet next to the refrigerator, and poured a scoop of it into Bramble's bowl. Then he filled the water bowl and set it beside the food. Bramble approached, his nose twitching.

"Here ya go, boy."

That was all the invitation Bramble needed, apparently.

Finn left him to it and went over to the coffee pot. He turned it on, then reached into the cabinet for two mugs. It wasn't long before the smell wafted through the air, and Finn smiled.

That might wake him up.

Sure enough, a moment later he caught movement above his head. "Do I smell coffee?" A pause. "Is that the time? *Christ.*" There came the sound of feet thudding down the stairs. "I *never* sleep this late." Joel burst into view, wearing only his jeans. "Bramble needs to—" He broke off at the sight of Bramble chowing down. "Oh. Great. But he has to—"

"Been there, done that." Finn gestured to the front door. "I took him out there."

"Thank you." Joel sniffed. "*And* you made coffee." He grinned. "A man who's house-trained. I like it."

"We aim to please."

"Of course, it's *your* fault I didn't wake up with the birds this morning."

Finn chuckled. "Did I wear you out last night?" He'd had the *best* sleep. Finn liked Joel in nothing but jeans. Even his bare feet were sexy, and Finn had *never* had a thing for a guy's feet. A wave of shyness broke over him. "Good morning."

Joel walked slowly to where Finn stood. Without a word, he leaned in and kissed Finn on the lips, a chaste kiss that still managed to light a fire in Finn's belly. "*Now* it's a good morning," Joel said as he drew back.

Finn couldn't resist. He put his arms around Joel and closed the gap between them, emboldened by Joel's kiss. "It could get even better."

Joel's eyes gleamed. "Well, seeing as you went to the trouble of picking up *all* those condoms, it seems a shame not to use them." He stilled. "That's if you—"

Finn stopped his words with a kiss. "Dumb question," he murmured against Joel's lips.

Breakfast would have to wait.

"You are a terrible distraction," Finn muttered as they walked back to Joel's car.

Joel blinked. "I took you for breakfast at Becky's Diner. How is that a distraction?" He gestured to the wharf that had been their view while they ate. "This has to be better than eating at my place."

It was a great view, and Finn had devoured every mouthful of his Hobson's Wharf Special, wolfing down sausage, scrambled eggs, French toast and home fries, and a lot of coffee. But there was a deck to finish, and so far his Sunday had been nothing but fucking and eating. Not that he'd said no when Joel suggested driving to Portland to eat. So what if it meant a thirty-minute drive? Becky's French toast was to *die* for. And he couldn't really complain about the fucking part either.

Warmth rushed through him. *Definitely not gonna complain about* that.

"I'd love to know what just went through your mind." Joel's eyes glittered.

Finn snorted. "I don't think it would come as a surprise."

"You said come." Joel bit his lip.

Finn rolled his eyes. "What is this—you get laid, and then suddenly you're a kid again?"

Joel laughed. "I feel young today."

Finn's heart soared to hear the words, and right then he yearned to be back in Joel's bed, on his knees, holding onto the headboard and impaling himself on Joel's meaty dick—again. And again. And again, with Joel's hand on his belly, the other on Finn's shaft. Damn it, he could still feel Joel's lips on his back, those gentle kisses that were the perfect accompaniment for the leisurely in-and-out motion of Joel's cock.

He expelled a breath. "Yep, you are a terrible distraction." And Finn couldn't have been happier about it.

Joel's breathing changed, and Finn knew he wasn't going to get any work done on the deck *that* day.

"Then let's go home so I can distract you some more."

"Joel?"

Finn knew that voice. Joel stiffened. "I do *not* believe this," he muttered. They turned around, and Joel sighed heavily at the sight of Megan and Lynne. "Hello there. What a surprise."

Finn chuckled at the lack of sincerity in Joel's voice. "Hey, you chose Portland. Did you figure the chances of running into your sister were slim?"

"What are you guys doing here?" Megan gave Finn a cheerful nod. "Is the deck finished?"

"Not yet. The base is down," Finn told her.

"We came here for breakfast," Joel added quickly.

Megan arched her eyebrows. "So you decided to call Finn and invite him to eat out?" Her lips twitched. "Or did you just roll over and suggest it?"

Joel narrowed his gaze. "In earlier times? They've have tried you as a witch."

She cackled. "I knew it!"

"Knew what?" Lynne demanded. "What did I miss?"

"Oh, not much, just Joel and Finn playing Hide the Salami." Megan's eyes gleamed. "Which I predicted," she added smugly.

Finn swore Joel was about to have a fit of apoplexy. "Will you keep your voice down?" Joel's face was flushed.

Megan beamed. "Wow. You took my advice. I'm dumbfounded. I mean, since when do you listen to a word I say? Next thing you know, you'll be busting pages of that novel you're—"

"We have to get going now," Joel interjected. "Finn has a deck to finish, remember?"

Finn wasn't certain if their plans had changed or if Joel was making an excuse to get them the hell out of there. The way he pulled his car keys from his pocket indicated the latter.

"Don't let us stop you. Good to see you again, Finn." That gleam in Megan's eyes hadn't diminished.

"You too." He gave Lynne a wave.

"See ya." Joel was already moving quickly along the sidewalk, and Finn had to sprint to catch up.

He snorted. "You *really* didn't want to talk to her, did you?"

"Are you kidding? I'm never going to hear the last of this." They reached the car, and Joel got behind the wheel.

Finn got in and fastened his seatbelt, his stomach roiling. "Hey… you don't regret…" He didn't know what to think. *Does he not want Megan to know about us?*

Then a wave of cold reality crashed over him. *What us? We've fucked twice. There is no us.*

Jesus. Seb really had him nailed. One night with Joel, and Finn was—

No. No. I am not *gonna fall for Joel like I fell for every other guy I had sex with.* Except he knew such vehement decisions were a waste of time.

Finn had already been falling before he'd gotten as far as Joel's bed.

Joel switched on the engine, but didn't take the car out of Park. "I don't regret a single second, okay? Last night was…" He swallowed. "Last night was amazing, and I don't care if I wear that word out. It was, truly. And I don't care if Megan knows things have changed between us."

The iron band constricting Finn's chest loosened a little.

"No, what pisses me off is that she's going to be saying I told you so for *weeks*. Because believe me, she's done it before." Joel laid his hand on Finn's thigh. "And by the way? You don't have to work on the deck this afternoon." He gave an adorable smile. "Not if there's something else you'd rather be doing."

Finn grinned. "I think I can come up with a few ideas."

Joel laughed and pulled away from the curb. As they drove along Commercial Street, heading for the 295, Finn pondered something Megan had said. He figured it was none of his beeswax, but his curiosity got the better of him.

"What was Megan talking about? What novel?"

"It's nothing." Joel kept his eyes on the road ahead.

As if Finn was going to be deterred by that. "Sure didn't sound like nothing."

Joel said nothing for a moment, and Finn got the feeling he'd pushed when he should have backed off. Then Joel sighed. "It's just that… I had an idea. I've always wanted to write a book."

Finn gaped. "I think that sounds awesome. How much have you written?"

Joel laughed out loud. "I haven't even started it. Every time I sit down to put my thoughts into words, the sight of that blank page terrifies me."

"But why? You won't know what you can accomplish till you try."

Joel jerked his head briefly to stare at Finn. "What if I suck?"

"What if you don't?" Finn retorted.

"Okay, fair enough. But I still don't have a clue where to start."

"The beginning sounds like a good idea."

Joel rolled his eyes. "Yeah, *big* help.

Finn sighed. "No, I mean *your* beginning. Start with the moment you first knew you were gay, and take it from there."

There was a pause. "Seriously? Who'd want to read that?"

"Well, I would, for one." Finn held up his hands. "Hey, it's only a suggestion. No one's saying you have to publish it, okay? But it might get you started. You know, get you into the swing of writing."

"I'll think about it."

That was an improvement on 'What if it sucks?'

Joel set the laptop on the kitchen table and fired it up. He could hear Finn singing outside as he screwed boards to the deck. Joel wasn't surprised Finn had elected to do a couple of hours of work that afternoon, instead of pursuing other… avenues.

He's a good guy.

Besides, when Finn was done, Joel would make dinner for them, and who knew where the evening would lead?

Joel already had an idea of how he wanted the evening to go, and he didn't think Finn would be averse to it. He glanced at the whiteboard he'd put up on the bathroom door, and chuckled.

If Megan came over and saw the words condoms and lube written there, would she be shocked? Who was he kidding? She'd probably send him a box for his birthday as a gag gift, along with anything else she thought might be appropriate.

Joel knew he was procrastinating. Finn had gotten him thinking during the ride home, and once he'd gone outside, Joel had seized the moment. The only thing was, that blank document was taunting him as usual.

Start with the moment you first knew you were gay.

Joel laughed. "Now *that* might shock her." Especially if he wrote about his late-night shenanigans during sleepovers. He smiled. *Fuck it.* Joel started typing.

A loud cough broke his concentration. Finn stood beside the table, grinning.

"Your dog thinks you don't love him anymore. That's the second time today I've had to take him outside to relieve himself."

Joel glanced at the wall clock. "Four-thirty? But…" It had been one-thirty when he'd sat down at the table.

Where did the time go?

Finn gazed with interest at the laptop screen. "Wow. I'm impressed." He peered at the bottom of the screen. "You've written over a thousand words."

I have?

Joel moved two fingers over the mouse pad, scrolling up. "Wow. I'm impressed too." A thousand words didn't sound like a lot for three hours' work, but hey, he'd take it. Like Finn said, it was a start.

"Can I read it?"

Joel bit his lip. "Would you be offended if I said no?"

Finn smiled. "Not at all. I'm just happy to see you writing." He bent over and kissed the top of Joel's head, and the intimate chaste gesture both surprised and delighted him.

"You done out there?"

Finn nodded. "I've cleared up. I meant to get more done today, but—"

"But I distracted you, yeah, I know." Joel chuckled. "There's always next weekend."

"I'll see what I can do after work too. An hour here, an hour there. It all adds up." Finn glanced at the clock, and Joel's stomach tensed.

I don't want him to go.

"Do you have to rush off? Won't you stay for dinner? Unless you've got things to do at home."

Finn smiled. "I'd love to stay." He pointed to the laptop. "Are *you* done?"

Joel nodded. Whatever muse had inspired him had taken their leave.

Finn's eyes sparkled. "In that case…" He leaned over once more, only this time his lips met Joel's in a slow kiss. "Save what you've written, turn off the laptop, and take me upstairs," he whispered in Joel's ear. "We've still got condoms left, remember?"

Joel could get behind that plan. Apparently, so could his dick. "Do you need a snack or something first?" Finn had expended a lot of energy that afternoon.

Finn moved to stand behind his chair, slid his hand down Joel's chest, and cupped his growing erection. "You have all the snack I need right here," he said in a gruff voice that send a shiver of anticipation trickling through him.

Joel had never shut the laptop down so fast.

As they headed up the stairs, Joel mused that at some point the shine would wear off and they wouldn't be fucking every chance they got.

He hoped that wouldn't be anytime soon.

Chapter Nineteen

By the time Wednesday night arrived, Joel knew he had a problem.

He was addicted to Finn.

Joel hadn't seen him since Sunday night when Finn had finally gone back to his place after they'd spent most of the evening in Joel's bed: they'd gone right back to it the moment dinner was over. Finn had apologized for not being able to work on the deck in his evenings that week, but Grammy's chair wasn't ready, and the party was drawing closer. And while Joel knew it made sense to not overdo things—and he'd totally agreed with Finn that four nights wasn't *that* long to go without seeing one another, and that they could get together Friday night for sure—he'd spent the intervening three days thinking of nothing but Finn.

Finn's smile.

His arms.

His laugh.

His butt.

His dick.

That last one, however, was the clincher. All through Wednesday, Joel had tried to push one thought from his head, but it wouldn't leave. He'd buried himself in phone calls and appointments, but his mind kept straying back to that tantalizing conclusion.

He needed Finn's cock in his ass. Like, yesterday.

Joel told himself this was the result of years of denying himself, that it would wear off, that he wasn't *always* going to feel consumed by the need to touch Finn, kiss him, fuck him… A consumption that sent delicious ripples of pleasure through him.

Friday, okay? You can wait till Friday night, surely. It wasn't as if there was no contact between them, right? They sent texts, Joel called, Finn called…

Finn's voice. Yet another thing to occupy Joel's thoughts. If Finn ever got it into his head to talk dirty, Joel had no doubt he'd come without so much as a finger in his ass.

And here I am again, right back to my ass.

He climbed into bed, reached for the lube, closed his eyes, and let his imagination take over. It wasn't Joel's fingers that penetrated his tight hole but Finn's, long and slick. Fingers gave way to Finn's tongue, and *sweet Jesus*, that was enough to bring him to the edge. Much as he tried to delay the inevitable, it wasn't long before he was stifling his moans for fear of disturbing Bramble, and coming into the towel that had become a regular fixture beside his bed.

As he lay in the dark, his heartbeat slowly returning to its normal cadence, Joel came to a decision. *Fuck waiting.* He'd stop by Finn's the following day when he took Bramble for a walk.

Just for a coffee.

Yeah right.

Bramble walked ahead of him, with less exuberance than he'd shown on the way to the beach. Joel knew from experience that within a couple of hours, he'd be pawing at the door, dragging his leash off the hook, and dropping it at Joel's feet with a look that said *Well? Are we going or what?*

Then Joel spied Finn's truck on his driveway, and his pulse quickened.

He's home.

It was absurd how happy that simple realization made him.

"Let's go see Finn, eh, boy?" Bramble tugged on the leash, steering Joel toward Finn's truck, and Joel laughed. Bramble was just as keen to see Finn as he was. He stopped at Finn's front door, striving to breathe evenly. Then he rang the doorbell.

Finn opened the door and smiled. "Hey. I owe you a coffee, don't I?" He cocked his head to one side, and stood very still. "But you didn't come here for coffee, did you?"

Joel locked gazes with him. "Nope. Is it that obvious?"

"I've been thinking about you. I *hoped* you were thinking about me." Finn glanced at Bramble. "On your way to or from the beach?"

"From."

He grinned. "Thank God for that. Get your ass in here."

No sooner had Finn closed the door behind him,

than he was tugging Joel out of his jacket, their mouths locked in a frantic kiss.

"Fuck, I've missed you," Finn murmured against his lips. "Shoes, off."

Joel chuckled. "Yes, sir." He toed them off, then shivered as Finn dove in and kissed his neck. "Christ, much more of that, and I'll shoot before you get anywhere near my ass." When Finn froze, Joel stared at him, his heart beating fast. "Have I said something wrong?" Then it hit him. "Oh God. Tell me you top."

Finn's eyes were so dark. "Oh, I top. And you have *no* idea how many times I've thought about this."

Joel caught his breath. "Seriously?" He liked being the object of Finn's lust. When Finn gave a slow nod, Joel smiled. "Then let's see if reality is better than your fantasy."

They stumbled toward the couch, and Joel fell backward against the cushions. Something caught his eye, and he laughed. A *very* large box of condoms and the biggest bottle of lube Joel had ever seen were sitting on the coffee table.

"I guess I'm not the only one who's been shopping."

Finn's eyes twinkled. "The way we're going? That's about a week's supply." He grabbed hold of Bramble's collar and led him to the kitchen, closing the door on him. "Sorry," he told Joel when he returned to the couch. "The thought of him watching us was too much for me."

Joel was glad of the moment's reprieve. "Hey... can we maybe slow things down a bit? I know I came in here with my engine all revved up, but—"

Finn stopped his words with a kiss. Then he drew back a little, his eyes gleaming. "Slow is good. Slow is *definitely* good." He removed his T-shirt and tossed it onto the floor, then sat astride Joel's lap and popped the buttons on his shirt, taking his time and kissing each newly exposed area of skin. Joel shivered with each electric touch of Finn's lips on his skin. When they were both bare above the waist, Finn looped his arms around Joel's neck and kissed his forehead, mouth, cheeks, brushing his lips over Joel's ear lobes.

"Have you noticed," Joel murmured, letting out a low moan when Finn kissed his neck again, "how much time we spend kissing? Not a complaint, by the way."

Finn gave a slow sexy smile. "Good, because I could kiss you all day, given the opportunity."

Joel chuckled. "I think your coworkers might have something to say about that."

Finn's grin made his stomach quiver. "I might start a whole new trend. Coffee breaks are out, kissing breaks are in."

"Why stop at kissing?" Joel shivered as Finn kissed his way down Joel's chest. "God, I like it when you do that."

"Then lie down and let me do it some more. This couch is plenty big enough for the two of us."

Joel got on his back, and Finn lay on top of him, licking a trail down Joel's torso, interspersed with kisses. When he reached Joel's pants, he raised his chin and looked Joel in the eye. "These need to come off."

Joel blinked. "Here?"

Finn chuckled. "You came over on a mission, didn't you? Does it matter *where* it happens? Don't tell me you've never fucked on a couch before."

"I never had the chance." He and David had fucked every opportunity they got, wherever they could find a place far from prying eyes.

Finn kissed him. "Welcome to the world of sex on a

sofa, on the floor, against the wall, wherever you want." He chuckled. "I draw the line at doing it in public. I don't want the cops to throw my ass in jail."

"Wouldn't be my first choice either." He waited while Finn unzipped his pants, then pulled them over Joel's hips, leaving his briefs in place. "They don't get to come off too?"

Finn laughed. "Patience. You said slow it down, this is me slowing it down. You never heard of delayed gratification?" He tossed Joel's pants onto the floor, then took his socks off. He ran his hands over Joel's bare feet, stroking the soles. "Anyone ever tell you what nice feet you've got?"

Joel laughed. "Christ, I'm suddenly in the middle of *Little Red Riding Hood*." Then the laughter stopped when Finn knelt on the couch, lifted Joel's legs, and brought his feet to Finn's crotch, pressing them against his obvious erection. Joel breathed a little faster as he moved them, a slow rub over Finn's shaft that pointed toward his hip. "God, that's a hard dick."

Finn's eyes glittered. "All the better to fuck you with." He let go of Joel's feet and unhurriedly lowered the zipper on his jeans.

Joel stared, his heartbeat increasing. "Don't you ever wear underwear?"

"Is that a complaint?"

"Fuck no." Finn's dick bobbed as he pushed down his jeans, and Joel gazed at it with fresh eyes. *That's going inside me.* His hole tightened at the thought. Then Finn pressed his naked body against Joel's, and Joel pulled him down into a kiss that sent the blood rushing to his dick. He moaned into the kiss as Finn undulated on top of him, rubbing his bare shaft over Joel's, which strained to be released from the cotton briefs imprisoning it. Finn's lips were soft, and Joel couldn't get enough of his mouth on his body. Finn shifted to lie at his side, stroking down Joel's torso till he reached his briefs, where he cupped and squeezed Joel's now fully hard cock.

Joel caught his breath, and Finn brought his hand to Joel's face in a soothing caress. "It's not your first time bottoming, is it?"

"No, but it might as well be, it's been that long." Joel shuddered. "So be gentle?"

Finn's lips on his was the perfect response. He slipped his hand beneath the cotton, and freed Joel's cock and balls, pushing his briefs below them. Then he shifted, and Joel arched his back as Finn's warm, wet mouth closed over his cock. Instinctively, Joel placed his hands on Finn's head and held him steady as he pumped, hips rocking as he drove his dick between Finn's lips. Finn moaned around his shaft as Joel went deep, but he made no effort to stop him.

"Fuck, you're gonna make me come," Joel cried out. The sensations were too exquisite, the wetness and warmth too fucking perfect.

Finn was off him in a heartbeat. He grasped Joel's briefs and tugged them, Joel's legs in the air as Finn removed them completely. Finn grabbed a cushion and stuffed it under Joel's ass, then gave his thighs a gentle yet firm push toward Joel's torso. His heart pounding, Joel held his knees to his chest, groaning at the first tentative touch of Finn's tongue to his hole. "Holy f-fuck."

Finn's only response was to keep right on licking, sucking, and working that pucker, his hands pulling Joel's ass cheeks wide so he could push his tongue into Joel's stretched hole. Joel trembled, and the muscles in his abs quivered. Watching Finn's eyes darken as he probed and licked was hotter than hell.

Finn finally raised his head, his lips shining. "Got a job for you." He flipped himself around, and Joel was confronted by the sight of Finn's hefty cock above him.

"I can do that." He took Finn's dick in one hand and brought the head to his lips. Finn pushed, and Joel had a mouth full of hot, hard cock. He moaned around it as Finn spread his ass cheeks once more and dove back in there, teasing and licking his hole.

Joel lost track of time, adrift in a world of spiraling intense pleasure and heat that came to a shuddering halt when Finn stretched his hand toward the coffee table and grabbed the box of condoms, followed by the lube.

Oh God.

Finn shifted again to kneel between Joel's legs. "*Now* we're ready." He squeezed lube onto his fingers, and Joel tensed as he rubbed them over his hole. Finn stilled instantly. "Breathe, okay? You know what to do. And trust me, your ass is gonna remember how amazing this feels."

Joel took a deep breath and willed himself to relax. Finn slid a finger inside him, and he winced a little, taking deeper breaths. Finn didn't rush things. He took his time and the burn faded. Joel curled his fingers around his dick and tugged on it, gentle strokes to match the motion of Finn's finger in his ass. Then Finn found his prostate, and Joel moaned.

"Don't stop. Don't stop." Joel rocked his ass a bit higher, riding that finger, seeking more of the sensations. Finn added another slick finger, and that stretched feeling was back. Finn didn't pick up the pace, but maintained that steady slide-in-slide-out motion, until Joel's need was white-hot.

Then Finn stopped, and Joel knew what was coming.

Finn grabbed a condom from the box, tore open the wrapper, and unfurled the latex over his dick. "How do you want this?" His hand was gentle on Joel's belly. "Your ass, your choice."

Joel didn't hesitate. "Can I ride you?"

Finn smiled. "You can do anything you want." He lay on his back and squeezed lube over his solid shaft, smearing it with his fingers. He set the bottle down and held his arms wide. "Come here."

Joel straddled his hips and leaned over. Finn wrapped his arms around Joel and they kissed, Finn's dick sliding through Joel's crease as Finn rocked his hips. Finn cradled Joel's head in his hands, and it made Joel's heart ache to feel so… cherished.

"When you're ready, guide me in," Finn whispered.

Joel swallowed. "I'm ready now." He reached back and brought the head of Finn's cock to his hole. He held it there, trembling.

Finn looked Joel in the eye. "Tell me I can move." Joel nodded, Finn visibly held his breath as he pushed—and Joel sighed as Finn's dick slid home.

They stilled, Finn's hands on his ass, Joel's on the seat cushion on either side of Finn's chest. Finn's soft sigh echoed his. "Oh my God. You're so tight around me."

"Are you all the way inside me?"

Finn nodded, his lips parted, his eyes shining. "So good."

Joel gave an experimental roll of his hips, and moaned at the result. "You were right. It does feel amazing." That glorious sensation of feeling full, of being stretched…

"Can I move some more?" Finn asked.

Joel claimed Finn's mouth in a fervent kiss. He leaned on his forearms that bracketed Finn's head, and Finn held him close as he moved in and out of him, a gentle pace at first, but picking up speed. And all the while they kissed, feeding each other soft noises that made no sense yet said so much.

Joel sat upright and rocked back and forth, his hands on Finn's chest, overwhelmed by the notion that Finn's cock was all that kept him on the ground, because damn it, Joel felt like he was flying. Then he reached for Finn once more, and their mouths reconnected in another kiss, both of them breathing rapidly, a sheen of sweat on Finn's chest,

"On your back, baby."

Joel complied, and Finn hooked his arms under Joel's knees, pushing them higher and driving his cock deep into Joel's ass, their lips locked in a kiss.

Fuck. The angle was just right.

Joel clung to him, riding out the waves of pleasure that zinged through him, buffeted him, sending him closer to the edge. He slid his hand between their damp bodies, reaching for his shaft, and Finn nodded again.

"That's it. Gonna watch you come." He claimed Joel's mouth in a heated kiss, and Joel tugged harder, a moan falling from his lips as warmth covered his stomach. Finn's nostrils flared, and he grunted as he picked up speed, thrusting deep. Then he shuddered, and Joel opened his eyes wide as Finn's shaft throbbed inside him.

Finn buried his face in Joel's neck, his breathing shallow and erratic. Joel locked his arms around him and held on tight, folded in two, the pair of them cinched into one mass of flesh, Finn's cock still buried in Joel's ass.

When Finn raised his head and kissed him, heat radiated through Joel's chest and his limbs felt light, almost weightless.

"Now *that* was worth waiting for," Joel murmured, breathing in the smell of Finn's skin, his sweat, his own natural scent that stirred Joel's senses.

Finn's eyes sparkled. "I suppose you want that coffee now."

Joel chuckled. "In a while." Right then he wanted to lie there, holding Finn, enjoying the moment.

He wanted to remember this feeling. He was sticky, hot, wrung out, he ached in places that hadn't ached like that for decades—and he'd never been happier.

"Joel?"

He gave a start. "Sorry. I must have zoned out there. Did you say something?" Finn was curled up beside him on the couch, and the TV was on, but Joel wasn't watching. Bramble lay on the rug, snoozing. Joel had taken him for the fastest pee break ever, but he knew it wasn't enough. At some point he needed to think about going home. Finn had shoved a frozen pizza into the oven, so dinner had been taken care of, but Joel knew the day had to end sooner or later. They both had work the next day after all.

"I said I'm going to get some juice, and I asked if you wanted some." Finn craned his neck to look at him. "Are you okay?"

"I was thinking about something, that's all."

Finn sat up. "Anything you wanna talk about?"

Joel regarded him in silence for a moment. "Remember the day I told you about my past? And I said my future was exciting, but scary?"

Finn nodded, his eyes warm. "You were thinking about your kids."

Joel blinked. "Yes. Yes, I was. And I've finally come to a decision." He took a deep breath. "I think it's time I told them. They need to know the truth." Not that he was completely happy about the idea, but he knew he couldn't put it off any longer. It didn't make sense to hide anymore.

"Do you want me to be there when you do? It's okay if you want it to be just the three of you."

Joel's stomach clenched. "I don't know *what* I want." He sagged against the cushions. "I mean, yes, I want you there for moral support, but—"

"But I'm not part of the family, and they might wonder what the hell this has to do with me," Finn finished for him. He laid his hand on Joel's knee. "I do get it, you know. This is tricky shit. And if it makes you feel better, I'm just as torn."

Joel frowned. "You are?"

Finn nodded. "I want to be there for *you*. I know how much you've dreaded doing this. And if having me there makes it even a tiny bit easier for you, then that's great. But at the same time… I don't want the kids to think I'm interfering." He sighed. "Maybe this is one we play by ear."

Joel was no clearer in his mind. On the coffee table his phone buzzed, and Finn lurched off the couch and grabbed it, passing it to him. "I'll go get us some juice." Then he headed into the kitchen, affording Joel the perfect view of that gorgeous butt in tight jeans.

His phone vibrated in his hand, and he clicked Accept when he saw it was Carrie. "Hey."

"I know it's late, but can we talk?"

Something in her voice had the hairs standing up on his arms. "What's wrong?"

"The last time Nate visited... how was he?"

Oh God. "He was okay," Joel said slowly. "They both were. Nate didn't say much, but then he hasn't said an awful lot lately."

Carrie sighed. "As I thought. Well, it's a different story now."

"What do you mean?"

"I guess he's been bottling everything up inside, because he just pulled the cork and I'm dealing with the aftermath."

Joel's chest tightened. "What happened?"

"He exploded, would be a fair description. He went on about how he didn't understand why we divorced. He talked about there being no fights, no real conflict between us. He can't understand why we act like we're friends. What it all boiled down to was, 'There's something you're not telling me. There's more to this than the two of you just *growing apart*.'"

"What did you say to him?"

"The only thing I *could* say—I told him the four of us needed to talk about this, face to face, as a family." She paused. "I told him it was time he knew the truth."

Joel expelled a long breath. "Your timing is uncanny. I just said the same thing to Finn."

There was a pause. "Finn's there?"

He let out a wry chuckle. "Correction—I'm at Finn's place."

"A little late for discussing deck-building, don't you

think?" There was a note of interest in her voice.

Here we go. "Well… to be honest, we weren't doing a lot of talking." Hell, she had a right to know. He knew about Eric.

"I see. Things *have* progressed, haven't they?" Another pause. "You happy?"

"I was—until *you* called. So did he agree to us getting together?"

"He wanted to know why I couldn't tell him right that second. I explained again that we needed to do this as a family, and said I'd ask you if Sunday was okay. Turns out Nate is meeting up with a college friend Saturday, so that works out for us. How about you?"

"Sunday's fine. Just let me know when you're on your way."

"Sure. And Joel?" Carrie's voice was warm. "I *am* happy about you and Finn."

"Hey, don't start picking out china or anything like that. We're just dating, all right? And it hasn't been that long." Okay, so he wanted more than Finn warming his bed, but he wasn't about to jeopardize the situation by moving too fast.

"In that case, I'll keep my fingers crossed. I like him."

At that moment, Finn walked into the living room carrying two glasses of juice, and Joel smiled. "I'm pretty fond of him too. I'll see you Sunday." He disconnected.

Finn sat on the couch. "Sunday?" Joel repeated the conversation, and Finn gaped. "Well shit. Talk about a coincidence." He squared his shoulders. "That clinches it. I won't be there."

Joel stilled. "Really?"

He nodded. "This moment belongs to you and

Carrie, and I shouldn't intrude." Finn gave a half smile. "No matter how much I wanna be there. Just promise you'll call the minute they leave."

"The second," Joel assured him. Then he smiled. "Come here. I need to hold you close."

Finn straddled Joel's hips. He bent down and kissed Joel on the lips. "This close enough?"

Joel's hands were on his waist. "Oh, I think we can get closer than this."

Right then he wanted to be so close that he couldn't tell where Finn ended and he began.

Where do you want this to go, Finn?

Not that Joel was about to ask him. He'd said as much to Carrie. This was a recent development, and much as Joel wanted it to continue, he wasn't going to make a move so soon.

No matter how much he yearned to do just that.

Chapter Twenty

Finn let out a sigh of sheer contentment. "I like it when Friday night spills over into Saturday morning." Especially when that meant snuggling in Joel's bed. There was even a foot warmer, in the shape of Bramble who had ventured upstairs. He'd gazed at them from the top step with those liquid brown eyes, and Finn wasn't surprised when Joel beckoned him onto the bed. Right then he was curled up at their feet, his eyes closed.

That would change in a heartbeat if either of us said walk.

Of course, snuggling was eating into his deck-building time, but hey, Joel was the boss, and Finn wasn't about to go against the boss's wishes. As if he could refuse anything Joel asked of him.

If he wanted my heart, I'd give it. Finn knew when he was smitten, and this was as smitten as he got.

"You do know we have to get out of this bed eventually, right?"

Finn blinked. "But why? We still have..." He counted on his fingers. "Thirty condoms left." He grinned.

Joel laughed. "Who was it who mentioned delayed gratification less than forty hours ago? Hmm?"

"Aw, come on. Can't we stay in here a while longer?

Please?" Finn wheedled, adding his fingers to the coaxing, loving how Joel's breathing hitched whenever Finn got near his nipples. Then he brought his mouth to one of them and flicked it with his tongue.

A gasp stuttered from Joel's lips. His gaze narrowed. "You fight dirty."

Finn bit his lip. "I can get dirtier, believe me."

"I don't. I demand proof." Then he gasped as Finn rolled him onto his belly, spread his ass cheeks, and speared Joel's hole with his tongue. "Fuck." Joel raised his head from the bed when Bramble let out a bark. "Bramble? Daddy's fine. Bed."

Finn chuckled. "I rest my case." He waited while Bramble jumped off the bed and trotted with extreme reluctance to the stairs, pausing to give them one last soulful pleading glance. Finn grinned. "So you'd better not make too much noise, or Bramble will think I'm doing something awful to Daddy."

"You'd *better* be doing something," Joel retorted.

Finn went back to fucking Joel's hole, loving how Joel's body danced on his tongue.

Yeah, he wouldn't be working anytime soon.

Joel went into the kitchen. "You hungry?" he called out as he poured himself a glass of water at the sink. Finn had taken a shower after spending a couple of hours adding more boards to the deck. Joel reckoned it would be finished by Sunday, providing there were no more distractions.

"What's for dinner? And am I invited?" Finn hollered from the bathroom.

Joel laughed. "Stupid question. Of course you're invited. And there are a couple of Hungry Man meatloaf dinners in the freezer." Moments later, Finn was at his back, sliding his hands around Joel's waist, one heading north, the other south. Joel chuckled. "I see you're hungry for something."

"Mm-hmm." Finn's breath tickled his ear. "I have an idea for an appetizer. Ever wanted to get fucked on the kitchen table?"

A flood of heat surged through him. "Not until you mentioned it." And suddenly Joel couldn't think of anything else. He caught his breath when Finn squeezed his stiffening dick through his sweats.

"Aha. You like the idea though." Another squeeze. "Hoo, yeah." Finn spun him around and locked his arms around Joel's neck, rocking his hard shaft against Joel's.

"Does that thing *ever* take a break?" Not that Joel's was any softer. He held on tight to his glass, doing his best not to spill its contents.

Finn leaned in, and his rough chuckle tickled Joel's neck. "Not when you're around. That's its perpetual state." Another roll of his hips, and his dick slid over Joel's. "Maybe I should just pick you up and carry you to the table, lay you flat and—" He stilled and jerked his head toward the back door. "What was that?"

"What was—" Joel followed his gaze, and froze.

Nate was standing at the screen door, his eyes huge, his mouth open.

Aw fuck.

Finn sprang back as though Joel had burned him and Joel dropped his glass to the floor, where it shattered instantly. "Shit."

"I'll get this—go talk to him," Finn urged. He began picking up the largest fragments of glass.

Joel took a step toward the door, but Nate beat him to it and pushed the screen door open. He came into the kitchen and stood there, still staring, his lips parted.

Fuck, he's shaking. Then it hit him. Nate was so pissed he was vibrating, anger pulsing through him. And Joel couldn't move, rooted to the spot.

"I thought you were coming tomorrow, with Mom and Laura." He fought to keep his voice even. "Did I get my days mixed up?" Joel listened but heard no voices outside. "It's just you, isn't it?"

Nate gaped at him. "*That's* how you wanna play this? Jesus, you got some nerve."

Joel bristled. "Hey."

"Don't you 'hey' me." His eyes flashed and his cheeks were mottled. "You wanna know why I'm here? There was no way I was gonna wait till tomorrow. So I told Mom I was meeting a friend. Yeah, I lied. I wanted to hear what you had to say." His gaze flickered to Finn and narrowed. "And *now* it all makes sense. Is *he* why you and Mom broke up? Is that it? You were cheating on her with him, and she found out?" The hard edge to his voice cut Joel to the quick.

"Hey, it's not like—" Finn blurted out, but Nate's eyes flashed again.

"I'm not talking to *you*, I'm talking to my dad."

Joel held up his hand. "I don't care how upset you are, you will *not* talk to Finn that way. I brought you up better than that." He did his best to keep his voice even, as cold inched through his body.

Nate's eyes bulged. "You expect me to be cool about this? When you *lied* to us?"

Joel's heart pounded. "I never lied to you. I just… didn't tell you guys everything. And for the record? I met Finn while I was walking Bramble—less than a week before *you* did." When Nate let out a derisive snort, Joel saw red. "You don't believe me? Ask your mom. Because why would she lie about that, if Finn was the reason we broke up?" He pulled his phone from his pocket and held it out to Nate. "Here. Call her."

"Sure. She'll back you up. The pair of you have been lying to us from the start. And for the *record*? I *never* believed that half-assed line you fed us." Nate made no move to take the phone.

Joel didn't break eye contact. "If *you're* not going to call her, I am. She thinks you're someplace else." He hit speed dial.

Nate's lips twisted into a sneer that sent Joel's heart plummeting. "Yeah, that'd be right. Pass the buck, get Mom to do your dirty work."

Joel had had enough. His arm fell to his side, the phone still in his hand. "*You* are going to calm the fuck down and get a hold of yourself. You're an adult, so fucking *act* like one." From his phone came Carrie's voice, but he ignored it. Nate's eyes were huge, his chest heaving. "Well?" Joel demanded.

Nate held out his hand. "Gimme the phone."

Joel held up one finger as he brought the phone to his ear. "Hey. Nate's here."

She gasped. "He's what?" There was a pause. "It's bad, isn't it?"

Joel looked at Nate's flushed cheeks, his hands clenching and unclenching at his sides. "Yeah, but that's no surprise."

"Put him on."

Joel held out the phone. "She wants to talk to you."

Swallowing, Nate took it. Joel's heart ached to see how stiffly he held himself. He prayed Carrie could get him to see sense.

"You don't have to lie anymore, Mom. I know the truth. I saw them, Dad and Finn." Nate glanced in Joel's direction, and his nostrils flared. "He can't lie his way out of that."

Finn dropped the shards of glass into the trash, then moved to Joel's side. "Let them talk," he said in a low voice. "Give him some space." He gave Joel's arm a tug. "Joel. Please."

Joel's heartbeat raced, and there was pain in his chest. He fought the urge to throw up. He tried not to listen, but it was hard to miss Nate's accusatory tone. "You should've told us, Mom. You should've told *me*. I'm not a kid, all right?"

"Joel. *Joel.*"

He blinked. Finn's gaze was locked on him, his hand on Joel's arm. "Let Carrie do what she can, okay? Come into the living room, sit down and let them talk."

Joel allowed himself to be led into the living room, where Finn walked Joel to the rocking chair and waited while he sat. Bramble was at his feet a moment later, letting out a soft whine. Joel stroked his head. "You know something's up, don't you, boy?" Out of sight around the corner, Nate was still talking, but at least his voice had lost its sharpness.

Finn crouched beside his chair. "Listen, I think I should go. When Nate finishes his call with Carrie, you both need to talk. And I don't think I should be around when you do."

"But—"

Finn stopped Joel's words with a finger to his lips.

"Look how pissed he was when I tried to explain. This is a time for a father and son talk. Me being here is only gonna complicate matters." He sighed. "Send me a text, okay? Let me know how it goes?"

Joel nodded. "Sure." Deep down he knew Finn was right. This was something he and Nate needed to sort out together. He leaned forward and kissed Finn on the lips. "Thank you."

Finn stroked his cheek. "Try not to worry, okay? It's gonna work out."

Joel wished he could be that certain.

Finn got to his feet and glanced at his body. "Just thankful I put on a pair of your sweats before I came out of the bathroom. Imagine if he'd caught me in a towel."

Joel sighed. "I don't think it would've made the situation any worse than it already was."

"I'll go get my clothes." Finn headed up the stairs.

Bramble pushed his nose into Joel's hand, and Joel stroked his soft ears. "This is a mess, boy," he whispered. Nate was still talking, but his voice had lost its vehemence and harshness. Moments later, Finn was back. He grabbed his boots from the mat and put them on, peering toward the back door. When he was ready he glanced at Joel.

Call me? he mouthed. Joel nodded. Finn opened the front door and stepped outside.

Now it was just Joel and his son.

He looked at the wall clock. Nate had to have been talking for about ten minutes or so, but whatever Carrie was saying seemed to be working. Nate spoke quietly, calmer than before, but Joel didn't dare move from his rocking chair.

The ball was in Nate's court.

Silence fell, and a moment later Nate walked into view. He came over to the rocking chair and held out Joel's phone. "Here."

Joel took it and shoved it into his sweats pocket. Nate stood there, his arms limp at his sides. When it became clear Nate wasn't going to break the silence, Joel sighed. "So now you know."

Nate swallowed. "But why didn't I hear this from *you*? Why did you hide it?" He widened his eyes. "Did you think I'd freak? Jesus, Dad, don't you *know* me?"

"I didn't know the person you'd become," Joel admitted. "You didn't talk, didn't share… I had no idea how you'd take it. Let's be honest here. Our relationship used to be better, but it's been in the shitter for a while." When Nate blinked, Joel chuckled. "Considering what I said to you earlier, I think that's mild, don't you?"

Nate bit his lip. "Kinda, yeah." He breathed a little easier. "Mom said to tell you she'll be here in the morning with Laura." He swallowed hard. "She also said I shouldn't blame you."

"That's because your mom is a sweet person and I don't deserve her." Joel's throat tightened. "She and I disagree on the blame part, however." There was something else he had to get out. "Nate… I never lied to you. I wouldn't do that."

Nate expelled a breath. "Mom called it a sin of omission. I guess you can't call it lying if you don't actually say anything." He glanced around. "Did Finn leave?"

Joel nodded. "He figured we needed a little space."

"I really laid into him, didn't I?" Nate's face fell. "I should go."

Joel was on his feet in a heartbeat. "Why? Your

mom will be here tomorrow. You might as well stay tonight." He took a breath. "I'm not happy about you driving all that way."

"I'm calmer now."

"Sure, but…" Joel strove to find the words. "Stay?" When Nate didn't respond, Joel pushed ahead. "The past six months have been tough on all of us. Maybe we need to spend some time together, just the two of us. You know, eat pizza, watch a movie, chill…" He locked gazes with Nate. "Talk, maybe, without all the strain, tension and repressed anger that's underlaid every conversation we've had since I moved out." Joel held up his hands. "I know, I know. If I'd just told you the truth, things might have been different. That's my fault. I told your mom I'd be the one to tell you everything." Joel swallowed hard. "I got scared, all right? I didn't want to lose you."

Nate stared at him for a moment. "I'll stay." He expelled a breath. "And I'd like to talk. I want to know more."

"Anything in particular?"

He nodded. "I wanna hear about you growing up. Shit, I wanna hear *everything*. I suddenly learned my dad is gay. You gotta know I have questions."

Joel didn't doubt that for a second.

Nate tilted his head to one side. "Mom said there was a boyfriend before she came on the scene. Is that true?"

"Yeah, it's true. We split when I started dating your mom."

"Well… can you tell me about him?" There was no trace of the rage that had contorted his features minutes ago, only an earnest expression that tugged at Joel's heart.

Joel had a better idea. He got up from the rocking chair and went over to the bookcase, where his laptop sat. Joel opened it and found the document, then handed the laptop to Nate. "Read this. It'll tell you everything you want to know."

"What is this?"

Joel smiled. "My first attempt at writing, so please, don't judge."

Nate inclined his head toward the kitchen. "I'll read it at the table, okay?"

That was fine by Joel. He didn't think his nerves could take watching Nate read.

He waited till Nate was out of sight, then sagged into the chair. His phone vibrated in his pocket, and he took it out. It was a text from Finn.

I'm going out of my mind here. Is everything okay?

Joel wasn't sure *okay* was the right word, but he was happy with the cessation of hostilities. Joel's thumbs flew over the keys. *Nate's still here. I think we called a truce. He's staying tonight. Maybe you can come over tomorrow?*

He won't mind?

Joel smiled. *Not now he won't. Carrie will be here too, and Laura.*

A moment later, Finn's reply pinged. *Okay. I'll come over tomorrow. I'll miss you tonight though.*

Warmth pulsed through Joel in a slow tide. *I'll miss you too.*

"Dad?"

Joel got up from the rocking chair and went into the kitchen. Nate sat there, his eyes wide. "Have you read it all?" Joel asked him.

Nate shook his head. "I'm up to the part where you went off to college. This… this is really good."

"You're the first person to read it."

Nate blinked. "Not even Finn?"

"Nope."

"Wow." He returned his gaze to the laptop. "I can't even begin to understand how you must've felt, having to hide everything. Not like nowadays, when people can just come out."

Joel sighed. *He is* so *young*. "Not *everyone* comes out, because even today, not everyone can."

Nate's stomach growled, and he flushed. He gave Joel a sheepish glance. "Hey, Dad? Did you mean it when you said pizza?"

Joel chuckled. "Yeah, I need to eat too. Pepperoni okay?"

Nate nodded eagerly. "My favorite."

"Mine too." Joel went over to the freezer to search for the pizza, his heart a little lighter.

Maybe Finn was right after all. It's going to be okay.

He wasn't about to count his chickens, however. He and Nate still had a lot of talking to do.

Chapter Twenty-One

"Nate? Coffee's ready." Joel poured himself a mug and went over to the back door to gaze out at the deck. *Almost finished.* A thought flitted through his head. *And what then? Will Finn stick around?*

God, Joel hoped so. Of course, he could just come right out and ask Finn if he wanted what they had to continue, but that raised a dilemma. Joel already knew he didn't want things to go on as they were—he wanted more. Only thing was, he was too shit-scared to reach out for it.

Nate came out of the bathroom and sniffed. "I like the smell of coffee. Laura thinks I'm weird."

Joel chuckled. "Wait till she's thirty. She'll change her tune." He nodded to the coffee pot. "Help yourself. Creamer's in the fridge and there's sugar in the canister." He didn't move from his spot.

Nate joined him once he'd poured himself a cup. He stood at Joel's side, looking out at the yard. "I should've told you I was coming yesterday. And I should've rung the doorbell too, but I went around the back to take a look at the deck. Then I had to look inside, didn't I? I got more than I bargained for."

Joel took a deep breath. "I'm sorry you had to find out like that."

"Hey, it could've been a lot worse. Then I'd be reaching for the eye bleach." Nate snorted. "Joke, Dad."

The fact that he could joke about it made Joel breathe that bit easier.

"Does Bramble need to pee?"

Joel laughed. "You were still asleep when I took him outside. He needs a walk though. We could do that before your mom gets here."

Nate's phone buzzed, and he took it from his jeans pocket. "No, we couldn't." He stared at Joel. "Laura says they just got off the turnpike."

Joel glanced at the kitchen wall clock. "They're about twenty minutes from here. That means they must have left the house before seven o'clock." Oh God. Carrie was *not* a morning person. Neither was Laura, if it came to that. And it was a miracle he'd gotten Nate out of bed so early. Joel had definitely not passed his early bird gene on to his kids.

Nate bit back a smile. "You got enough eggs? Because I can't see Mom making breakfast before they left."

Joel laughed. "Forget that. I'll take us all out for breakfast. And I know the perfect place." He inclined his head toward the futon. "But you might want to unmake your bed before they get here."

"Good thinking." Nate lowered his gaze to his cup. "Can I at least finish my coffee first? I'm not even awake yet." He grinned. "I'm really in bed. What you see is a hologram."

"How do you cope when you have early classes?"

That grin didn't fade. "Get notes from my friends."

Joel shook his head. "You drink, I'll clean up." They'd gone to bed without clearing away the dishes.

He got on with the task, while Nate sat at the table and drank. There wasn't that much to do, but Joel wanted the place to be spotless before Carrie and Laura walked in.

"Dad? Can I ask you something?"

Joel smiled. "You mean you still have questions?" They'd talked until late, but he'd gone to his bed feeling as though they'd cleared the air.

"Something I forgot to ask last night. Do my grandparents know? That you're gay, I mean." Nate bit his lip. "Still sounds weird to say it."

Joel came to a dead stop and gazed at him. "I haven't changed," he said quietly. "I'm still Dad."

Nate sighed. "I know. Just takes a little getting used to, that's all." His eyes met Joel's. "But it's okay, really. I can deal with having a gay dad."

Joel's heart was lighter than it had been the previous night.

"To answer your question, I haven't told them. They don't need to know. When I told them your mom and I were getting a divorce, they weren't happy. They told me I hadn't tried hard enough to make it work, that I was giving up too easily... Imagine how they'd react if they knew the truth."

Nate nodded. "Then I won't say a word when we visit next time."

Joel couldn't help himself. He walked over to Nate's chair and kissed the top of his head. "Love you."

Nate gazed up at him. "I still have questions, but I'll wait till Mom and Laura get here. That way, you don't have to say everything twice." When Joel gave him an inquiring glance, Nate smiled. "Nothing heavy. I figure Laura will have the same questions." His eyes glittered. "Who am I kidding? Laura will have *tons* more questions." They both chuckled at that.

By the time Carrie pulled onto the driveway behind Nate's car, the house was spotless. Laura was the first through the door, and Bramble was dancing around her before Carrie had closed the screen. Then Laura launched herself into Joel's arms.

"Hey, Dad. Do you have *any idea* what time Mom dragged me out of bed this morning so we could get here this early?"

He laughed as he hugged her. "Hey, munchkin." Carrie leaned in and he kissed her cheek. "Help yourself to coffee. You could probably use some. I made fresh."

"You are a lifesaver. I've been running on fumes." Carrie made a beeline for the coffeepot, but came to a halt when she saw Nate. She folded her arms, the coffee apparently forgotten. "And as for *you*, young man…"

Nate held up his hands. "Mom, I'm sorry, okay? I had to talk to Dad on my own."

Carrie's gaze went from Nate to Joel.

"We're good," Joel told her.

She expelled a breath. "Okay." She narrowed her gaze. "You're still in trouble for lying to me."

"He's a little too old to be grounded," Joel observed. "And we did a lot of talking."

Laura walked into the kitchen. "Why isn't Finn here?"

Joel frowned. "Why should he be?"

She blinked. "Isn't he your boyfriend?"

Three pairs of eyes bulged. Joel's mouth fell open and he gaped at Carrie. "Did you—?"

"Not a word," she replied vehemently.

Laura rolled her eyes. "Oh, come *on*, Dad. I might be fifteen, but I'm not stupid."

"But... how did you know?" Joel demanded.

She shrugged. "I pretty much figured it out on my own."

"And he *is* your boyfriend, right?" Nate commented. "Well, based on what *I* saw."

Joel supposed he'd have come to the same conclusion if he'd caught *his* dad making out with a guy.

Nate frowned at his sister. "But how did *you* work it all out?"

Another impressive eye-roll. "Nate, you've been a real jerk ever since Dad moved out. And if you'd only stopped being so angry, and done what *I* did, you'd have come to the same conclusions."

"Why, what did *you* do?"

Laura gave a superior smile. "I just started watching. Amazing the things you notice. Like the way Dad was looking at Finn. *And* I heard Aunt Megan and Dad talking. That kinda made it obvious." She glanced at Carrie. "What?"

Carrie laughed. "Nothing, sweetheart. You never fail to amaze me, that's all."

Joel was past amazement and up to his eyeballs in dumbfounded.

Carrie cast longing glances at the coffee pot. "*Now* can I have some caffeine?"

Joel took pity on her. "Sit. I'll pour. Juice for you, Laura? Nate, you want more coffee?" His head was still reeling, and dealing with practicalities was the only way he could function.

It wasn't long before all of them were seated at the kitchen table. Carrie gave Joel a glance. "You want to go first?"

He wasn't sure what she meant for a second, until it dawned on him Carrie might have a secret of her own.

"Sure. Though it sounds like they know everything already."

Laura widened her eyes. "What? But I wanna know how you and Finn met, when you're getting married, do I get to be a bridesmaid—"

"Whoa there." Joel's heartbeat quickened. "First of all, about Finn… he's…" What the hell *was* he? That word *boyfriend* had been a bolt from the blue. *But is he?* Finn was more than a friend, and *definitely* more than the carpenter who'd turned up to assess Joel's busted deck.

He gazed into the faces of his children and his ex-wife. He had to be honest with them.

Joel took a deep breath. "Truth is, I don't know where this will go."

"You mean, you and Finn?" Nate asked. When Joel nodded, Nate cocked his head. "But you *do* hope it will go somewhere, right?"

The truth, remember? He gave another slow nod. "Yeah, I do." He gazed at Nate and Laura's faces. "And you'd be okay with that?"

Laura beamed. "Of course. I like Finn."

"So do I," Nate added. "Is he gonna come over later? Because I need to apologize." Carrie gave him a quizzical glance, and he sighed. "I was a jerk yesterday."

Carrie squeezed his shoulder. "I think he'll forgive you." She met Joel's gaze. "Why not call him?"

"Dad says he's taking us out for breakfast," Nate said quickly. "We could ask Finn to come too. Couldn't we?"

Joel liked the idea, even if the thought of Laura grilling Finn about his intentions gave Joel a severe case of butterflies. "I'll ask."

"Before you do that, there's something I'd like to share." Carrie took a couple of quick breaths, and Joel reached across the table for her hand, squeezing it.

"Just tell them." He smiled. "Just be prepared for them to tell you they know already." They had an awesome couple of kids.

She shuddered out a long breath. "The thing is… I've been seeing someone too."

Nate and Laura stilled in an instant.

"Seriously? How long for?" Nate demanded.

"About a month."

"And you're only telling us *now*?" His voice rang with incredulity. "Why didn't you say anything?"

"What's his name? Do we know him?" Laura demanded. "Do we get to meet him?

Carrie held up her hands, and they lapsed into silence. "His name's Eric, I met him at the Tennis Association, and I wasn't going to introduce him until I knew it was serious."

"I'm guessing since you're telling us, it *is* serious," Nate concluded.

Carrie glanced at Joel before responding. "I think it's definitely heading in that direction. That doesn't mean things can't change, okay? Right now, we're both happy with the way it's going. And yes, now I've told you, I'll invite him over for dinner one weekend, so you can interrogate him—I mean, get to know him."

Joel chuckled. "I think you nailed it with 'interrogate'."

"Dad?" Laura's brow furrowed. "Do I tell my friends you're gay, or bi?"

Carrie chuckled. "Over to you, Joel."

Joel took a drink from his mug, but before he could speak, Nate got in first. "Dad's gay. He's *always* been gay, since he was your age. Actually, since he was younger than you." Nate glanced at Joel, his eyes warm.

"He just couldn't live the way he wanted, but now he can."

Joel's throat tightened, and tears pricked the corners of his eyes. "You got that right."

Carrie gave Joel a dazed stare. "That must have been some talk you two had last night." Her eyes glistened, and she wiped them quickly with her hand.

Nate glanced at Joel. "Dad let me read something that made things a whole lot clearer, that's all."

"And don't forget *you* played a part in this." Joel gazed fondly at Carrie. "I don't know what you said to him on the phone, but you sure talked him down."

"I knew he'd be okay about it, once he got over the shock."

Nate coughed, then speared Joel with a look. "Dad? Finn, remember? Call him."

Smiling, Joel pulled his phone from his pocket and called Finn's number.

"Hey. I wanted to call, but I figured it would be best to wait." Finn paused. "You okay?"

"Yeah, I'm fine. Have you eaten yet?"

"Not yet. I'm on my third cup of coffee though. Does that count?"

Joel laughed. "Be ready in about ten minutes. I'll drop by to pick you up. You're invited to breakfast." This time he paused. "A family breakfast."

Crickets.

"Finn? You still there?"

"Yeah, still here. You sure you want me there?"

Joel smiled. "*All* of us want you there. And I hope you're hungry. I'm taking us all to Becky's."

Finn cackled. "What's the likelihood of Megan turning up again?"

"Don't say that. Don't even *think* it." Joel just

wanted some time with Carrie, his kids—and Finn.

Chapter Twenty-Two

Finn gazed at the finished deck with a smile. *Good job.*

It had taken Finn all week to finish it, coming over as soon as he finished work, but it was finally done. Joel had protested that completion could have waited till the weekend, but Finn had suffered a major attack of the guilts. Too much time in Joel's bed—or his, if it came to that—meant too little time spent on the job Joel was paying him for, and that wouldn't do at all.

And now it's finished? Where does that leave us?

Of course, once the deck-building activities were done for the night, other activities took precedence. It wasn't as if he could work in the dark, right? And if Joel wanted to get in a little naked time, Finn wasn't about to say no.

Except it hadn't all been hot, sweaty sex. There had been a couple of evenings on the futon while they watched movies, and one night spent entirely at the kitchen table, when Joel had brought out a board game he'd found when he'd bought the house. Marvel Villainous was one of the coolest games Finn had ever played, and he took great delight in scuppering Joel's plans. It was overwhelming at first, due to its many layers, but they'd soon gotten the hang of it, and had played it three times in succession.

The one thing he'd always remember about that night? Their laughter. Finn couldn't recall the last time he'd laughed so much. *Gotta love a man who makes you laugh.* And there it was, the crux of Finn's dilemma.

He was falling in love with Joel, and he couldn't see into the future to know how it was going to end. Sure, he knew how he *wanted* it to end, but he wasn't the only one in this relationship. And it *was* a relationship from his point of view.

How Joel saw it? Finn had no clue, and was too scared to find out. *Besides, what's wrong with what we have? It works, right?* Joel seemed happy to continue, so why rock the boat? *Not everyone wants commitment, right?* And Joel was just starting on his journey of discovery. Surely he wouldn't want to be tied down as soon as he stepped out of the gate.

Of course, he could just *ask* Joel, but the thought of Joel's face, that look of *what the hell do I do now?* he wouldn't be able to hide…

Then Joel opened the screen door, and Finn pasted on a smile. "Ta-da!"

Joel stepped out onto the deck, beaming. "This looks great." He ran his hand down the nearest post, one of the six that supported the pergola. "I had no idea you were putting this up too."

Finn smiled. "I knew when I drew it that you loved the idea. So I adjusted my calculations for the delivery. You don't pay for it though."

Joel blinked. "Say what?"

He shook his head. "You wanted a deck. The pergola was *my* idea, to show you what you could have out here, how it could look. So think of it as a deck-warming gift from me." It wasn't as it had been a great expense, and he'd put the whole thing up in less than thirty minutes.

Joel's eyes were soft, his face glowing. "Aw, thank you. I… I don't know what to say."

Finn didn't want words—he wanted Joel's kisses, for as long as he could have them.

He closed his toolbox. "So now you can order whatever patio set you want out here. And maybe a grill?" He glanced at the yard. "This place could use a grill."

"I'll add it to the list." Joel's gaze flickered to Finn's toolbox. "Are you going home?"

Not if you don't want me to.

"Been a long day, and I need a shower." Finn willed Joel to say something, anything, to give him an excuse not to leave, but Joel merely nodded. Finn picked up the toolbox and carried it through the side gate to his truck. Once it was stowed, he turned to say goodbye, only to find Joel walking toward him.

"When you've had your shower… want to come over for dinner? I'm making lasagna."

"Is that the lasagna Nate was telling me about, that time when Carrie brought her casserole? He said it was awesome."

Joel smiled. "It was always my go-to meal."

Finn would have said yes if Joel had been dishing up fried boot leather with marinated shoe laces. "If you're sure it's no trouble, I'd love to. Gimme thirty minutes?"

Joel's eyes shone. "Great. I'll start chopping. And seeing as tomorrow's Saturday… want to stay the night?"

Finn grinned. "I'll bring a toothbrush." He got behind the wheel, his heart singing.

More time with Joel. Perfect way to end his week.

Finn did *not* want to move.

He sat on the futon next to Joel, his bare feet in Joel's lap, and Joel was giving them the *best* rub *ever*.

Okay, the *only* foot rub ever.

The movie had finished, followed by a show all about funny commercials.

Joel snorted. "I love that one." On the screen, a couple in bed were discussing condoms. The guy was saying they never fit, so the girl covered her hand with one. "This is from years ago, though. You don't see a lot of condom commercials these days."

Something had niggled Finn ever since that first time together, and he couldn't wish for a better opening. "Can I ask you something?"

Joel picked up the remote and lowered the volume. "As if I could stop you."

"Back at MaineStreet, when I said I didn't have any condoms at home, for a second there you had this look on your face… almost like panic."

Joel stilled, then switched off the TV. "I guess we can talk about this. You know more about me than any other person, except perhaps Carrie. The thing is… I might not have had sex with a guy for twenty years, but using condoms is sort of ingrained in me. That's what comes of growing up in the AIDS era, I guess. I've never had sex without one, and when you said you didn't have any…"

Finn nodded slowly. "You thought I was gonna

suggest we bareback?"

"Yeah. I did wonder if that was because you were on PrEP. I see it in commercials all the time."

He shook his head. "Not me. I know I haven't had many relationships, but the guys I was with all used condoms, at least in the beginning." When Joel cocked his head, Finn sighed. "I know a lot of guys my age wouldn't agree with me, but for me, commitment isn't a dirty word. And when I give my heart to someone, I give them everything else—and that includes trust. So yeah, when I thought a relationship was gonna go the distance, we both got tested and gave up using condoms." He exhaled. "The problem was, I picked the wrong guys to give them up for."

Joel rubbed the sole of Finn's right foot. "Part of me hates that those relationships didn't go the way you wanted. You don't deserve to be messed around like that." He smiled. "Then again, if one of them *had* gone the distance, we wouldn't be sitting on my couch right now, and I wouldn't be taking you upstairs in about ten minutes."

Finn blinked. "I never thought of it like that." Then Joel's words sank in. "Ten minutes, huh?"

Joel grinned. "Unless you don't want to watch the rest of this show."

Finn was off the couch in a heartbeat. "What show?" By the time his feet hit the stairs, Joel was already hot on his trail. "Last one on the bed gets to bottom."

And there was Joel's laugh again, filling Finn with a lightness he wanted to hold onto for as long as he could.

Joel opened his eyes, not entirely convinced he wasn't still asleep. Because the most delicious smell of cooking bacon was everywhere. Then he realized Finn wasn't lying next to him, and Bramble wasn't at his feet.

"Finn?"

From below came Finn's chuckle. "It works!"

"What works?" He got out of bed and pulled on his shorts.

"I've discovered another Joel alarm clock."

"You're making breakfast? What did I do to deserve this?" Joel grabbed the T-shirt he'd removed the previous night.

"Reminds me of that meme I saw on Facebook," Finn called out. "It said, 'Masturbated so good last night, my dick was in the kitchen making breakfast.'"

Joel laughed as he headed down the stairs. Finn stood at the table, whisking eggs in a bowl, and Bramble sat nearby, licking his chops. Then Joel took in Finn's attire. He wore Joel's apron, but that was *all* he wore—the apron strings dangled over his bare ass.

"Oh, if this is how you make breakfast, I need you to do it more often." Joel walked over to him, grabbed Finn's firm ass with both hands, and squeezed.

"Hey. No distracting me."

Joel kissed Finn's neck, loving the shivers that coursed through him. "Where's the bacon?" He kissed Finn's nape, heading lower.

"In the oven, keeping warm."

"Good." Joel slowly undid the apron, then sank to

his knees behind Finn.

"What's going on behind my back?"

"Put the bowl down, Finn, and bend over the table."

Finn's loud gasp filled the kitchen. "Fuck, you're not gonna—"

"Fuck, yeah. You gave me the idea, remember?" He chuckled at the speed with which Finn followed his instructions.

"Remind me to share more of my ideas with you." Then he let out a low guttural sound as Joel's tongue found his hole. "Jesus."

That was *all* kinds of gratifying.

Joel closed his laptop and glanced at the wall clock. Time for a break.

It became apparent Bramble had the same idea: he got up from his spot at Joel's feet and went to the front door. Joel laughed. "Okay, okay. I get the message." He could do with a walk. He'd been working all morning, and Bramble had been very patient.

"Let's go see if Finn is home, eh, boy?" Then he remembered. Finn would be working. It had been three days since Joel had seen him. They'd spoken on the phone, and Finn had sent photos of the rocking chair. It looked beautiful. But Finn's voice was no substitute for the real thing.

Dear Lord, I've got it bad.

Sunday afternoon, when they'd gone for a walk on the beach with Bramble, seemed a lifetime ago. Warmth filled him at the thought of strolling along the shoreline, Finn at his side, talking, laughing, throwing sticks for Bramble… What he recalled most vividly was the desire that seized him, the need to hold Finn's hand but not possessing the courage to do so. Especially when Finn showed no inclination to do the same.

Which was all the evidence Joel needed that Finn didn't feel the same yearning that tormented Joel. Sure, Finn couldn't keep his hands off Joel when they were together, but Joel wanted more than that.

His phone buzzed, and Joel snatched it up from the table. It was Carrie. "Hey," he said as they connected.

"You okay? You sound… I'm not sure *how* you sound, just… not like you."

"I'm fine," he lied. Having his head full of Finn was *not* fine, not when Joel really wanted him—

In my arms. In my bed. In my life.

Joel pushed such thoughts into submission. "So, what's up?"

"I'm just calling to let you know… Eric came to dinner on Sunday."

"Oh, great. How did it go?"

"Well, I think. He was playing chess with Nate. Eric paid you a compliment. He said you were obviously a good teacher."

"That was nice of him. Does Laura like him?"

Carrie laughed. "She says he's sweet." She paused for a moment. "So… about Finn…"

"What about him?"

"Well, it's been almost two weeks since we were there. Are you any clearer on where this is going?"

I wish.

Joel let out a sigh. "I'm not sure it's going anywhere. Finn… Finn isn't looking for a relationship." That was what his head told him in the middle of the night, when he lay in his bed that felt *so* empty without Finn.

"And you know this how? Did Finn say that?"

"Well, not, but—"

"Have you even *talked* about this with him?"

"No." He couldn't… just *couldn't*.

"Why not?"

"Because I'm scared, okay?" That came out louder than he'd intended, and Bramble let out a bark. "Come here, boy." When Bramble reached his chair, Joel stroked his head. "Daddy's all right." He took a breath. "I'm sorry. It's just that I've been thinking a lot about him. I love being with him. I love it when he comes over to watch a movie. I love the way he makes me feel."

"It's okay to say it, you know." Carrie's voice was soft.

"Say what?"

"That you love him."

He opened his mouth to deny it, but the words wouldn't come. *Because you know she's right, don't you?*

"I see you together," she continued, "and it makes me *so* happy. I don't know if it will last, any more than I know if Eric and I will last. There are no absolutes. But if he makes you happy, then go for it. Tell him how you feel." She paused again. "Don't let fear hold you back."

Joel shuddered out a breath. "Is it that obvious?"

"Only to me, but then, I *know* you, sweetheart. So here's my advice. Call him, text him, whatever, and invite him to dinner. Make it special. And then sit him down and talk to him."

He could make Finn dinner. As for talking… *Let's see how the wind is blowing after we've eaten.*

"I'll think about it." Except Joel knew he'd do more

than that. "But now I really need to walk the dog."

"That's you saying 'Shut up, Carrie.'" She chuckled. "Go for your walk. But please—"

"I said I'll think about it, and I will. So let me get off the phone and walk my dog. I *can* think and walk at the same time, you know."

"Wow. A man who multitasks. I must call Guinness."

"And on *that* note…" Joel said goodbye. He stroked Bramble's silky ears. "Walk?"

Bramble's joyous bark was answer enough. Joel had one more task to do before they left the house. He scrolled through *Contacts* and quickly composed a text to Finn.

Friday night, dinner at my place? Come over as soon as you're ready.

Then he clicked *Send* before he had a chance to change his mind. It was just dinner, right? No big deal.

Except Joel knew it was a huge deal.

Chapter Twenty-Three

Finn pulled the drapes back and groaned. "Well fuck."

The sky was the color of lead, and the clouds looked as though they were about to disgorge themselves within minutes. The forecast the night before had mentioned rain, sure, but this went beyond a shower. Finn knew the guys would turn up to work, just like he was going to do, but if the weather got dicey, that would be an end to it for a while.

Why couldn't it wait till the roof was on?

By the time he arrived at the site, the rain was coming down heavily, and Lewis and Ted were covering up the piles of rebar with a tarp. As Finn walked over to them, Lewis's phone rang, and he put it to his ear under the humongous hood that covered his head.

"Hey, Jon. Yeah, it's bad here." Just then, thunder rumbled, lasting several seconds, and Lewis scowled. "Scrap that—it just got worse." He listened intently, while the others stood around, the rain pelting their coats and hitting the ground so hard, it bounced. "Okay, sure. Yeah, I got that. You never know, this might pass." Then Lewis cackled. "Yeah, I know, ever the optimist. I'll let you know." He disconnected.

"What did Jon say?" Max demanded.

"He says to keep working. A little rain never hurt nobody. Just be sure to dodge the lightning." When Max's jaw dropped, Lewis cracked up. "Are you fucking kidding me? He said go home. The forecast is shit, this storm is coming in fast, and we don't wanna be around when it hits." Lewis grinned. "So, ladies, go home and bang the girlfriend—or girlfriends—or boyfriend, as the case may be." He speared Finn with a glance. "Well, he sure won't be walking the doggy in *this* crap."

Lewis had a point.

Finn walked back to his truck, jumping when a roll of thunder reverberated through the heavens. He got behind the wheel and stared out at the driving rain. Much as he loved the idea of paying Joel a surprise visit, he wouldn't do that, not when Joel was working. There was dinner the following day to look forward to, right? *I can wait that long, right?* His stomach clenched.

I can't go on like this.

It wasn't that he didn't fucking *love* every minute he got to spend with Joel—what was killing him was the not knowing if they were ever going to pass Casual and reach Commitment. He wasn't going to tell Joel how he felt, because that would only put pressure on him, but Finn couldn't leave this hanging. He had to know if they had a future.

Because dear *Lord*, Finn wanted one with Joel.

What I need right now is some good advice, from someone whose first response won't be to just fuck Joel's brains out. And he knew just who to get it from. Finn pulled his phone from his pocket and hit speed dial. "Hey. I haven't caught you in the middle of a video call or something, have I?"

Levi chuckled. "No, that was last night. And the

good thing about being a social media manager is I get to take breaks when I want. What's up?" Then thunder rumbled overhead, and Levi gasped. "Tell me you're not out in that."

"I know it *sounds* like a torrent of bullets, but that's the rain pelting the roof of my truck. No work today. And I'm calling because…" Finn sighed. "Because I need to talk to someone, and you're the first person I thought of."

"Well, do you want to talk over the phone, or do you want to come over? Seeing as you're not working. And Grammy just baked."

Finn stilled. "What did she make?"

"Chocolate chip and pecan cookies." He paused. "She made your favorite lemon cake yesterday."

"Christ, you fight dirty. I'll be there as fast as I can."

"Hey!" Levi's voice rose. "Be careful, okay? Don't go breaking any land speed records, not in this weather."

Warmth radiated through him. His friends were the best, always looking out for each other. "I'll drive safe, I promise. See you soon." Then he disconnected.

Finn pulled away from the curb and turned the truck around. Thank God Wells was less than a half hour's drive.

Well—maybe a little longer in this *weather.*

Before Finn could ring the doorbell, the door swung open, and Grammy stood there, beaming. "Finn! Come on in, you big galoot."

He stepped out of the rain and into her hallway, then bent down and kissed her cheek. "Who you calling a 'galoot'? You still sore about that cup I broke last time I was here?" He grinned. "Either I'm standing on a box, you're standing in a hole, or you're shrinking, Grammy."

"You little article!" She whacked him on the arm, then chuckled. "I've lost a couple of inches. They must be around here someplace." She peered over his shoulder. "Lord, it's wicked out there. Let me close the door." Once it was shut, she narrowed her gaze. "Coat and boots off, before you drip all over my hall floor."

Finn shrugged off his coat, and she hung it over the mat. Then he toed off his boots and left them there. "Now give me a proper hug. Haven't had a Grammy hug for months, and they're the best kind."

"Aw, aren't you some cunnin'?" A loud crack of thunder shook the glass in the door, and her eyes widened. "My, this weather. Did you ever?" She wrapped her arms around him and hugged him tight. "I swear, you're gettin' bigger every time I see you." She released him. "Go on into the dining room. Levi's in there, workin'. I'll bring you both some hot chocolate and cookies." Grammy patted his arm. "Good to see you, sweetheart." Then she disappeared through the door that led to the kitchen.

Hot chocolate and cookies. *Gotta love Grammy.*

Finn went into the dining room, where Levi sat at the table, his gaze focused on the screen, his brow furrowed. He glanced up as Finn entered, and the frown vanished, replaced by a broad smile that reached his eyes. "You made it." Levi got up and came over to give Finn a hug. Finn held him close, and Levi stilled.

"Hey, you okay?"

They parted, and Finn pulled out the chair next to Levi's. Levi sat beside him.

"Not really." He glanced at Levi and despite his churning stomach, he smiled. "It's official. You got the best beard of all of us." Dylan had joked at the wedding that except for Ben, they were all sporting beards of one description or another, but most of them were little more than scruff. Levi's was the fullest, and the neatest.

As if *that* was any surprise.

Levi arched his dark brows. "I'm pretty certain you didn't come here to talk about my beard."

Then Finn realized Levi knew nothing about Joel. "There's something I need to tell you. The thing is… I've met someone."

Levi's face lit up. "Oh wow. When did this happen? That's awesome." Then his smile faltered. "I'm guessing it's *not* awesome, or else why would you be here needing advice?" He closed his laptop. "Okay, you've got my undivided attention. Tell me everything."

"There's not that much to tell. His name's Joel, he's amazing…" Finn's throat seized up.

Levi's mouth fell open. "Oh my God. Hoist the flags. Finn's in love." He tilted his head to one side. "And does Joel feel the same?"

"*That's* the part I don't know." And the part that was killing him.

"Don't you guys talk?" Levi snorted. "Stupid question. Of course you don't. You're guys. Heaven forbid you actually say how you feel." Then he sighed. "As if I'm any better." Before Finn could ask what he meant by that, Levi plowed ahead. "*Have* you talked to him? Or at least tried?"

"I wouldn't know where to start." Except he knew

exactly what he wanted to say—the problem was, he was too scared of Joel's response.

Levi leaned back in his chair. "Tell me about Joel."

"He's forty-two. He was married for twenty years—just divorced—and he's got two great kids, Nate and Laura. Nate's eighteen, Laura's fifteen. He had a boyfriend back in his late teens and early twenties—a secret boyfriend—but then family pressure got too much, so he started dating girls. And now he's single, out, and living for the first time as a gay man." Finn swallowed. "Which is why I can't tell him how I feel. He's just discovering life—he won't wanna be tied down."

"What kind of a dad is he?"

Finn's face grew warm. "He's a great dad."

"And all that time he was married... he didn't cheat with guys?"

Finn shook his head. "He's not like that."

Levi stroked his beard. "Doesn't sound like he's the kind of guy who would go for a string of hookups either." He raised his eyebrows again. "Dude, you need to tell him. I'm not suggesting you come out with 'Hey, Joel, I wanna move in with ya and get married,' okay? But at least let him know how you feel about him."

"And if I do that..." Finn took a deep breath, willing himself to stay calm. "I don't wanna be his transition guy, all right?"

"His what?"

"You know—the guy who shows him the ropes, the first guy he goes with—and then dumps when he feels ready for more. What if that's all I am to him?"

Levi narrowed his gaze. "Do you feel like he's the type of person who'd treat someone like that?" He gave Finn a thoughtful glance. "Is he the type to hang out in all the gay bars, and spend every waking minute on Grindr?"

Finn shook his head. "No." That wasn't Joel.

Levi balanced his elbows on the arms of his chair and laced his fingers. "Then maybe you need to stop playing the *What-if* game, and find out what *he* wants?" He bit his lip. "Because it sounds to me as though it's time for *That Conversation*. You know the one. 'What are we doing? Where are we going?'" He smiled. "But you can't assume he's some all-knowing, all-seeing guy who has the answers. This is something you'll need to work out together."

They both jumped when Grammy called out in a loud voice, "Oh Jeanie Crummel!"

Levi was on his feet in seconds. "You okay, Grammy?"

"I'm fine. Just dropped an egg on the floor, that's all. I'll be in with the cookies—that's assumin' I don't drop them too. Dear Lord, I hate gettin' old."

Finn was trying not to laugh. "Jeanie Crummel? She still says that?"

Levi chuckled. "You know Grammy. That's as close as she gets to swearing." He sat once more. "She says her fingertips are drying out, she can't grip anything anymore," he said under his breath. Then he cleared his throat. "But enough about Grammy. Talk to Joel. Don't put it off, because you *know* there will never be a perfect time. You just need to seize the moment."

Finn had been thinking about that. "He's invited me to dinner tomorrow night." *And what do they say? No time like the present?*

Levi's eyes sparkled. "That sounds like a God-given opportunity." The door opened, and Grammy came into the room, carrying a tray.

Finn was at her side in a heartbeat. "Here, I'll take that." He took the tray from her and set it down on the table.

Grammy cackled. "What you *really* mean is, you want to drink your hot chocolate, not wear it." She reached up and patted his cheek. "Some cunnin'." Then she walked slowly from the room, closing the door behind her.

Finn gazed after her. "She looks a bit frailer than when I saw her last."

"She had a rotten cold. She's still getting over it. And don't worry about Grammy. She's as tough as an old boot." Still, Levi stared at the door too.

Finn picked up a cookie and bit into it, relishing the crunch of nut pieces and the chocolate that melted on his tongue. He sighed happily. "She still makes the best cookies."

"And you know that before you leave here, she'll be at the front door with a box full of them for you." Levi smiled. "You always were one of her favorites." He speared Finn with a look. "Can I ask you something? If you and Joel do work out… how do you feel about getting involved with a guy who has kids?"

Finn frowned. "What about it? They're great kids."

Levi nods. "And if you and Joel get serious, they'd be a responsibility. You up for that?" He held up his hands. "I'm just trying to be realistic here, and make sure you see the big picture."

Finn didn't even hesitate. "I'm more scared of losing Joel than I am of suddenly gaining two kids." Breakfast at Becky's had been great. The way Nate and Laura just accepted him being there…

"You *are* going to talk to him, right?"

Finn nodded. "But I wanna do it *my* way."

"And what does that mean?"

The seed of an idea had taken root in his mind. "I want him to be in no doubt how I feel." That seed swelled, and the first tendrils of a plan uncurled themselves, filling his head with a delicious notion that sent shivers of anticipation through him. "Do you think Grammy would lend me something for a couple of days?"

"What did you want to borrow?" When Finn told him, Levi burst into laughter. "What on earth…? Sure, I can't see her minding that. I'm dying to know what you're going to do with them."

Finn tapped the side of his nose. "That's my secret." Except for his plan to work, he was going to need help—very specific help.

"Levi? You got a minute?" Grammy called from the kitchen.

"Coming, Grammy." Levi got to his feet. "I'll be right back." He gave Finn a mock glare. "Don't eat all the cookies." He left the room, pulling the door to after him.

Finn pulled his phone from his pockets and called up the White Pages website. He did a quick search, smiling when it produced results. Then he dialed, his heart pounding.

Please be the right person. There couldn't be *two* Megan Halls in Portland, could there? And that assumed Megan had kept her maiden name and not taken Lynne's.

"You're lucky I'm in a good mood." Thank God, it was her. "I don't usually answer calls when I don't recognize the number."

"Megan? It's Finn."

Her tone changed instantly. "Hey, Finn," she said in

obvious delight. There was a pause. "Why are you calling? Has something happened to Joel? Is he okay?" A note of panic crept into her voice.

"He's fine," Finn assured her. "And I'm calling because I need your help."

"Well, now you got me curious."

He outlined what he needed her to do. "Think you can manage that?"

Megan's cackle filled his ears. "Definitely. Are you going to tell me what this is all about?"

"If this comes off, you'll know soon enough." *Please, let this work.* "So you know what to do, and when?"

"Yup."

"And you're sure he'll do it?"

Megan laughed. "I'll give the performance of my life. I'm still dying of curiosity though."

So was Levi, but Finn wasn't sharing.

He thanked her and disconnected, just as Levi came back into the room.

"Crisis averted. Grammy wanted a box from the top shelf of the cabinet, and she couldn't reach, not even with the little step I got her for stuff like this." Levi gave him a quizzical glance. "What are you up to?"

"Making plans."

And praying they would bear fruit.

Grammy poked her head around the door. "Finn? Do you have someplace you gotta be, or can you stay for lunch? It's only soup, but I made it yesterday. And there's lemon cake for after."

Finn glanced at Levi, who nodded eagerly. Finn smiled. "I'd love that." There was nothing he could do at home to advance his plans, and he hadn't seen Levi since the wedding. Besides, if she agreed to his request, Finn would have to go up into Grammy's attic to find what he needed. He could already picture the results in his head.

Now all he had to do was make it happen.

Chapter Twenty-Four

By the time Joel pulled onto Megan's driveway, he was cursing his sister with everything from hemorrhoids to a plague of frogs. He had things to *do*, dammit. He'd finished work for the day and was about to get the place ready for Finn's arrival when Megan had called in an obvious blind panic saying she needed help, and for him to get his ass over there ASAP. Had it been any other time, Joel wouldn't have hesitated. The coming evening had been on his mind for the last two days, however, and the last thing he needed right then was a mercy mission. Especially when he had no clue what Megan's emergency was. He hadn't been able to glean much, except that she sounded pretty distressed, and that wasn't like her. And seeing as she'd *never* called on him like that, it was enough to get Joel reaching for his car keys. He'd only just gotten home after an appointment, so he hadn't had time to change out of his suit. He'd sent Finn a text before leaving the house, telling him dinner would be delayed. Then he reconsidered and told Finn where to find the key. Bramble would be glad of the company, and Finn could take him for a walk while he waited.

So much for his plans to make a special dinner.

The curses were nothing to do with Megan's

emergency, and everything to do with whatever the fuck was going on with the 295 heading into Portland. He'd gotten as far as the turnoff, but the exit was closed. He was forced to stay on the turnpike for ten miles, all the way down to Falmouth, and then back south to Portland on 295. By the time he reached Megan's house, over an hour had elapsed since her call. More than *one fucking hour* to get there, and yet another to get back, providing the traffic wasn't snarled up any worse than it had been on the way there.

Why today? Why the fuck did this have to happen today? Then he stopped. *Don't be such a selfish dick. Megan needs you, asshole.*

Joel switched off the engine, got out of the car, and ran to Megan's front door. It opened as he raised his hand to bang on it, and Megan stood there, a cane in one hand, and her left ankle bound up in a bandage.

"Oh, thank God you're here." Megan gave him a one-armed hug as he stepped into the house.

Joel glanced at the white bandage. *"Tell* me you didn't drag me over here because you sprained your ankle. And when did you do that?" He'd half-expected to find Lynne on the floor with a broken leg, or something equally catastrophic.

"Wednesday."

He blinked. "Wednesday? Okay then, what's the emergency?" Her lack of panic sent a small measure of relief flooding through him. "Why am I here?"

She dragged him through the house to the back door and pointed at the yard. "Midge is out there. She's been out there for two days."

For a moment, Joel was lost. "Midge?" Then he remembered. "What's happened? Has that damn cat got herself mauled by some dog? And why call me for that?" He grimaced. He didn't want to be the one to pick up the pieces of Megan's mangled cat.

Megan rolled her eyes. She yanked open the back door and tugged him outside, then hobbled to the tall tree at the far end of the yard, dragging him with her. She pointed up into its branches with her cane. "See? She's stuck up there."

Joel squinted. Sure enough, a black and white face stared down at him, and seconds later Midge gave a plaintive *meow*.

He blinked. "You called me over here to rescue your damn cat? Why couldn't you guys do it?"

"Lynne isn't here. She's visiting her mom this week. And… and I can't stand heights."

Joel gaped. "Since when? You were always climbing trees when you were a kid. Mom and Dad could never get you to come down out of them."

"Yeah, but I'm older now. I can't climb a tree at my age. What if I fall?"

He stared at her. "Oh, but it's okay if *I* do?"

Megan's eyes bulged. "Can we go back to the part where I have a *sprained ankle*?"

Then he noticed the ladder, its top rungs leaning against the thick branch on which Midge was perched like a goddamn huge furry sparrow.

Megan coughed. "She's been stuck up there since that storm hit yesterday morning, and I couldn't get her to come down. I tried, okay? But I… got dizzy. That's when I called you," she added. "So can you *please* get your ass up there and rescue Midge?"

There was nothing for it but to climb.

Grumbling, Joel carefully made his way up the ladder, keeping his eyes locked on the cat, willing it not to decide to move any higher before Joel reached it.

Midge meowed as he leaned against the top rungs and stretched out his hands toward her. "Here, kitty. Nice kitty. Don't be an ass, kitty."

Midge didn't move as he grabbed her and tucked her under his arm. "Christ, what are you feeding her? She weighs a ton." Now one-handed, he made his way to the ground, with a great deal more care than he'd used on the way up. At last his feet touched the earth, and he shuddered a sigh of relief.

Megan scooped the cat out from under his arm, and held her against her chest. "You bad kitty, scaring me like that."

If she'd been scared, she deserved an Oscar for that performance, because Joel had seen no trace of fear. Then he noticed her cane lay on the ground, and he picked it up. Midge chose that moment to squirm out of Megan's grasp and make a dash for the house.

"Poor thing. She must be starving." She smiled as Joel handed her the cane. "Thank you *so* much. I had visions of her starving to death up there."

Joel snickered. "Seems to me that cat is way too fond of her food to let that happen." He brushed cat hair off his suit jacket. "*Now* can I go home?"

Megan widened her eyes. "Don't you want to stay for a coffee or something?"

"No, I do *not*. It's getting late, and Finn is coming over for dinner. Thanks to Midge here, I haven't prepared so much as a carrot."

Megan bit her lip. "I'm sorry. You should've said."

Joel regarded her in amusement. "Why—would it have done any good?" He sighed. "I'm glad Midge is down safe and sound. Next time, call a neighbor? You know, someone who lives closer than I do?" And with that, Joel hurried around the side of the house to his car. As he got behind the wheel, he sent up a silent prayer.

No more surprises, please. Tonight is important.

Maybe the most important night of his life, and so much was riding on it.

His phone buzzed, and Joel pulled it hurriedly from his pocket. He smiled when he saw it was Finn.

"Hey. Where are you?"

Joel sighed. "Megan's. I'll tell you all about it when I get there. It's going to take me at least an hour to get back." He paused. "I'm sorry. This is *not* how I wanted tonight to go."

Finn chuckled. "Don't worry about it. Bramble's been on his walk, and now I know approximately when you'll get here, I'll make dinner. It won't be your lasagna, but it'll be edible—I hope."

"The whole point was, I was supposed to be cooking *you* dinner."

"Hey." Finn's voice softened. "It's okay. I'll see you when you get here." He disconnected.

Joel took a deep breath. *Okay, Plan B. So what if Finn cooks? He's still going to be there, right?*

And they had things to discuss.

Seventy-five minutes later, Joel pulled onto his driveway behind Finn's truck. As he switched off the engine, his phone pinged.

Go to the side gate.

He frowned. *What the hell?* Joel got out of the car and went toward the gate. There was music coming from somewhere, and as he opened the gate and walked through, he realized the source was his own backyard.

What is going on?

Joel rounded the corner—and came to a dead stop as hundreds of white lights blinked into existence. They were everywhere: in the trees, along the top of the fence, and wound around the deck railing. Lights hung from the pergola's top beams, and more lights snaked around all the posts.

It was like walking into a fairy grotto.

Then his heartbeat raced when Finn stepped into view. He wore a tux, and Joel had never seen him looking so good. "Welcome home." Finn walked to the steps, clearly waiting for him, and Joel went around the deck, his heart still pounding. Finn held out his hand and Joel took it, climbing the steps.

"You did all this… for me?"

Finn smiled. "With a little help from Grammy. I borrowed every set of Christmas lights she's got, and believe me, we're talking *thousands* of lights." His eyes sparkled. "And of course, your sister helped a bit too."

Joel froze. "My…"

Finn grinned. "I needed you out of the way while I set all this up."

He let go of Finn's hand, pulled his phone out and dialed. Before Megan could say a word, he got in first. "You used your cat?"

She chuckled. "Hey, it was all I could come up with on short notice. Do you know how long it took me to get her to stay there? I had to put pieces of tuna all along the branch."

"Wait—you *put* her up there?"

"Yup, about half an hour before you arrived. You took so long getting here, I was starting to panic. I was sure she'd find a way down before you walked through the front door."

"And the sprained ankle?"

Another chuckle. "It had a miraculous recovery as soon as you left. Go figure."

"You sneaky—and was Lynne really at her mom's?"

Megan snorted. "She was hiding in our bedroom the whole time, trying not to laugh her ass off."

"You do know I'm never going to believe a word you say, ever again. And—"

"Hey!" She interjected. "Let's not forget, I climbed a tree for you. If that isn't love…" Megan cackled. "Have a good night." Then she disconnected.

Joel pocketed his phone. Finn was gazing at him in obvious amusement. Joel raised his eyebrows. "You've gone to a lot of trouble." What made his heart beat so fucking fast was the feeling that this whole scenario screamed *romance*.

Then Finn sealed the deal. "I wanted tonight to be special."

Jesus fucking Christ.

Joel couldn't have named the song playing as he'd approached, but he certainly knew the next one. Etta James's beautiful voice filled the night air with those perfect opening words. *At last…*

Words that spoke to his heart.

Finn stepped closer. "May I have this dance?"

Joel bit his lip. "There's not a lot of room out here for dancing."

Finn's smile lit up his eyes. "Then we'd better dance real close." Joel caught his breath as Finn looped his arms around his neck, their bodies almost touching. "Like this," Finn murmured. Joel placed his hands on Finn's waist, and they moved together, a gentle sway that made his heart sing.

"Love the tux," he murmured.

"It's rented. I had to drive all the way to Alfred to a bridal shop yesterday to find one."

Joel chuckled. "When do you have to return it?"

Finn snorted. "Tomorrow, so make the most of it. I don't put on a tux for just *any* man, y'know." He paused. "I'm glad you like it."

"You have *no* idea what the sight of you in it is doing to me. And that's not my dick doing the talking." Joel stroked Finn's back. "You look amazing." The tux added to the magic—to the *romance* of it all—and Joel allowed himself to fall under its spell. "And it *is* a special night." A night where Joel might finally find the courage to open his heart.

Finn leaned in and brushed his lips over Joel's ear. "You remember when we talked about my past relationships, and you said I didn't deserve to be messed around like that. Well, the truth is… that's not how it was, not really."

"Oh?"

Finn drew back, nodding. "They didn't mess me around. I just moved too fast, that's all. I was *so* in love, I didn't stop to check they were too. Which brings me to you."

Joel's breathing quickened and his pulse sped up. "Okay."

"I didn't want to make the same mistake. I wasn't gonna rush in and bare my soul, if there was even a chance you didn't love me…" Finn's gaze met his and he swallowed. "The way I love you."

Holy fuck.

Joel stopped dancing and brought his hands to Finn's face. He looked him in the eye, shaking a little. "You love me?"

Finn nodded. "And I gotta tell ya, I'm scared to death right now."

Joel couldn't leave him hanging. "Don't be. Because I love you too. And—"

Finn's lips met his, and Joel lost himself in the sweetest kiss he'd ever known. Etta sang on, oblivious to them, as Joel held Finn under a ceiling of white lights, growing brighter still against the sky that was turning all shades of orange and gold, just for them.

When they finally parted, Finn murmured, "Wow."

Joel found his voice. "Wow indeed."

Finn smiled. "Not talking about the kiss, although it *was* pretty epic. That was sort of a whoa-he-loves-me-back wow."

"Need to hear it again?" Joel cupped Finn's head and drew him closer, until their lips were almost touching. "I love you," he murmured against them before taking Finn's mouth in a lingering kiss.

When they parted, Finn let out a sigh. "Still wow."

"I couldn't agree more."

Finn cleared his throat and pulled back. "Well… now we have the important stuff out of the way… are you hungry?"

He laughed. "Starving. What's for dinner?"

"Lobster and salad."

Joel gaped. "You cooked me a lobster?"

Finn chuckled. "No, I bought one from Wolff Farm, ready cooked." He stilled. "You do like lobster, right?"

"Love it." He had to say the words again. "Love you."

Finn's face glowed. "Love you too." He smiled. "I think I'm gonna be saying that a lot tonight."

Joel didn't think he'd ever tire of hearing it.

Finn wiped his lips with a napkin. "That was delicious." Eating it on Joel's deck under all those lights had been magical enough. Those moments when they stopped to share a kiss or a squeeze of a hand added to the wonder of it all, and Finn knew he would never forget this.

"When you asked me to come to dinner tonight…"

Joel sighed. "Carrie told me not to let fear hold me back. So I decided to tell you how I felt." He gazed at Finn. "As to why I was afraid? The difference in our ages. I'm continually amazed you'd be interested in a guy who's forty-two."

Finn arched his eyebrows. "Okay… One? You are the *perfect* age for me, and that's the last time we're gonna mention that. Two, unlike one particular friend—who I'm not gonna name because I don't need to—I like commitment, all right? That's why my relationships were so messed up. I wanted commitment, they didn't."

"And I should have realized that, because you said as much." His eyes twinkled. "Carrie always said I was crap at reading between the lines. Now tell me what stopped *you*."

Finn bit his lip. "I was your first guy in twenty years. I figured it was all about the sex. And how would it have looked if the first guy you lay suddenly declares you're the one he's been looking for his whole life?" He froze. "Okay, that was more than I intended to reveal."

Joel reached across the table and took Finn's hand. "On the contrary. I needed to hear that. And while the sex has been amazing…" He swallowed. "God, there's so much more to us than that."

Finn decided to go for broke. "Listen… I was

thinking of taking an hour or two off work next week. I need to go to Portland. To visit the Franny Peabody Center."

Joel smirked. "Have we run out of condoms? That's what drugstores are for."

Christ, his heart was hammering. "That's not why I'm going. I visit the center every three months… to get tested."

Joel was so still. "I see. It's not something I've ever done."

Finn nodded. "Which is why I thought you might wanna come with me. We could get tested together." *Come on, Joel, read between the lines…*

"Oh." Joel's breathing quickened. "*Oh.*"

Thank God, he got it. "Is that something you might wanna do?"

"Yes." Joel smiled. "Oh yes." He glanced at the table. "Are we done here?"

"Why—you got something in mind?" As if the same thought wasn't already in Finn's head.

"We haven't run out of condoms, have we?"

Finn chuckled. "Between the ones *I* bought, and the ones *you* bought, I think we've got plenty." He couldn't resist. "Enough to last us until we get our results back, at any rate."

Oh fuck. Joel's pupils were huge. "Then let's go inside."

He grinned. "I'd had enough of the tux anyway."

The dishes could wait.

Finn moaned into Joel's kiss as Joel gently fingered him, Finn's hands on Joel's head and neck, both he and Joel in constant motion and neither in a hurry to reach their destination. Finn wanted to enjoy the journey: the feel of Joel's hands on him; Joel's hot shaft sliding over his own; Joel's sighs as Finn curled his fingers around both their lengths and gave them a leisurely tug; and the look of wonder in Joel's eyes as he eased his gloved dick into Finn's body.

Then his heart stuttered when Joel stilled, balls deep inside him, kissed him, and whispered "I love you." Their lips met, and Finn held him close as they rocked in harmony, Finn's legs wrapped around Joel's body, wanting him deeper.

Time lost all meaning as they rolled together in Joel's bed, and all that mattered was their connection. When Finn got on all fours, and Joel knelt behind him to slide into him with an exquisite languidness, Finn bowed his head and closed his eyes, letting the sensations wash over him. He arched his back and Joel laid a trail of kisses up his spine to his nape, one hand stroking Finn's cock with infinite gentleness, as though Finn was some fragile creature to be cosseted, caressed... worshipped.

Joel slipped an arm across Finn's chest and held him close, and Finn turned his head to meet Joel's kiss as Joel rocked into him with consummate speed.

"Oh, just like that," Finn murmured, pushing back to meet Joel's thrusts.

"Can't last much longer," Joel gasped out. He covered Finn with his body, pinning him to the mattress as he picked up the pace, their flesh meeting in slap after sharp slap. And when he felt the throb of

Joel's cock inside him, Finn sighed.

One day soon, there would be nothing between them.

The thought was enough to bring him to the edge, and Joel clung to him as he shuddered through his climax, their bodies locked together.

Joel kissed his nape. "And I thought it couldn't get any better."

"You and me both."

Joel chuckled. "We've only gotten started."

Finn smiled. *Now it's* we. Us.

There were never sweeter words.

"You got anything planned for next weekend?"

"Hmm?" Joel caressed Finn's back, enjoying the feeling of mellowness. "Apart from spending as much of it with you as I can, no. Carrie's taking the kids to visit my parents in Boise for a week, now school's out. Why? You got something in mind? Apart from the obvious."

Finn chuckled. "Mind out of the gutter, please. Next weekend is Levi's party for Grammy's birthday, and I wondered if you wanted to come with me. My friends will all be there—I hope—and I want you to meet them."

Joel shifted in bed to lie facing him. "Really?" Joel was no fool. He knew what Finn's friends meant to him, and this was a huge deal.

Finn nodded. "I've met *your* family—now I want *my*

family to meet the most important person in my life." He bit his lip. "Well?"

Joel's heart was doing a happy dance. "I'd love that. Would we just stay for the party, or had you planned to spend the night there?"

"I *was* going to stay at Seb's, with as many of the others who can make it." He smiled. "Time for a catch up, and boy, will I have a lot to tell them."

"Then you don't want me around."

Finn stroked Joel's cheek. "Oh yes I do. We can stay at the Colonial Inn in Ogunquit. Dylan—another friend—works there. He can give us their friends-and-family rate, so we might end up with something pretty special. And I'll have plenty of time to catch up with the guys at the party." He grinned. "Besides, that'll give them the chance to talk about us during their little sleepover." Finn's eyes glittered. "Just not the kind of sleepover *you* had, dirty boy."

"Do you remember everything I say?" Joel marveled at his retention.

"Only the important stuff. But the thing is?" Finn leaned in, his lips almost touching Joel's. "Everything you say is important." Then Joel shivered as Finn grabbed his hand and brought it to Finn's stiffening cock. "You got someplace I can put this?"

Joel grinned. "I have the perfect spot."

Chapter Twenty-Five

Finn switched off the engine. When Joel made no move to get out of the truck, Finn stroked his thigh. "You okay?"

"A little nervous." His gaze met Finn's. "This is important."

Finn's heart went out to him, and he leaned across to kiss Joel on the lips. "They are gonna *love* you," he assured Joel. "And they don't bite." He grinned. "Well, not so sure about Seb, but let's not go there, okay? Hey, at least you've already met one of them. And Grammy is gonna love you too."

"Grammy sounds like a tough cookie."

Finn laughed. "She's that, all right." He squeezed Joel's thigh. "Come on, let's get in there. And just think. When this is over, we get to spend the night in that gorgeous room." They'd checked into the hotel before coming to the house, and Finn had to admit Dylan had done them proud. The king room was on a corner with an ocean view, and the bed looked *so* inviting.

Joel chuckled. "We'd still be there if I hadn't dragged you away. It doesn't take much to distract you, does it?" He drew a deep breath. "Okay, I'm as ready as I'll ever be."

"That's my man." Finn kissed him again, loving the

way Joel cupped his cheek. "Now help me get the rocking chair out." They got out of the truck, and Joel helped him lift the chair onto the sidewalk. Together they carried it to the front door, which opened before Finn could ring the doorbell.

Levi gaped at them. "Oh, that's awesome. Quick, bring it into the dining room. Grammy's in the backyard, holding court like she's the queen of England." He gave Joel a smile. "Hi, Joel. I'm Levi. Welcome." Then he stepped aside, and they carried the chair into the house. Levi went ahead and opened doors for them, and they set it down in the dining room.

Finn pulled a wad of wide red ribbon from his jacket pocket. "Thought you might wanna put this around it."

Levi beamed. "That's sweet."

Finn inclined his head toward Joel. "It was his idea."

Levi held out his hand, and Joel shook it. "It's good to meet you, Joel. Finn's told me a lot about you. I'm glad you could come today."

From his kneeling point in front of the chair, Finn chuckled. "He's feeling a bit nervous about meeting the guys."

Joel stared at him. "Sure. Tell everybody."

Finn got to his feet and squeezed Joel's hand. "Levi isn't 'everybody'. He's one of my closest friends, and he's not gonna walk out there and tell the world, okay?" He knew Joel had been on tenterhooks the moment he'd woken up, and Finn had done his best to take Joel's mind off of it.

Sex was the best therapy sometimes.

Levi led them through the house and out of the French doors onto the patio, where Grammy was sitting in a high-backed basket-weave chair. Guests sat on the patio furniture, chatting with her, and yet more people stood on the grass, talking and drinking. The smell of grilled meat filled the air. Shaun was busy turning sausages and slabs of beef, and he waved to Finn, his eyes widening when he saw Joel. *Who's that?* he mouthed.

Finn grinned and mouthed back *Later.* He leaned into Joel and murmured, "By the way, I didn't tell the guys I was bringing a guest, and it looks like Levi didn't share that either."

Joel jerked his head to stare at him. "Way to go to make me feel more nervous."

Finn took both Joel's hands in his, and looked him in the eye. "Relax, okay? Come meet Grammy. Then I'll introduce you to the gang."

"'Gang', huh?" Joel was smirking. "Makes you sound like a bunch of teenagers."

Finn laughed. "Trust me. Once you've spent a little time around them, you'll see why gang is the perfect word." He wasn't nervous about them meeting Joel. He knew they'd love him.

Just not as much as I do.

Joel sat on the patio sofa, gazing at the backyard a damn sight emptier than it had been six or seven hours ago. The sun had dipped out of sight and the sky had darkened but lights illuminated the yard: among the flower beds, along the paved paths, and at the base of the trees, lighting up their trunks. Most of the guests had left, and Grammy had said goodnight. Finn had been right—Grammy was a force of nature. He loved the way Levi took care of her, making sure she was comfortable, bringing her food and drink, and generally looking out for her.

"Levi seems like a good guy," he murmured.

Beside him, Finn sighed. "One of the best." He chuckled. "I think Grammy loved her rocking chair."

"Whatever gave you that idea? Apart from the fact that she demanded it be taken outside so she could sit in it. And then she *stayed* in it for the rest of the afternoon and evening." He nudged Finn's arm. "You did good."

"Hey, it was Levi's idea."

Joel nodded, then took Finn's hand in his. "But these talented hands fashioned it from lumps of wood." He raised Finn's hand to his lips and kissed his fingers. "These talented fingers." He grinned. "These *multi-talented* fingers."

Finn snatched his hand back. "Down boy. Don't think I don't know what you're doing. Do *not* go there. Save it for when we get back to the hotel."

Joel chuckled. "Payback is a bitch, huh?"

"Excuse me?"

"Oh, I'm sorry. That wasn't you calling me during a break Tuesday? To tell me *exactly* what you planned on doing to me when you got to my place? Six hours. I had to wait *six freaking hours* for you. Talk about blue balls."

"Yeah, but I made it worth your while, right?"

Joel couldn't deny that. The combination of anticipation and the sight of Finn turning up still in his work clothes, that tool belt slung around his waist, had led to him going off like a rocket.

Then they got to do it all over again. And again, this

time *without* the work clothes.

He took another drink from his bottle of beer. "Someone has good taste." It was from one of his favorite microbreweries.

Finn coughed. "That would be me. I picked some up the other day." When Joel stared at him, he shrugged. "I just happened to be passing through Portland, and when I saw the name of the place, I remembered where I'd seen it before. It was one of the beers you gave me that time. So I thought I might as well pick some up and bring it along as my contribution."

Yeah right. Joel smiled. "You weren't just *passing through*, you went there especially."

Finn widened his eyes. "How did you know?"

Joel sighed. "Because it's the sort of sweet thing you would do."

Finn leaned against him. "You having a good time?"

"It was a great party. And Grammy is quite a character."

"I meant to ask. When I got back from taking a leak, you two were deep in conversation. What were you talking about?"

"You." When Finn gave him a quizzical glance, Joel smiled. "I think it came under the heading of 'checking my intentions'."

"Really?"

Joel took Finn's hand in his once more, and they laced their fingers together. The intimate gesture warmed him. "She was looking out for you, that's all." He wasn't about to share her exact words.

She'd speared him with a sharp look. *"You break his heart, you'll have me to deal with, you got that?"*

Joel had assured her he'd do everything in his power to make Finn happy. She'd gazed at him for a moment, then gave a satisfied nod.

Then he remembered. He had a message to pass on.

"Carrie called while you were talking to Levi earlier. She said I was to give you her love, and to say Nate wants to teach you to play chess when they visit next time."

Finn snorted. "Yeah, good luck with *that* idea." He beamed. "Your kids like me."

"Of course they do. They have great taste—just like their dad."

Finn chuckled. "Not gonna argue with that."

Joel glanced at the far end of the patio, where seven guys sat around the fire pit, talking and laughing. He made his way mentally around the group, attaching names to faces, relieved he recognized them. He'd been introduced to all of them at some point during the afternoon, and the conversations had varied in length. Some of Finn's friends were a lot quieter than Joel had expected, but all of them seemed happy to meet him. No one had teased Finn or made jokes.

Joel had a feeling he'd gotten off easy, not that he expected that state to last.

He nudged Finn. "I'm ready."

Finn gazed at him, his brow furrowed. "For what?"

Joel inclined his head toward the group of guys. "My trial by fire." He got up from the patio sofa and held out his hand. "Come on. Let's do this."

"You sure?"

Joel laughed. "No, but I'm doing it anyway." Finn grabbed his hand, and Joel hauled him to his feet. "You can lead the way. I'm not *that* brave."

Finn chuckled and led him across the patio. The guys fell silent as they approached, and then Seb grinned. "Took you long enough."

Joel smiled and seized his courage. "Not all of us have your balls, Seb." That earned him a ripple of chuckles. Finn dragged a couple of chairs over, and the men shifted to make room for them. Their faces glowed in the firelight.

"Dude, your guy is a fast learner." That was Ben, who seemed to be the youngest. He had a shock of longish brown hair swept through with highlights that he was constantly pushing away from his chocolate-brown eyes.

"How's the room?" That came from Dylan.

Joel smiled again. "It's great. I take it we have you to thank for that."

Dylan waved his hand. "It's nothing. You're not the first I've done it for. And at least you guys booked it in Joel's name." His eyes twinkled. "*Someone* recently reserved a room under the names of Mr. and Mr. Smith."

It cracked Joel up that all heads swiveled immediately in Seb's direction.

Seb glared. "Hey. None of you guys ever done any role-playing before? He wanted to make believe we were on honeymoon, and it was our wedding night."

Aaron guffawed. "Nearest *you'll* ever get to one of those."

"Hey, you want to watch it, Seb." That was Noah, the only one of them who wore glasses. "He might decide you're the one, and that he wants to try it for real." He gave an impish grin.

Seb snorted. "Yeah right. Never going down *that* road."

Finn coughed. "Don't say never, man. Because you don't know what's coming at you, from right around the corner." His eyes met Joel's, and there was that fluttering in Joel's stomach again.

"Oh my God, the pair of you are so freaking *cute*." Ben raised his bottle to them. "Welcome aboard, Joel." The others followed suit.

"Kinda gives you hope, don't it?" Aaron winked at them. "Because if *Finn* can find a guy…"

Joel laughed, the last remnants of his nervousness finally slipping away.

"So is Finn moving in with you, or are you moving in with Finn?" Ben demanded.

It was kind of funny, how he and Finn both burst out with 'Whoa!' at exactly the same time.

Finn gaped at Ben. "We only just got together. It's been one week, dude."

"So?"

"So how about you let us get used to the idea of being a couple before you have us moving in together?"

Joel said nothing. He was surprised to find that once he'd gotten over the shock caused by Ben's suggestion, he didn't mind the idea of living with Finn at all.

Not going to rush this though. They had plenty of time.

"How's your dad, Shaun?" Finn asked.

Shaun leaned forward, his elbows on his knees, holding the bottle between them in both hands. "I had to find a new in-home nurse. Susie dropped a couple of bombshells. She's pregnant, and her husband wants her home, building the nest. *She* wants to work, but apparently he's the kind who worries, so…"

"Is the new carer okay? What's her name?" Levi asked.

"*His* name is Nathan." When they stared at him, Shaun rolled his eyes. "Jeez, guys, there *are* male nurses, y'know." He took a drink from his bottle. "He's good with Dad, that's the main thing." He swallowed a mouthful of beer. "First weekend I've been away from him since Teresa's wedding."

Noah squeezed his shoulder. "Nothing wrong with taking a break, dude."

Shaun turned his head to stare at Noah. "Dad doesn't get to take a break, so why should I?" He expelled a breath. "Sorry, guys. That came out wrong."

"It's okay." Dylan's voice was gentle. "We know how it is."

Joel didn't say a word, recalling Finn telling him Shaun's dad had dementia.

"Guys, I almost forgot." Ben's eyes sparkled. "I've got a job interview next week."

Joel loved the hoots and whoops of obvious delight that filled the night air.

"That's great," Levi exclaimed. "What's the job?"

"Working in a gift store—*and* it's right on my doorstep, in Camden. Apparently, this place has been owned by the same family for eighty years. Not that I've ever been in there. What do I want with a gift store for tourists? It's owned by the Pearsons." He grimaced. "That's a popular Maine name, right?"

Noah widened his eyes. "Oh God, I hope so."

Joel frowned. "Am I missing something?"

Finn scowled. "There was an asshole in high school—Wade Pearson—who made Ben's life hell, all because he got it into his fat head that Ben was gay."

When Joel gave Finn a puzzled glance, Ben burst out laughing. "Okay, so I *am* gay—now—but back then I was still figuring stuff out. Fucking homophobic asshole." His eyes gleamed. "Pity he was such a *good-looking* homophobic asshole, because in another life, I would've been all over that guy like a rash. And I'm not even gonna *entertain* the possibility that these Pearsons are remotely related to him. God wouldn't be that cruel."

Noah shook his head. "Which God are we talking about here?"

Seb held up his hands. "Nope. We are *not* gonna talk religion."

"Not even to say a quick prayer?" Ben asked. "Because I *need* this job, guys."

Seb raised his eyes heavenward. "Hey, God? Make sure Ben gets this job. And while You're at it, don't let whoever's gonna interview Ben be in any way connected to that asshole Wade Pearson. You got that?" He gave Ben a smug smile. "That oughta do it."

Ben rolled his eyes. "Yeah, thanks for that, Seb."

Finn laughed. "If Grammy heard you, Seb, she'd take her broom to your ass."

Seb looked quickly toward the window behind them. "She sleeps on the other side of the house, right?" Everyone laughed. He peered at Aaron. "Must be getting into your busy season right about now."

Aaron snorted. "Don't I know it. What is it about the summer that brings out all the idiots?"

"Aaron's a ranger at Acadia National Park," Finn told Joel. He grinned. "I think he's lost count of how many times visitors makes jokes about Thunder Hole."

Joel blinked. "Seriously? That's a place?" He'd heard the name before. When the kids were growing up vacations were a visit to Boise to stay with his parents. They hadn't explored much of the northern part of Maine, much to his regret.

Aaron nodded. "It's a giant cave that belches seawater up in the air, sometimes as high as thirty or forty feet." He snickered. "Sort of like a college frat party." He shook his head. "All those forests and miles of rugged coastline, and *that's* all people talk about?"

Noah got to his feet. "I'm going to get another beer." He touched Levi lightly on the arm. "You want something?"

"I'm good, thanks," Levi told him with a smile.

"You gonna ask us too?" Seb grinned. "'Cause I sure could down another cold one." He tapped the label on his bottle. "Specifically, *this* one. Somebody actually brought some decent brew to this shindig."

Joel bit back a smile. "Oh, I don't know. Some folks are happy with a Bud."

Seb snorted. "Training beer, I call that. Tastes like—"

"Don't!" Shaun interjected. "We all know what you think."

"And *why* do we know?" Finn grinned. "Because you've only told us about a million times. And I happen to *like* Bud, so shut the fuck up." That raised more chuckles.

"Hey, Seb. School's out for summer, right?" Aaron asked.

"You know it. I spent the last week there, getting all my stuff ready for the next semester. So now it's time to kick back and party *all* summer long."

"Well, you can't party on your own. Hey, Joel?" Dylan laced his hands behind his head, and Joel steeled himself. "Know anyone else your age who might be interested in Seb?" His eyes gleamed. "Because we *all* know Seb wants a Daddy."

Both Finn and Seb glared at him, but Joel laughed. "Okay, I'm no Daddy, and I wouldn't *dream* of assuming to know what kind of guy Seb likes." He gave Seb a sideways glance. "Although after seeing him in action, I do have an idea."

"Okay, we're done here." Finn got to his feet. "Time we were going to the hotel."

Ben cackled. "Which translates as… Finn has an itch, and he wants Joel to scratch it." Everyone laughed, including Finn and Joel.

"It was good to meet you all," Joel said as he stood. "Finn talks about you a lot."

"Whereas we didn't have a clue you existed until today," Shaun said with a smile.

"Speak for yourself." Seb's smile was still smug. He looked at Finn. "Are you guys coming to my place for lunch tomorrow? There'll be plenty of food. And then we can talk some more."

Finn glanced at Joel, and he nodded. "We'd love to." Now he'd dipped his toes in the water the idea of going deeper caused no trepidation. He grinned. "But now we'll leave you to talk about us behind our backs."

There was a moment of silence which was broken by Finn's laughter, and the others joined in.

"Okay, he'll do," Aaron said with an emphatic nod to Finn, who rolled his eyes.

"Gee, thanks. Not that I need your approval, but hey, don't let *that* stop you." Finn grabbed Joel's hand. "See you tomorrow."

"Enjoy the hotel," Ben called out to them as they walked toward the house.

"We will," Finn murmured. He led Joel through the hallway and out of the front door. When they reached the truck, Finn stopped and kissed him.

"I've been waiting *hours* to do that."

Joel chuckled as he pulled Finn close. "You could have kissed me in front of them. They wouldn't have minded."

Finn snorted. "Are you kidding? Seb would've sold

tickets."

"Just so you know?" Joel leaned in to whisper. "I really like your friends."

Finn's face glowed. "I'm glad." Their lips met in another kiss. When they parted, Finn swung his keys around on his finger. "The hotel is about fifteen minutes' drive from here. I want you in that bed within twenty. Think that's doable?"

"Oh, I think we can manage that. In fact, I think I can have my tongue in your ass within twenty-five."

Finn's eyes glittered. "You're on." As he got behind the wheel, he let out a happy little sigh.

"What was that for?" Joel asked.

Finn reached across and took his hand. "For weeks, you were nothing but a fantasy. A guy I dreamed about, but never thought I'd find the courage to speak to."

"And now?"

Finn squeezed his hand. "I couldn't dream of being with anyone else."

The End

Coming next in the Maine Men series…

Ben's Boss (Maine Men Book Two)

A painful history
Walking into the job interview confirms Ben White's worst fears. It's been eight years since high school, yet he can still recall Wade Pearson's taunts.

There's always a chance Wade isn't the same homophobic asshole Ben knew. *Yeah right.*

Pity, because the boy Ben remembers has grown into one seriously hot, brooding man. In another life, Ben would have climbed him like a tree. Wade's gaze still makes Ben shiver – although now for entirely different reasons.

A secret longing
As soon as Wade read Ben's application, he knew he had to see him. Ben's still as gorgeous as Wade remembers. It's obvious he doesn't expect to get the job, given their history.

But Wade has an agenda. He has to make it up to Ben for treating him so badly – not that Ben will ever know why he acted like he did. Seeing him every day only heightens Wade's regret. If he'd had more courage back then, maybe he and Ben could have been something.

The least he can do is show Ben he's changed. There's no way Wade can get what he *really* wants – Ben's heart.

About the author

K.C. Wells lives on an island off the south coast of the UK, surrounded by natural beauty. She writes about men who love men, and can't even contemplate a life that doesn't include writing.

The rainbow rose tattoo on her back with the words 'Love is Love' and 'Love Wins' is her way of hoisting a flag. She plans to be writing about men in love - be it sweet or slow, hot or kinky - for a long while to come.

Available titles

Learning to Love
Michael & Sean
Evan & Daniel
Josh & Chris
Final Exam

Sensual Bonds
A Bond of Three
A Bond of Truth

Merrychurch Mysteries
Truth Will Out
Roots of Evil
A Novel Murder

Love, Unexpected
Debt
Burden

Dreamspun Desires
The Senator's Secret
Out of the Shadows
My Fair Brady
Under The Covers

Lions & Tigers & Bears
A Growl, a Roar, and a Purr

Love Lessons Learned
First

Waiting for You
Step by Step
Bromantically Yours
BFF

Collars & Cuffs
An Unlocked Heart
Trusting Thomas
Someone to Keep Me (K.C. Wells & Parker Williams)
A Dance with Domination
Damian's Discipline (K.C. Wells & Parker Williams)
Make Me Soar
Dom of Ages (K.C. Wells & Parker Williams)
Endings and Beginnings (K.C. Wells & Parker Williams)

Secrets – with Parker Williams
Before You Break
An Unlocked Mind
Threepeat
On the Same Page

Personal
Making it Personal
Personal Changes
More than Personal
Personal Secrets
Strictly Personal
Personal Challenges

Personal – The Complete Series

Confetti, Cake & Confessions

Connections
Saving Jason
A Christmas Promise
The Law of Miracles
My Christmas Spirit
A Guy for Christmas

Island Tales
Waiting for a Prince
September's Tide
Submitting to the Darkness

A Material World
Lace
Satin
Silk
Denim

Southern Boys
Truth & Betrayal
Pride & Protection
Desire & Denial

Kel's Keeper
Here For You
Sexting The Boss
Gay on a Train
Sunshine & Shadows
Watch and Learn
Double or Nothing
Back from the Edge
Switching it up
Out for You

State of Mind
My Best Friend's Brother

Anthologies

<u>Fifty Gays of Shade</u>
Winning Will's Heart

<u>Come, Play</u>
Watch and Learn

<u>Writing as Tantalus</u>
Damon & Pete: Playing with Fire

Titles also available in French, German, Italian, and
Spanish.

Printed in Great Britain
by Amazon